What people

IRREVOCABLE

"Modern fiction seems to careen back and forth between mindless fantasy and dystopian depression. *Irrevocable* is a bright ray of redemptive light in the dark. Don't miss this engaging new novel."

Mark Rutland, Former President Southeastern University, Oral Roberts University, author of *NY Times* Best Selling book, *Relaunch*

"Stories of grace and second chances never get old. When they're told with captivating drama and page-turning curiosity, they spark life within. Do yourself a favor and grab a copy of this book, a cup of good coffee, and get ready to be entertained and inspired."

Dr. Douglas Witherup, Senior Pastor of The Multiply Family of Churches and Author of *Interrobang Preaching*

"This work masterfully captures the agony of a broken heart and the joy of a redeemed soul as it sheds light on the indefinite space between the fragile, sinful nature of man and the irrevocable call of God."

Terry Allen, Founder and President of MVP Leader Group dedicated to honoring, encouraging, and connecting leaders

"It was Joe Phillips' voice—nearly 40 years ago—that provoked, affirmed, and stewarded the call on my life. He has done that again with this brilliant, creative, and anointed offering. This book is a reminder of God's relentless pursuit and His wind in the sails of a weary heart."

Teri Furr, Executive Pastor Refuge Church Kannapolis, NC

"This work is another example of God working. It is a God thing when His Grace saves and redeems the life of a weary and distressed soul. I've been leading the rescue prayer team for JPM for 13 years. I can tell you that Joe believes what he preaches.

He loves ministers. Through this book he hopes to inspire people to continue in all manner of callings that God has given them. I highly recommend it."

Jewell Massey, Leader of Rescue Prayer Warriors

"Sixteen years ago I invited Joe Phillips to be part of evangelistic endeavors in North Carolina. Neither of us had any idea where that phone call would lead. I have witnessed Joe use the creativity that God gives in a variety of artistic endeavors. Each effort points people to the life-changing message of Jesus. *Irrevocable* is no exception in this pursuit. This novel flows from page to page outlining the heartache that can come from pursuing God's will and His everlasting pursuit for our destiny. I have dedicated my life helping ministers achieve their very best in life. However, this book is not just for ministers. It is for <u>anybody</u> that wants to walk in their divine assignment."

Dr. Rick Ross, Superintendent, North Carolina Ministry Network, denominational Executive Presbyter

"Even though the character is fictional, the story is real. I have been blessed to watch the grace of God capture thousands of hearts as Joe opens the altars at camps and churches after speaking God's story. Now you will also experience the genius of grace as you read this written tale both raw and refreshing, and take this profound journey. So get ready for an experience that will also move you to IRREVOCABLE hope".

Jeff Kennedy, Lead Pastor Southgate Church, South Bend, IN

"A gem that will be hard to put down, as John Mark Wright struggles through life, like many he does not realize that God is working behind the scenes in his life. A story of abundant grace that God has for us all."

William Pittman – Managing Director, Local Hotel Adventures Kiawah Island

"Joe Phillips has written a story that will remind you of God's irrevocable call on your life. It shares disappointment, heartbreak, and defeat—it also shares that the restoration of God's call is waiting for those who need it. It's never too late to return to your Father's house."

Dr. Ken Draughon, Superintendent, Alabama Ministry Network of AG

"Insightful, inspiring, interesting and illustrative is the book, *Irrevocable*. Joe has captured what it means to be called by God! His storytelling inspires the reader to meet the challenges of life."

Bob Sandler, Superintendent, South Carolina Ministry Network

"Joe Phillips is the right person to write on the irrevocable call of God. I have personally experienced how he has a passion for encouraging people to walk in their own unique call of God. Joe embodies in his own life experience what it is to face many challenges and remain steadfast. In his book, Joe delivers a realistic and authentic story. Most start ministry with hopes, dreams, and high expectations—and the toils of life happen. Through the pages you will discover that no hurt, rejection, or adversity can cancel God's favor on you. No person or trouble can bury your calling. God's grace breaks through all barriers.

Whether you are walking in your call or just starting out, I strongly encourage you to read *Irrevocable* because you will gain valuable nuggets of insight that you will be able to apply to your own ministry call."

Rev. Guadalupe Sanchez, Lead Pastor, Sunnyvale
International Church, Sunnyvale, CA

"This book is written by a man with trials, challenges, scars, and tribulation clothed with triumph and inspiration; Founded upon a life lived with people—not above or below. Joe has inspired and changed lives by speaking to others—not above or below. This work and life personify a man of Faith and Faithfulness. I treasure my friendship with Joe and his family and value all that they have done and continue to do to help many."

Gardner A. Altman Jr., Attorney, NC and District of
Columbia Bar Association, Chapel Hill, NC

"Joe Phillips, my mentor and dear friend for fifty years, has once again listened to the tugging of the Holy Spirit and poured his heart into a project which captures the Grace of God. Through a riveting storyline, Joe brilliantly exposes the heartaches and hardships of how John Mark Wright, a powerful and anointed preacher, walks away from his life's calling to escape the hurts, the infidelities, and the betrayals caused mainly by his parishioners. Pastor John wanders aimlessly for the next thirty years without hope or purpose. BUT GOD. . . . never stopped interceding on behalf of Pastor John. God never took His Watchful Eye off this man. Through a series of divine appointments, God rescues Pastor John from his tormenting despairs, forgives him, and restores him by His Grace."

Penny Romine, Retired English Teacher

"Where is God and what does one do . . . When surrender doesn't lead to success, when vows have exceptions, when the soul is bruised so badly that it never takes its original shape again? What one does in response to these events and seasons is important, but who God is and what He does in them is primary and has the last say. This book will be like a roaring fire, hot soup, and a secure place to hope again, for all who have experienced hard winters of the soul."

John Wood, Founding Pastor Christ Chapel, Macon, GA

"Joe Phillips is more than a minister. He's a gifted entertainer, author, motivator, mentor to many, a husband, father, grandfather, and friend. This piece of creative artwork will provoke you to pause, meditate and graduate from where you currently are in life to another level of glory. As you read, you'll be riveted by the words penned on each page and receive a personal message that you are unconditionally and irrevocably loved by God. Enjoy."

Nikita Koloff "the Russian Nightmare", minister and
retired World Champion Professional Wrestler

"This book portrays "real life" experiences of HOPE and REDEMPTION. What God ordains, He will accomplish. We can run away from God and fall hopelessly into the pit of shame and despair, but God never gives up or lets go of our sin-stained souls. This book reveals the resilience of God."

Linda Campbell, Successful Realtor for 45 years –
multiple years #1 in Columbus, GA market

IRREVOCABLE

Joe Phillips

Romans 11:29

ARROWS & STONES

OTHER BOOKS BY THE AUTHOR

3 for 30 - Three-word devotionals for thirty days.

Fundamentals in Family Life - Funny stories and practical principals offering families hope.

The Third Chair - Implementing lasting change.

To learn more visit
www.joephillipsministries.com

This novel is dedicated to every wanderer who has been beaten to a pulp by circumstances, yet somehow found their way back to life and purpose.

PART 1

CHAPTER ONE

I t was four o'clock in the morning. John Mark Wright slumped in his chair. In front of him, on a crappy table used at a cheap hotel, sat four objects. Legal pad. Pen. Loaded nine-millimeter Glock. Half-empty glass of Hennessy cognac.

John Mark was fifty-five years old, but had high mileage—he looked not a day under sixty-eight. Underneath his sparse one-room apartment was a smoky jazz club. This particular night was the weekly all-night spoken word open mic. He was used to the muffled noise. Stopped noticing long ago. He fidgeted with the pen. He pulled the pad towards him. Then he played with the pistol. Took a long drag from the cognac. Repeated this pattern. He contemplated his life as one does during such existential crises. It seemed like a blur to John Mark. There were a couple of good memories that fought to bring a smile to the corners of his mouth. But the bad memories quickly overtook them like a thick fog. Good ones were out-manned by bad ones twelve to one. So much potential. So much loss. John Mark took another gulp of the cognac. He fiddled with the pen. Another memory came to mind.

At exactly 4:13 a.m., his cheap cell phone rang, rattling the wooden table in front of him. He nearly jumped out of his skin. On the second ring, he picked it up and shouted, "Hello!... Wait, slow down. What the heck are you talking about?... Oh, no. When? How?"

The semi-hysterical voice on the other end was Sandra, his baby sister, and only sibling. He hadn't seen her in years but faithfully spoke to her once or twice a year—briefly. She had just informed him that their mother had unexpectedly died. She had fallen on the way to the restroom and hit her head. Before she lost consciousness, she'd had the presence of mind to call her daughter. Sandra immediately called the attendant on call who rushed to the room and found her dead. After 911, the next call was to her big brother.

Promising to come soon, John Mark took his hands off the objects and then put his face into those hands and wept for a good long time. This night belonged in the bad memory column.

CHAPTER TWO

Thirty Years Earlier

Reverend John Mark Wright looked crisp in his clergy collar, standing in front of around a hundred worshippers at St. John's Church in the sleepy little town of Smithville, Georgia. Actually, he looked crisp *and* cool. His formal collar was juxtaposed with his faded jeans. His flock seemed infused with joy. No one was sleeping. John Mark's conversational, passionate, and sincere style captivated them.

He smoothly and vulnerably closed his homily. "That's it. I don't know if you want that, but I can tell you that your pastor certainly does. Peace. Peace that passes all understanding." A few "amens" rang out. "While Cheryl plays something softly, join me here, and let's ask the Prince of Peace to give us some of it. He has a lot of it."

Almost half the people in the congregation stood and walked down to the front as Cheryl, a matronly forty-year-old, gently played "Softly and Tenderly Jesus is Calling." Grown men knelt at one of the three altar benches in the sanctuary as brilliant light streamed through old stained glass. A young mother clutched the hand of her ten-year-old son. People were standing, kneeling, crying. Some comforted each other and softly prayed. It was a scene. But though it was a scene that Rev. Wright often experienced, he felt continually in awe of such responses to his ministry.

As a small boy, his mother had taken John Mark and his sister to a neighborhood church with a vibrant Sunday School program for children. The siblings had loved it. The stories captured John Mark's imagination. The plump ladies serving red Kool-Aid in Dixie cups exuded love and care. There were flannel boards with whales and swords, sea waves and boats, and all manner of mysterious items.

It was during a summer Vacation Bible School that John Mark Wright had experienced his "calling." He had been listening to the story of Zacchaeus, and in his heart, he'd known something. There hadn't been a voice or a vision. Like the water balloons that had fallen on him earlier that day during the games portion of the programming, something had dropped and then exploded in his little spirit. He had just known that he was supposed to dedicate his life to telling the stories from that mysterious book.

John Mark would tell his mother about it later that day. He matter-of-factly reported, "I am going to be a preacher." She had heard similar declarations before: "I'm going to be a cowboy," "fireman," "toy store boss," and "baseball guy," to name a few. This one seemed different to her, however. It rang a little differently in her ear and her mind would often meditate its meaning.

In the lobby of St. John's, a man walked up to the pastor. This individual looked more like he was at a country club than a house of worship. He was wearing lime-colored golfing pants and a pinkish polo. The golfer offered his hand. "Pastor, you have no idea what these services have meant to me. My buddies think it must be my secret weapon."

John Mark shook the hand. "How so?"

"I've been blistering them on the links. They bust my chops telling me that 'getting religion just ain't fair.' Hey, I felt prompted by something to hand this to you. No strings attached. Use it for the church if you like. I'd rather you use it for you and the missus."

John Mark accepted an envelope and graciously thanked the man for his thoughtfulness.

"Great service," the golfer continued. "One day, I'm going to get you out there on those fairways."

Laughing, Pastor John Mark replied, "Well, you may be right." He promised to contemplate a golf match soon.

Layla Wright was standing in the lobby holding court with three ladies. She looked like a ray of sunshine. She was the same age as John Mark, twenty-six. She was wearing a yellow sundress. Her hair was glistening in the sun. She saw her husband and excused herself from the sweet ladies around her. Walking up to the pastor she said, "Nice job, Rev."

John Mark gave her a formal handshake and a very pastoral, "Why thank you, dear Sister. I am so glad you enjoyed the worship experience." He winked at her, and they both chuckled as he bent over and kissed her on the cheek. Looking left and right like he had been paid off by a mafia boss instead of blessed by a congregant, he whispered the news. "You know that weekend we've been putting off because of our . . . "—here he cleared his throat—"budgetary constraints?"

"M-hmm."

"Well, Sister, the Lord gives us our heart's desire. Like the kid with the loaves and fish, there are leftovers. I think probably enough for the dress I saw you looking at."

He showed her the envelope and let her peek at the contents inside.

Layla was used to stretching a dollar and rarely had anything left for herself at the end of the month. This was a tantalizing windfall. Her heart seemed to race a little as her eyes widened.

"How? Who?" She was impressed and curious.

John Mark said, "The Lord hath provided." Then, leaning in, he added, "Actually, that golfer who started coming a couple of months ago. He said to use it for me and the missus or the church. But he emphasized us, and since the church is doing so well. . . ."

Looking at the time on her phone, Layla interrupted and said, "Let's go home, Pastor."

CHAPTER THREE

The young couple had been married three years. They didn't go the traditional route in ministry: college or university, seminary, internship at a hot church, associate position (often youth ministry), and then, after the boxes were checked, submitting resumes to churches, culling out the goats and only interviewing with the sheep—the good ones.

Instead, John Mark Wright finished college early and cut seminary short by doubling up on classes and cramming in the maximum effort every twenty-four hours. He skipped internship and took a position at the first little church that had an opening. His whole life up to that point had been about trust. He considered all factors but didn't over-analyze them. His life philosophy was simple. *God called me to tell the great story, and He will take care of the details.*

From the first day on the job, it was as if John Mark had the ministry "Midas touch." He was handsome—and honestly, that hurt nothing. People were more attracted to his effect—his heart—than anything else. He had a natural ease with all manner of folk. He exuded care and concern.

John Mark's grandfather, Cless, loved John Mark seemingly above all the other grands. He saw the brightness of his intellect from an early age.

John Mark had an uncanny ability to exercise inductive and deductive reasoning to solve little problems and riddles around Grandpa's house.

When John Mark expressed interest in law, he held out hope that they might finally have a lawyer in the family. He got extra excited when John Mark joined the debate team. "You know, this family could use a good lawyer," he said on many occasions to anyone who would listen.

When he announced his "calling" to full-time vocational ministry, Grandpa could scarcely hide his disappointment. That reaction did not go unnoticed by the sharp-minded grandson.

After a little time to process the situation, Grandpa came by to have a chat with the boy. He said, "John Mark, I have been thinking about it." John braced himself.

"If you want to be a preacher, I 'spect you'll be a good 'un, because you've got a winning way with people." John Mark started believing those words immediately, and they manifested in his life—especially in that tiny, disheveled congregation. His pastoral care didn't exude from a manual or a seminary class. His peers would say things in ministry or pray a certain way because they knew they were supposed to do so. After all, it had been on page eighty-seven of the manual. John Mark's ministry was more instinctual. It was natural—even supernatural.

His seminary buddies ragged on him by calling him "Gamaliel" from the New Testament—a reference that pegged him as a theologian's theologian. "You're the Michael Jordan of ministry," they would say. John Mark didn't let these comments go to his head. He was too concerned about telling as many people as possible the stories which had changed his life.

CHAPTER FOUR

The couple walked into their simple, two-bedroom home. It was well-kept and organized. The furnishings were sparse. They ate on a coffee table for about a year until they could buy a decent, actual table at a thrift store. They picked off one necessity at a time, like runners in a race, passing competitors one by one. John Mark tossed his bag on the couch, and they walked into the kitchen.

Life was good for this young ministry couple. There was a tangible joy in their days. They bickered on occasion, as all couples do. But there wasn't much drama, and John Mark Wright was just fine with that.

They'd met in high school. Life was good now, but it certainly hadn't always been that way for Layla. She had been raised by divorced parents. It hadn't been an amicable divorce. They'd used her like a bargaining chip. Each parent had threatened to hold her hostage if they didn't get their way. She'd lived out of an overnight bag, splitting time between them for most of her childhood.

Because of this difficulty, she hadn't been dialed in with religion like her husband had. It hadn't been practical to be part of any kind of church because of the judge's custody edict, which split her time down the middle. She'd had friends, but not the type of friends who would cultivate relationships, sharing experiences day in and day out. To compound her angst, she was an only child. The only love modeled for her was a vindictive sort with complex motivations and manipulations.

When Layla met a handsome, young man with a calm demeanor at school, she developed a quick and deep attraction to him. He was an oasis for her, tranquility in her storm. John Mark was a veteran when it came to the church. He always seemed to be centered. He invited her to the high school homecoming dance. It went well, and then he invited her to his church. She had only been to any kind of church twice in the past: once for a wedding and once for a christening.

Layla liked John Mark's church. More serenity. The lines were straighter. She didn't feel the wormy motivations or the weird manipulations there. She'd liked it, and she'd begun to love the boy who'd invited her.

They'd continued their love story through college and had married right before seminary. Before proposing, John Mark Wright had been very clear about his life goals. He communicated directly about the ministry and the kind of life it entailed. He told Layla on many occasions that ministers got the "portion of the Levites," and that had to be enough.

After hearing this two or three times, she'd finally summoned the courage to say, "Hey, Church Boy, I don't really know what that means." His explanation was plain, like his life philosophy. He told her that all the tribes of Israel got land and stuff. However, the tribe of Levi got their portion, which consisted of the priesthood and whatever came from that simple service. No land. Not much stuff.

Layla had considered the implications of that, but her love for the boy had overpowered any desire for stuff. "If that's enough for you, John Mark, it's enough for me. Because you are enough for me."

They sealed the deal and set off to change the world. And it was working.

Layla pulled the oven door open. "You did it again, Preacher. Had them on the edge of their seats."

Falsely pious, John Mark responded, "We've talked about this, Sister Layla. I'm just a humble country boy. If anything good happened, it did not come from me." He laughed.

"Regardless, John Mark, it was the Good Lord that used you, but it absolutely was you He used."

He pulled up a chair and sat with his stomach at its back and his elbows resting on the top. "Something smells good. What are you going to dazzle us with today, Chef Layla?"

Now Layla was being playfully pious. "Actually, Pastor Wright, this roast won't be finished for another forty-five minutes. While it does its thing, I was wondering if you might have time to counsel one of your congregants?"

She sauntered across the kitchen, grabbed his clergy collar, and nearly pulled him off his chair. As they moved down the narrow hallway, John Mark grinned widely and said, "Please allow me to check my calendar and see if I may be of assistance to you . . . Yep, I'm free." They shut the bedroom door, giggling and laughing.

CHAPTER FIVE

The couple arrived early for their "urgent" appointment to meet with the presiding bishop. When his secretary called, it was evident that the meeting was not optional.

The office was clean but a little dated. John Mark and Layla were seated in the lobby. Mary, the receptionist, was pleasant and went about her tasks with professional joyfulness. The little couple was pleasant in return, even as the young pastor tried to suppress the evidence of his nerves.

They had never been in the bishop's office. To be summoned here usually meant bad things. John Mark had heard of some legendary dressings-down. Self-confident and fully actualized ministers had been reduced to tears as the wise, old bishop "explained the way of the Lord more perfectly."

John Mark wasn't looking for that kind of infamous legacy. He took a mental inventory of what possible infraction could have landed him on this couch. He knew he wasn't perfect, but he was coming up blank for any potential cause of this meeting.

Layla had been through too many minefields for this to register, even as a blip, on her radar screen. The family dynamic Layla had been raised with produced regular mini-melodramas. She seemed content thumbing through a couple of old denominational magazines, and John Mark was impressed with her calm demeanor. Maybe he was subtly annoyed that she wasn't freaking out a little.

Mary broke his awkward introspection. "Reverend and Mrs. Wright, the bishop does apologize for your wait. There has been an unexpected crisis that is demanding his full attention. It wasn't on our calendar. With four hundred churches to oversee, I suppose we should schedule a crisis—or maybe three of them—per week." She laughed. John Mark tried to do the same. "He should be ready soon," Mary concluded.

"I understand. It's just fine. Maybe you could give me a hint about why I'm here? I don't mind waiting, but I admit that I'm a bit nervous." Layla raised an eyebrow as John Mark continued. "When the bishop calls you in, you kinda feel like you're going to the principal's office."

Mary leaned forward, smiling broadly. "Yes. I get that a lot."

The office door abruptly opened. An older gentleman emerged through it. He was wearing his ministry collar, a crisp pair of dress pants, and sensible—though out of fashion—shoes. The old preacher filled up the doorframe. Bishop Floyd Johnson boomed, "John Mark! Layla! So sorry to keep you waiting. Half of my job is racing from one fire to the other. Come on in, John Mark, with my apologies. Layla, I'll have him back to you before you know it." Layla smiled her dazzling smile at the kind, old bishop.

The bishop was beloved in the denomination. He was a large man with an ample core. He loved the church, and he loved fellowship—especially fellowship that involved the *coup de grâce* of fellowship, the "covered dish." He never appeared as an out-of-control glutton. He just really enjoyed his life, his food, and his calling. Although jolly, the bishop's mind and resolve were both sharp. With a shock of white hair on top of his head, there was something almost statesman-like about him.

Bishop Johnson put his arm around young Pastor John Mark. "Take a seat, Pastor Wright."

The office was nice—smartly furnished. The desk had several mounds of papers and files. They were neatly arranged, but the volume of them made an impression on the young pastor. The bishop grabbed a legal pad and pen and moved from behind the desk to a seat facing John Mark, who nervously offered, "It's good to see you, Bishop."

"Well, it is always great to see you, my friend, and your sweet wife. I know you're wondering why you've been called to the principal's office."

John Mark said, "Do you have the office bugged?"

"Ha! Hey, that's not a bad idea. Actually, my comment is inspired by occupational awareness."

John Mark laughed. "Well, I am a bit curious. Maybe a little more than a bit."

"I'm not trying to go all cloak-and-dagger on you, but I couldn't say anything before it was officially announced."

John Mark adjusted in his chair at this cryptic response.

"As you can see, we have to douse the flames around here from time to time. I need a fireman to help me put out a big wildfire."

"Okay," John Mark offered, now even more curious.

"How rude of me—John Mark, would you like a coffee or some water?"

No. John Mark just wanted this mystery to get solved, and quickly, so he could get back to Smithville and back to work.

"John Mark, I would like to recruit you to help me. I want you to be a part of a 'last days' ladder company,' so to speak."

"'Last days' ladder company," he repeated. "I like that. How can I possibly help?"

"You can help me indeed. John Mark, you've done a remarkable job in Smithville. That little church was a dead end to some fine ministers. A real preacher-eater. But somehow, under your leadership, there is new life. I had Mary triple-check the numbers. Everything is up. The attendance. The giving. The morale. Through it all, you have maintained a humble posture, and I appreciate that."

"That's very kind of you, Bishop Johnson."

"Just stating the facts," Johnson said. "I like to deal with the truth around here. Look, I have an assignment I'd like you and Layla to pray about together."

"Okay."

"John Mark, you're familiar with St. Mark's Church in Columbia?"

"Of course. Great, historical house of worship. It's iconic."

Johnson sighed. "More like ironic. The keyword you just spoke is *historic*, John Mark. Its best days seem to be behind it. It used to have such a huge footprint in Cumberland County. Now, its influence is minimal at best." Bishop took a long sip of his coffee. "John Mark, you're sure I can't get you something?"

"I'm sure, but thank you."

"I need you to go in and put your touch on that dry, old place. I want to send you there to bring some life to it. Whatever you're doing in Smithville, I need you to do it in Columbia, and the sooner, the better."

The assignment stunned John Mark. If his contemporaries had been sitting in his chair, they would have already been updating social media and calling their proud mothers. But John Mark felt a little sick to his stomach. He hadn't entered into this role thinking of it as a profession. There had never been any imaginary ladder to ascend. He thought of what he did as a calling.

John Mark's mission statement, values, and core strategies all melded into a simple premise. He wanted to tell people good news and love them ferociously. When he visited a family in the emergency room and stayed with them all night waiting for word about their loved one, he wasn't doing it to score points. He visited people, wrote notes, dedicated businesses, mourned with the mourners, and celebrated with the celebrators. He didn't do it to tally marks in some imaginary leger. He didn't think things like, "If I can get twelve more visits, three more hot sermons, and a top committee chair, I can advance to the next level."

This was not a video game to John Mark, and he sat there in his precious bishop's office, truly torn. If John Mark was anything, he was loyal. Loyal to his wife. Loyal to family and friends. Loyal to his calling. Now, his loyalty was effectively on a train track, and it was being pulled in two directions. His nature was to submit and be loyal to Bishop Johnson. He also felt a tenacious loyalty to the church into which he had poured years of his life. Before his introspection became too conspicuous, he gave a response to the offer. "We will certainly pray with you. But you're kinda like the white smoke from the Vatican, aren't you? Doesn't whatever you say go?"

"Ha! Maybe. But Pastor, I don't like ruling with an iron fist. The older I get, the more I realize that moving a family is a great strain and, in some cases, a big sacrifice. I would love for you to go, but only if you and Layla are completely on board with the whole program. I need your buy-in."

The bishop took another long pull on his coffee while he assessed John Mark's demeanor. Bishop Johnson had always been gifted in discerning things. He could walk into a tense conference room and almost immediately figure out where the trouble was sitting, as well as in which chair the solution was sitting.

He continued. "Some in the Conference want to close St. Mark's because it has tremendous real estate value. I am not so inclined. We aren't running an investment bank, for heaven's sake!" At that, he loudly slapped the arm of his leather chair.

The slap seemed to reverberate throughout the entire office. It was unusually loud and the abruptness of it truly startled John Mark. The whack seemed to come completely out of the blue. Now, John was longing for some discernment. This was something the bishop was obviously passionate about, but was it right for his wife and his own life?

"I want to see the shine back on that church. I don't want to be stuck in the mud of history. I'm not longing for 'the good old days.' I am longing for the good, bright future! I know it is there. I know it is possible!"

All Pastor John Mark could say was, "Refreshing perspective, Bishop."

CHAPTER SIX

Three men sat in a large conference room at one end of a powerful table. There were supposed to be five men in the room. Two members were not in attendance. They were not invited. The official board of St. Mark's was in session. Later, there would be some kind of administrative adjustment to the minutes regarding the other two men, in order to put the group into compliance with church bylaws.

Bill Nella presided as chairman and called the meeting to order. Bill was successful in the community, and he was proud of his accomplishments. He bragged about being a "self-made success" and used the "pulling myself up by my bootstraps" metaphor with anyone who would listen. He translated his business acumen to all facets of life, especially the local church. In Bill's mind, the functionality of the church didn't need to be subcontracted to any denomination or professional clergy. Who knew better how to run the show than the people in the community—in the marketplace? Who better to do so from that pool than the ultra-successful? If he could run a couple of multi-million-dollar businesses, he certainly had no problem with the budget and personnel of this beautiful, old church. Some people liked to go boating, skiing, hunting, and fishing. Of course, Bill did all of that, but his real hobby, his favorite hobby, was running stuff. Tonight, he was running a meeting.

Stan Overton, mid-forties, sat to Bill's right. Stan was a moderately successful accountant, but his main utility on this board was his ability to say "yes." Put all the "yes men" together in a line-up, and Stan would stand out as one of the most prolific. He could give a preemptive yes. He could provide a regular yes. Or, on some occasions, he could provide a long, pregnant pause before dramatically offering his yes. It seemed to be his mission statement. He existed to go along.

Larry Poser, a fifty-three-year-old businessman who lived up to his name, sat to Bill's left. His business in Cumberland County was floundering, but no one knew it. Larry presented all the trappings of success. He drove a luxury sedan and belonged to the best country club. Only the club's management knew that he struggled mightily to find the money for the dues each year. His clothes were the best, and his kids went to the best private schools. It was all a house of cards. Larry wasn't a "yes-man" like Stan. He would posture, postulate and try to exert his intellect. The "yes" didn't roll off his tongue. But because being in the know and circling with the rich and powerful was so important to him, he always found his way back to Going Along Boulevard. He didn't want to lose his spot at the club, the council, or the committee. He was blustery but could be easily controlled by a strategist like Bill.

"This meeting is called to order, having an official quorum," Bill coolly said.

Jim Graham and Chuck Woods hadn't made this meeting. After all, it is hard to make a meeting when you don't know anything about it.

Jim was an environmental contractor. He often joked that he was just a landscaper with better equipment. He was in his forties and had energy for days. His projects included beautifying interstate exit ramps—he called them "gateway projects." Universities used him for design work. He made a decent living but had to keep feeding the beast. He turned most of his profits back into the business and tried to satisfy a business partner who was difficult to satisfy. Through all of it, Jim maintained two things: a killer tan and a joyful spirit.

Jim had never been notified of this meeting.

Chuck Woods, in his mid-sixties, was a truly humble man. His humility was a part of the folklore of the church—and even of the community. That shared knowledge, when presented to Chuck, made him quite uncomfortable. He owned a simple sign company. He made a living, but not much more; the giant billboard conglomerates were taking over the industry.

Chuck was a hold-out who hearkened back to another time. He had broad shoulders that were rock-hard from decades of using post-hole diggers. He didn't adorn many billboards with signs these days. But if you needed a beautifully-crafted sign in front of your business, you could count on him to make it. He was an artist. He honored his work because he was an honorable man. He'd lived through the glory days of St. Mark's. Chuck was a key leader in some of their historic growth and outreach—a gentle giant who attracted all kinds of people. The wealthy loved him as well as the poor. The elderly, the children, the religious, and the irreligious loved Chuck Woods. Pastors loved him because he loved and advocated for them. Even when Chuck had voted "no" to something, the pastor had known he was loved by him.

Chuck had never been notified of this meeting.

"Gentlemen, we only have one agenda item tonight," Bill began. Stan was itching to shout "yes," but there was nothing to rubber-stamp yet.

He always had his finger on the yes trigger. "The pastoral vacancy is one of concern for all of us."

"I agree," Larry confirmed. "Did you find out more about protocol from the denomination?"

Stan said, "They've always just placed a candidate before the congregation for us to ratify. Right, Bill?"

Bill answered, "That is my understanding. The bylaws are a little murky. I think we can guide the process a little better than in times past."

"How so?" asked Larry.

"Well, I've been pretty successful getting around zoning ordinances in business with some—shall we say—creative language." Stan and Larry had heard this "bootstrap" theme many times over the years. "If I can do that, I think we can protect protocol, bylaws, and history with a little creativity."

"How do you recommend we do that?" Larry wanted to know.

Bill answered, "Well, I suppose we need to ask this question: what kind of pastor do we want at St. Mark's?"

"Good question," said Stan. "What do you think?"

"I'm just your humble servant, fellas. I want to hear what *you* think."

"Not a boring guy," Larry offered. "I don't want to take a nap every week. If I wanted to do that, I'd stay at home and not worry about putting on pants." He was pleased with this witty contribution.

"I'm with Larry on that," said Stan. "Someone good at the stuff. You know, the public stuff. Funerals, weddings, baby dedications, community prayer things—all that."

"Do we want a strong leader?" asked Bill.

"Yes-Man-Stan" was quick with the trigger here, thinking that he had the desired response. "Yes!"

Larry asked, "Doesn't that go without saying? Of course we don't want a weak leader."

"Let's think this through, gentlemen," replied Bill. "If effective leadership is sitting at this beautiful conference table already, why shouldn't that be a strength we pursue?" Bill's question hung in the air as the other two board members straightened their backs a little at the suggestion that they had leadership prowess.

"Never actually thought about it like that," Larry said.

"What do you think, Bill?" Stan wanted to know.

"Well," Bill said, "we can't do all that 'stuff' you talked about, right, Stan? I don't want to give a thirty-minute speech. Or conduct funerals and weddings."

"Me either," agreed Stan.

"I'm better serving behind the scenes," continued Bill. "I can—that is, *we* can—guide the ship just fine. The three of us—the five of us, I mean. We can handle the budget, personnel, and the big decisions."

"So what are we asking the denomination to send us?" Larry inquired.

"Let's get a thoroughly adequate shepherd," Bill replied. He was already prepared for this moment. He rarely went into any meeting without his own agenda up his sleeve and was truly deft at not showing his cards.

The members present enthusiastically nodded their heads at this response.

Bill continued, "Let's find a man who will marry us, bury us, dedicate us, give us the homilies, and smile in the lobby. We run the organization from behind the scenes, and he is the spokesperson out front."

"He or she," amended Larry.

"She?" asked Stan.

"You know, there are women clergy in the clergy club. What if they send us one of them?"

Bill's answer was simple, but not soft. "We want a shepherd that is not a leader, per se, but let's be honest, guys—a woman? Really? We aren't looking for that level of passivity."

All three men burst into laughter as if they had just heard an absolutely hilarious bit in the hottest comedy club and not misogynistic tripe.

"Then, for the record, it is agreed. We will put in our order at head-quarters and see what they send us. The old man running the thing is tricky to read, and I'm usually good at reading people," Bill concluded. "I think I can persuade him, but we'll see."

Larry wondered aloud, "Well, our track record hasn't been too good here. The other preachers wanted to run stuff—in the wrong direction—and we haven't been able to keep them here."

"Or find good ones," Stan added.

"Leave it to me," Bill suggested. "If you boys trust me."

"Hey," asked Larry, "what about Chuck and Jim?"

"They'll play ball. Let me work my magic."

That was that. Bill Nella planned to work his magic with the bishop, the board, and—eventually—the congregation.

CHAPTER SEVEN

"I am committed to this, John Mark," Bishop Johnson said. "I am prepared to put my money where my mouth is. I control the purse strings, more or less, and I am prepared to invest in this if it is the last thing I do on this earth before they carry my pine box up the hill."

John Mark noted sincerity in his words, gestures, and countenance. If there was something John Mark appreciated as much as loyalty, it was sincerity.

"If I were a betting man," the bishop continued, "I would put my money on the horse right here across from me. You would get a significant bump in salary, as well as a few other perks."

John Mark replied, "I know this sounds cliché, but honestly, all I want is the will of God in our lives and in the lives of both churches. We have invested blood, sweat, and tears in Smithville . . . and a lot of love. We have a genuine love affair going on with the congregation, and that's a lot more meaningful than a salary bump."

The bishop abruptly leaned forward and gave a loud clap. John Mark was startled again, even if he didn't show it. "That attitude right there! That attitude is why I would bet on you, my young racehorse! I need to let you go, but I want to pray for you, for both churches, and for Layla.

Let's get her in here and read her in. I didn't want to worry her with this if you weren't interested. Let's pray together—if you're okay with that."

"Absolutely. We're always up for prayer. Thank you, Bishop."

Bishop Johnson stood his big body up and shook John Mark's hand with his big hand. His heart was bigger than his body or his position. He walked out the door to collect and escort the young pastor's wife into the office for the news and for a prayer.

On the drive home, it was quiet between the couple. Layla wasn't sure about the pastoral protocol with something like this. She wanted to give space for the conversation to breathe a little. She sat on a hundred questions, just waiting.

John Mark just drove, looking straight ahead with a serious, contemplative expression. He didn't seem the least bit likely to break the ice and share his thoughts and feelings.

Finally, there came a tipping point in the silence, and Layla detonated a question explosion. "What about Smithville? We worked so hard, and doesn't that bother you? Do you even know anybody in Columbia? Not that I care that much, but do you get a pay raise? Is this our lot in life—never putting down roots?"

She barely took a breath between questions. Some men may have been annoyed at such a plethora of inquiries. This innocent, intelligent, and unbridled curiosity is what had made him fall in love with Layla. So the more she peppered him with questions, the bigger he smiled.

The smile actually annoyed her. "Take this seriously, John Mark! This is our lives we're talking about."

"Honey, I'm just processing," he responded gently. "It's a very serious matter. Now, rewind and ask me one question at a time. I probably don't have the answers, but I'll do my best."

"Thank you. I want to be included in your processing."

The rest of the drive, John Mark did his best to answer questions. Many he did not know, as he predicted. Even so, he at least tried his best to answer her, one question at a time.

CHAPTER EIGHT

Three months later, John Mark found himself on the deck of a beautiful lake house. He normally felt at ease with all manner of people. He could have a comfortable conversation with a homeless man and, five minutes later, engage in meaningful dialogue with a successful businesswoman. He interacted with children and the elderly.

Three men were seated with John Mark, enjoying the soft jazz music playing from a hidden speaker in the landscaping. For some reason, he was unsettled. He felt on his heels. The back-and-forth dialogue seemed forced. He couldn't put his finger on the reason or the reasons for his discomfort.

On the upper part of the deck, the wives enjoyed the weather and the conversation. They adjusted the table décor, laughed a little, made small talk, and sipped their wine—except for Layla. She enjoyed some iced tea.

Bill Nella pushed past the small talk and got down to business. "Well, gentlemen, this is Reverend John Mark Wright. Do you go by John Mark or John?"

"Yes," said the pastor, and gave a nervous laugh. "I answer to both."

"Well, which do you prefer?" asked Bill.

"I am fond of both," was the reply.

"Very well. I'll just call you Reverend Wright. So I go by Bill in case you have forgotten my name."

"No, sir," John Mark said, "I have not forgotten your name. Reverend Wright is too formal. Just call me John Mark and make it simple."

"Okay. Would you like some wine, Reverend?"

"No, thank you, I'm fine with the Diet Coke."

Bill asked if he was a "religious objector." John Mark still felt a little uncomfortable and divulged more information than he usually would. The whole gathering seemed awkward.

"Not so much religion. More like history. My family has a long pattern of addiction, and I never wanted to repeat that. But that's just me. You guys go ahead."

Bill looked puzzled. "The full board is looking forward to more formally meeting with you. We are three of the board members who also serve as representatives of the personnel committee. Two of our board and committee members, Jim Graham and Chuck Woods, couldn't make it."

Stan Overton and Larry Poser looked at each other with wry smiles and simultaneously sipped their wine glasses. Somehow, the email informing Jim and Chuck about this meet-and-greet had been sabotaged into the spam folder—or some similar excuse to be fabricated later.

"These two upstanding gentlemen are Stan Overton and Larry Poser—two very successful men in our community and pillars in the church."

John Mark leaned forward and shook hands with the men. "Very nice to meet you, gentlemen. Looking forward to working together."

Larry smiled and asked, "The bishop is high on you. He filled us in on your resume and all of that professional stuff. But I'd like to know what made you want to move all the way over here to the big city of Columbia."

"The short answer is that the bishop asked me to accept the position. All of you have met Bishop Johnson—I assume all of you, not just Bill. He's a pretty persuasive guy."

"Sounds a little like you may not have wanted to move," Stan said.

"Oh no," said John Mark. "Don't get me wrong. The preachers in this Conference have known all about St. Mark's since we were young bucks. It's a great honor even to be considered." He reflected for a moment and continued, "To be completely honest. . . ."

Bill Nella cut him off. "Sounds like a 'but' is coming."

"No buts. We just have some serious momentum in Smithville. The Apostle Paul had to slay some wild beasts in Ephesus, and I feel like we had slain most of our wild beasts there. God is doing some amazing things in that little community."

Stan continued the interview. Bishop Johnson had already made the decision. These men felt like they had the power to override it and to not ratify what had already been put into motion. "Well, you've driven around town and walked our campus. What are you feeling in your gut about this place?"

"I believe that God wants to do some great things here."

Larry objected to the young preacher. "'Do some things'? What does that mean? Are you implying that God has not already done great things here?"

"Not at all," John Mark pushed back. "He's always at work. Maybe I should have said that I believe He wants to do 'even greater things,' as Jesus talked about in John 14. Redeem lost and broken things. Lost people. Broken marriages and families. Deliver addicted people. You know, some of the New Testament stuff."

Bill looked over his drink towards the men with a profoundly skeptical expression.

"Yuck," Stan said. "That's not really what St. Mark's emphasizes. We sort of recruit the put-together, not the broken. The successful and not the addicted. Not trying to be rude."

John Mark was a little stunned but held steady. "With respect, that is exactly what St. Mark's should be doing. In fact, it is the very DNA of the place. I learned about this church in our required history and polity classes. I'm not trying to go back to the 'good old days' of outhouses and no A/C. But . . . "

Larry cut him off. "This preacher has lots of buts."

"You got me. Okay, but . . . " After a brief, reflective pause, John Mark continued, "If the history of St. Mark's were a passport, it would be stamped with renewal." He mimicked a stamping motion after that word, and each word that followed. "Refreshing." Stamp. "Fruitfulness." Stamp. "Revival." Stamp. "Revival in its most organic definition." Stamp. "This church had a supernatural origin and has had an unbelievable impact." The juxtaposition of Reverend Wright's enthusiasm and their skepticism was stark. "What you have done over the years to improve lives with social programs and in the area of social justice is astounding."

Stan could only offer two words. "I suppose."

"People change." John Mark took a drink of his Diet Coke. "Institutions change. Mission statements change. God does not change."

CHAPTER NINE

T ina Nella was the forty-five-year-old, doting wife of Bill. She had been described as "a little mousy," which was an apt description. She had now turned her attention to the pastor's wife.

"Ladies, in case you haven't officially met her, this is Layla. It is so wonderful to spend a little time with you. Thank you for coming to our little congregation. It seems like we've had the hardest time the past few years finding or keeping good pastors."

Marie Overton was also in her forties, but would never offer the exact number willingly. She had an opinion about everything, even if it was an uninformed one. "Well, finding them is one thing. Keeping them? That's another. These preachers come in with a lot of ideas, bluster, and 'vision.'" She made some quotation marks with her hands. "Then we turn around, and they are gone!"

Sheryl Poser was the prize of Larry. She was a little older and a little more highbrow. "Out of vision. Burned out. Wiped out. Rusted out. Flamed out. Spun out . . . "

Marie interrupted. "We get it. Out is out any way you frame it."

Tina tried to get things back on track. "Ladies! Please. Let's not scare this sweet little thing *out* the back door before they even get started. For heaven's sake." She grabbed Layla good-naturedly by the arm. "You're not getting away from us! Ha. It took too long to find y'all."

Sheryl said, "Besides if we have to hear our husbands in hushed, late-night conversations like middle-school girls for one more week, we're gonna pull out our hair."

Three ladies giggled. One tried but couldn't.

Marie furthered their plight. "Well now, that's the truth. They act more like senators making backroom deals for their constituents than board members of a church."

Almost under her breath, Sheryl added, "More like CIA operatives straight out of a Clancy novel."

Noticing Layla's expressionless non-participation in the banter, Marie said, "Honey, we're glad to have you."

Layla didn't want to seem aloof, so she smiled. "I don't know what to say. John Mark has told me what an incredible place this is." She looked down at her tea. "Frankly, I love all the stores. I'm like the middle-school kid you talked about. On Christmas Eve, at that. Smithville only had one big box place and a half-empty mall."

Across the vast dock, Bill Nella turned his attention away from the menfolk. He sipped his drink and let his eyes linger on the lovely Layla. Her yellow sundress sort of glowed and fell just so around her shoulders. The view over his right shoulder was vastly more attractive to Bill than the gorgeous lake over his left shoulder.

His lewd perusal lingered a long time, but he regained his focus on the current audience in front of him—before it became too apparent that he had taken a little mental field trip.

CHAPTER TEN

J ohn Mark Wright was in the pulpit of St. Mark's. The church was more ornate by far than anything he was accustomed to seeing. The lights were small chandeliers suspended from an enormous ceiling and spread throughout the vast sanctuary. The windows were costly stained-glass, imported a few lifetimes ago from Austria. Light from the beautiful windows and dangling chandeliers illuminated stately oak pews with thick burgundy cushions.

The congregation was enthralled with every word coming from their new shepherd. He wore well-worn yet clean and crisp jeans with a black, long-sleeved shirt and a white clergy collar. The church wasn't familiar with this kind of ecclesiastical uniform. Previous pastors had been more formal and buttoned up. Most wore stately clerical robes. The congregation, by and large, didn't seem to mind this shift.

They were captivated with his sincerity more than anything. Reverend Wright didn't have a booming baritone voice, nor did he utilize oratorical tools that others employed. He spoke deeply from the heart but not from the hip. He was always prepared and took his responsibility to feed the flock extremely seriously. However, his speaking was seasoned with a natural and effective sense of humor.

There was a guarded sense of enthusiasm in the house of the Lord. The congregation had ridden this ride before, but this felt different. Organic. Sincere. Real. The room lightly buzzed with excitement.

"Layla and I are just so excited to be here. We really loved our people in Smithville so much. But week by week, we are growing in our love for all of you." Music backed up the pastor's words. But it wasn't just any music. This music came from professional and talented musicians. John Mark usually heard music from dedicated laypeople. Some of them had a bit of talent, but not many were trained musicians. His new people responded with smiles. It was hard for folks to be too guarded or cynical when someone expressed genuine love toward them.

Every week, there seemed to be more people in front of John Mark. Word was getting out that something was happening in the old, stuffy church. Curious gawkers came in to check it out. Some of the sightseers never left.

In the church world, success was measured primarily by two "n's": nickels and noses. By that matrix, St. Mark's was becoming a rousing success under this new administration. The offerings went up each week. The strange part about that increase was that money was rarely addressed. There had been one teaching about the importance of stewardship, but it certainly hadn't been a month-long emphasis on the topic.

John Mark used a variety of creative methods to communicate truth. They weren't just the typical oratorical techniques such as voice inflection or dramatic pauses. The congregation might come one week to find their pastor in a full-blown firefighter's uniform, complete with a ladder and ax.

"The Bible says something about rescuing others from the fire," John Mark would bellow. How better to show people the importance of rescue than with a rescuer's wardrobe?

Another week, he simulated a weatherman in a storm accompanied by an assistant holding a fan and sprinkling water into it, thus spraying the preacher. He stood there in his rain slicker with severe storm sound effects in the background. In his way of thinking, that was an effective way to teach about Jesus calming the storm.

No one in the church would ever forget the day he spoke about the "root of bitterness." He had assistants bring in various-sized roots and went through them each, until coming to the last one. The final root was brought in by two strong men and was the size of a huge oak branch, balanced on their shoulders. The massive root was covered with dirt that resisted efforts to be knocked free.

As the men stood onstage, the pastor became more animated. "Now, if you don't take care of these roots," he said, pointing to the various smaller-sized roots on the platform, "you will have to have an outside force to dig up this bad boy. Before it gets to that point, reach down into your heart and pull out that young root. Quick. Don't let it so get so big that you have to hire equipment to help you."

He had different names for the roots. "Finger and thumb." "Full pull." "Glove required." "Elbow grease." "Chain needed." He called the last one the "Laughs-at-your chain root."

A couple of old saints grumbled that they felt like they were in children's church. They didn't particularly like the object lessons. The gripers were in the extreme minority. The majority responded to it positively, as evidenced by how many people were inviting their friends.

However, included within that extreme minority were individuals that could cause disruption—and not a small amount of it. One might say that their root was daily growing into "chain needed" or even worse. Their grumbles included words like "circus," "laughingstock," "spectacle," and "bizarre."

CHAPTER ELEVEN

J ohn Mark and Layla stood in the middle of a substantial kitchen with boxes of various sizes shoved against the walls. The center of the kitchen was a makeshift dance floor. Blasting from an old record player was Ja'Net DuBois, singing the famous song that she co-wrote with Jeff Barry: "Movin' On Up." She and the choir belted out:

"Now we're up in the big leagues
Gettin' our turn at bat
As long as we live
It's you and me, baby
There ain't nothin' wrong with that." [1]

John Mark Wright had told Bishop Johnson that the perks of moving to St. Mark's were not that important to him. However, at this moment, as he danced with his beautiful wife in a parsonage grander than anything he'd imagined he would ever have, he had to admit to himself that he was enjoying the perks.

He especially enjoyed them because Layla did. He saw the countenance of his loving wife light up. More appreciated than the material possession of having a beautiful home was the stability it offered. Roots. Constancy. Such stability had been elusive in her childhood—for most

---

1 Ja'Net Dubois and Jeff Barry. "The Jeffersons (Movin' on Up)," *Television's Greatest Hits: 70's and 80's*, 1975.

of her life; it had been absent. Layla liked the idea of the white picket fence and planting gardens. A real anchor. No overnight bag and shuttling between homes.

She took her head off of John Mark's chest. "Did we move on up?"

John Mark answered playfully and matter-of-factly, "Yep. And we are getting our turn at bat!"

The couple swayed together and softly sang, "It's you and me, baby; there ain't nothing wrong with that."

The music ended, and they looked deeply into each other's eyes. "John Mark, this place is beautiful."

"Not bad."

"Not bad?! Look at the place. I have a real kitchen. We have room to raise a family one day." She pulled him closer.

John Mark said, "Well, it is nice, but you know we didn't come here just to move on up, right?"

"Of course. But it's not a badge of honor to stay broke and small, right?" asked Layla.

"Layla, you're right. I don't happen to have the gift of voluntary poverty if that's what you mean. Nor do I have the spiritual gifts of martyrdom, nor celibacy."

"I'm well aware," said Layla. The couple heartily laughed.

"I'm glad you like this place, honey. I could live in a lean-to shanty as long as I'm with you," John Mark said. Layla assured him that this big, beautiful parsonage in the suburbs would be just fine by her.

Everything seemed to be an upgrade in their lives. Layla had better stores to do her shopping. Even the grocery stores were elegant to her.

John Mark had a hearty increase in salary. More poignantly, there was an upgrade in the influence of his ministry.

An old man back in Smithville had made a habit of saying in board meetings, "Pastor, there is no problem in this church that money can't fix." John Mark had respectfully taken umbrage with the statement. "Earl, all the money in the world can't buy the healing of diseases with no cure," John Mark would argue.

The old man would always offer refutation. "That's the exception. Name another problem this church has. Need a roof? Parking lot? A staff member? Money solves all of that."

Back and forth they would go. "If we were divisive—thank God we aren't—you can't buy unity, Earl."

Now, in Columbia, John Mark often felt like calling Earl to express his conviction and regret for arguing with him. Having endowments was a complete novelty to him. Those endowments, combined with the bank balance, gave margin to launch programs that he had only previously dreamed about starting.

A new feeding program was provided for the underserved in the community. He staffed a tutoring program for at-risk children. He paid college kids to come alongside and help disadvantaged youth with math and history, simultaneously teaching them life skills. Reverend Wright established what he called "The Justice League," a program that enlightened the community about the angst of racism. Each week, a different lecturer would present. The lineup included a former federal prisoner wrongly accused and exonerated with DNA evidence. He gave lots of melancholy statistics. The program may have had a cornball name, but it was very effective.

White people at St. Mark's started to get "woke" about systemic racism, the historical plight of Black and Brown brothers and sisters. From The Justice League, other programs were established—"spin-offs." There was a deliberate effort to reach out to prisoners. The church became vocal about housing and zoning issues that affected minorities.

John Mark had a financial margin to help—truly help—unwed mothers and their children. He boomed from the pulpit, "The American Church cannot march against abortions without offering solutions. This program is one solution." People offered hearty "amens" and presented healthy checks. It just made sense to them.

Though John Mark was rarely animated, this pregnancy issue was a personal soapbox of his. He would thunder, "How can we say that abortion is barbaric and then put a scarlet letter on these frightened mothers? At this church, we have no scarlet letters. In fact, sins that are as dark as scarlet are washed as white as snow by these mammas' heavenly Father!"

"Amens" in the pews. Checks in the plates. The preacher was riding a wave of momentum. He had change in his pockets, so to speak. Leverage. He was savvy enough to use that change to affect change. Change was long overdue.

CHAPTER TWELVE

It was a crisp autumn Sunday in Georgia, and all the converging circumstances lined up for a perfect Sabbath. The Chamber of Commerce couldn't have asked for better weather. By eleven o'clock, it was 61 degrees, the perfect temperature to wear a light sweater and pair of boots to kick fallen leaves. Sunshine lit up the sanctuary. The Georgia Bulldogs won a nail-biter in overtime against the hated Auburn Tigers. Folks were in a good mood.

These exigent circumstances pushed people into worshipping. They just felt like it. There were many people at church on this particular Sunday. The old-timers remembered a time, way back in their childhoods, when the balcony had been used. That had been the true heyday of St. Mark's—exciting times. For the last two decades, the balcony had been used to store excess chairs, dusty Christmas decorations, and other junk.

Today, John Mark wasn't on a soapbox. He was on his regular box of unpacking a God who loved people ferociously—a God who wanted a relationship with them.

"We don't claim to have it all together," he conversationally spoke into a handheld microphone. "But I want to. Paul said, 'Not that I have already attained, or am already perfected; but I press on, that I may lay hold of that for which Christ Jesus has also laid hold of me.'"

So often, people look at their watches during the homily portion of services. Or they make grocery lists, play games on their phones, catch up on sleep, or just daydream. That never seemed to happen during a John Mark Wright homily.

"Now, 'lay hold' means to seize or grasp. I want to grasp the thing Jesus has grasped for me.' There was a "Wow, Pastor" from the congregation. Others offered grunted words of affirmation.

"I want to speak to the men. Are you like me? Do you want to be a better husband? Press in. Want to be a better father? Press in. Do you want to be a better grandfather? Seize it. Businessman? How about just a better man? Press on. Press in. Join me here, and let's tell Him that we want this. For His glory."

The talented musicians played softly. The gifted singers sang quietly. The pastor walked from man to man and put his hand on shoulders. He offered quiet prayers for every single person.

It was a moving scene. The church wasn't used to these types of responses. Emotional responses were compartmentalized to football games and the occasional funeral. There seemed to be an invisible presence of something—something like the feeling of love—in the room.

Bill Nella, Stan Overton, and Larry Poser were moved in a profoundly different way. They were moved to the back of the sanctuary. They moved into an unholy huddle, and they were not talking about football.

"How long are we going to put up with this?" asked Larry.

"Yeah, it's getting out of hand, Bill," Stan chimed in. He studied Bill's face just to make sure that he hadn't offended him.

Bill answered, "I've tried to be patient, boys. Y'all are right. But I've got some ideas."

Jim Graham was volunteering as a sound booth assistant and saw the alliance forming in the back corner. He slipped out of the booth and tapped Chuck Wood on the shoulder. He nodded his head in the direction of the three, and then both joined the huddle.

"You boys didn't tell me about our board meeting," Chuck said.

"No official meeting," Stan said over the soft music coming from the stage.

"Looks serious," Jim offered.

Larry snorted. "We have a serious situation, I think." Stan always hoped to be conciliatory, but Larry liked to flex.

Jim asked, "What's the situation?"

"Do you need to ask? Look around," Bill answered.

"Looks more glorious than serious," Chuck said. "More people than I can remember—and more energy too."

"Looks like a d . . ." Bill began and stopped. He took a breath. "It looks like an ecclesiastical circus. Frankly, I am embarrassed and flummoxed that you two don't seem to be."

"If flummoxed means happy, count me in," Jim said.

Larry raised his voice a little, saying, "This is not a joke, Jim. I don't even know half of these people. It's getting out of control."

Chuck asked evenly, "Is this the serious situation, Larry? That you aren't in control?"

Bill answered before Larry could form a refutation to the accusation. "We were elected to be in control. That's our job—and, yes, we do take it seriously, even if you don't."

"With respect, Bill, we weren't elected to run anything. First of all, it's not ours to run—or his," Chuck said, motioning to the pastor walking from man to man praying for them. "This is the Lord's church, and He has entrusted us to be His servants. That means we serve the Lord and people—not lord over them."

"He's right," Jim said before they could unleash their furious rebuttal. "And look at all the people coming that we can serve. Our job is to grab a towel and imitate Jesus."

Bill glared. "Doesn't the good book say something about leaders not acquiescing to wait tables?"

Stan and Larry nodded their heads as if they were familiar with that ancient passage. They assuredly were not.

Jim, however, was familiar with it. "Bill, you read it right. Just didn't interpret it right. The apostles said that. They were preaching—their highest call to service. We don't preach. He makes signs, I cut grass, and you guys do other non-preaching stuff."

Larry had to flex. "I'm not grabbing a towel and wiping tables. I am going to do what I was elected to do: protect this organization!"

"Yeah, I saw a hole in the wall downstairs near the children's department!" Stan interjected. "A hole! And I saw cigarette butts in the parking lot. It's getting out of control."

Jim stepped to the three. "Thank God it is! It has been dead as a hammer for too long. Holes in the wall mean kids are coming and playing. Butts in the parking lot and butts in the seats mean something. It means that the city is coming here. Isn't that who we're supposed to reach?"

Pastor Wright was walking from man to man, his eyes closed the majority of the time. He was in the spiritual sweet spot and oblivious to carnal happenings like the insurrection brewing in the back.

Almost no one noticed Bill Nella close the distance with Jim Graham. *Almost* no one. Bill's young son, Rob, had come into the sanctuary with a couple of his buddies. The service was always long over by now. Not today, though. The little boy looked around and saw his dad. The look on his dad's face stopped the eleven-year-old in his tracks. He had seen it before, but not often. It was scary. His oblivious buddies ran to their parents, some of whom were crying tears of joy. It was a curious scene.

Pastor Wright didn't see Bill poke his finger into the chest of Jim Graham and wave his hands like someone out of control. Eleven-year-old Rob saw it. He turned his little head to the stained glass. He studied the ancient faces of men with flowing, white beards and elaborate head coverings. He tried to pronounce the word at the bottom of the glass. He couldn't quite say "Pharisee," and it would be years before he knew what the word even meant.

CHAPTER THIRTEEN

It was just another monthly board meeting. The meetings were usually low-key, somewhat boring but not altogether unpleasant. The agenda consisted of the usual parliamentary stuff. Call to order. Reading of the previous minutes. Old business. New business. Financials.

In the short time John Mark had been there, he'd tried to liven it up with testimonials from people in the congregation. Chuck and Jim actually loved them. He also had a dinner catered. He explained that the purpose of breaking bread was fellowship and relationship.

Stan was concerned about the financial toll the catering decision would put on the congregational budget. He was always worried about his constituents. In truth, there were accounts all over the place designated for this and that. Memorials. Pet projects. They had enough money to cater the city's lunch a couple of times a year.

This particular meeting started as normally as the rest. Quick meal. Call to order. At the new business portion, the train began to shake before eventually coming off of the tracks.

Bill Nella addressed the group first. "We didn't want to have this conversation, but alas, we must. Reverend Wright, we don't like the direction that you are taking our church. . . ."

Chuck Wood interrupted. "What direction is that, Bill? Up?"

"Well," Bill answered, "that is a matter of interpretation."

Jim Graham chimed in. "No, seriously, Bill—interpret it for us. Which direction do you object to? The astronomical increase in donations or the exponential rise in our attendance?"

Larry Poser startled everybody as he pounded the table, red-faced. "But at what cost?!" He had a talent for going from zero to sixty in two seconds. This particular escalation was faster than the others in his resume.

Chuck coolly responded, "What does it cost us, Larry?"

Stan saw a chance to offer a meaningful answer. "Our identity. We are becoming the laughingstock of Columbia."

Reverend Wright inserted himself into the discussion. He was the pastor, after all. Sincerely and not argumentatively, he asked, "Who is laughing at us? And what are they laughing about?"

Bill Nella was duly appointed to restore order, to control the narrative. "That is not our primary concern, though it is troubling. Our focus should be on what St. Mark's is all about and why we are becoming so far removed from that."

"Just what are we about, per se?" Jim pushed back.

Bill answered, "We are about balance. Family. Tradition. Safe worship in our community."

John Mark said, "Gentlemen, I am taken aback. I thought things were moving in a great direction."

"They are!" Chuck exclaimed.

John Mark continued, "I am trying to understand your concerns. What is happening at St. Mark's that makes the community feel unsafe?"

Bill began his answer in an even-keeled manner but became more and more agitated the longer he spoke. "Frankly, Reverend Wright, your charismatic tendencies. I mean, really, do we need a fireman outfit to convey a sermon point? Since I have been here, we have never had an 'altar call' or whatever those things are called. That is, until you came."

Larry and Stan nodded their heads in agreement.

Bill continued. "You seem not to be able to present one simple homily without parading people with problems in front of gawking eyes."

Larry continued to tremble moderately. "There are so many new people that we don't even know in our own church."

Stan bemoaned, "And nobody knows who we are, either."

Cool-headed Chuck spoke up. "Ah ha. I think we've landed on the problem. Boys, first of all, I thought it was God's church. Second, are you concerned about losing St. Mark's identity or losing your own?"

Bill offered his own brand of logic, "Well, isn't it the same thing? We've been carrying the water around here for years and years. We are not about to let this young, hyperactive preacher screw up what we have worked at for so long."

John Mark said, "Bill, people are coming. Families are reuniting. Addicts are getting clean. Sometimes it got messy around Jesus, and sometimes, when Jesus does stuff . . ."

Now it was Bill's turn to pound the table. "Young man, you are not Jesus Christ!" He took a breath to regain his composure. He was trembling. "I know you must be aware of that. This board is officially, on the record, admonishing you to tone down your rhetoric. . . ."

At this point, Jim Graham wasn't going to pound the table but did have a keen interest in pounding any of the three antagonistic board members. He could always ask God to forgive him later. "Or what? This guy doesn't speak for everyone on the board, Pastor John Mark."

"I beg to differ," Bill said. "Last time I checked, I am still the chairman. As I was saying, tone it down, Reverend. Back to more traditional services. Lose the props. Lose the gimmicks. For God's sake, lose the altar call prayer times."

"I hear you. I'm not sure I can be authentic to my call by changing my entire approach now. I tried to explain my ministry philosophy to you when you hired me."

Louder now, Bill said, "We didn't hire you! You were force-fed to us by Bishop Johnson."

"I'm sorry you have that perspective," John Mark said.

"Since we're laying all our cards on the table," Bill continued, "in addition to the previous admonition, you need to control that trollop of a wife. . . ."

At that moment, Jim Graham came as close to smacking someone in the mouth in a church building as he ever had. He did have some experience with such activity on his job sites. It was a vocational hazard. To feel this way in the church was entirely inappropriate for him. "You're out of line, Bill!"

John Mark's composure and patience evaporated. "Yeah. You are way out of line. Do you know what a trollop is?"

Bill fired back, "I absolutely know what it means, but I'm not out of line. *You* are out of line. We didn't ask the Conference to send us some kind of weird faith healer." At this point, Bill was trembling and didn't even try to fake being in control. "I suppose I can't help you if you're too dense to comprehend that we are telling you to . . ."

Reverend John Mark Wright jumped to his feet. There was a collective gasp. The group didn't know what was about to happen. John Mark had occasionally talked about his scraps on the basketball court in his sermon illustrations. He certainly had the physique to handle himself in any fair confrontation—especially with these guys. He may not have won all of his fights, but the other guys had always known that they'd been in one.

Bill ordered him, "Sit down!"

"You know what, Bill? I am not going to sit down. There is one person on this earth that is allowed to speak to me the way you just did. I call him Dad. I certainly do not call you that."

"I said to sit down!"

John Mark gathered his computer and backpack. "I don't believe I will sit down, Bill. You're welcome to try to make me. I will excuse myself before I say or do something that I will regret. Tonight, I have been called dense, and my wife has been called worse. This has not been a very productive meeting, gentlemen. Good evening."

CHAPTER FOURTEEN

The Reverend had a difficult time sleeping that night. In fact, sleep would be elusive for many nights. Layla knew something was wrong. She had never seen John Mark like this. He tried to put on a brave face and act like it was "nothing, really," but she knew that something was off.

Sunday was coming. Sunday was always coming, and the pressure of it was just a professional hazard in ministry. Along with the regular sermon prep pressure, now an accompanying pressure presented itself. John Mark had to make a decision.

He had to decide if he would heed the board's advice—after all, they were the fiduciary head of the corporation—or if he would continue serving within his basic DNA in the manner that had been working up until the last board meeting. He didn't even know if "dialing it back" was in the realm of possibility. He believed in the biblical mandate to submit to authorities. He also had a ferocious belief in the New Testament reality of encountering God.

It seemed to John Mark that these three board members wanted him to water down the message. In fact, it seemed like they just wanted to hire a chaplain. Someone who would give a lovely homily, bury folks, marry folks, dedicate babies, and just be an overall nice guy. Vanilla. Milk toast. A Milk Dud without the milk.

There were only a couple of times in life that John Mark had felt this stuck. Once, he had tried to decide whether to continue his education in the medical profession. He had dreamed of being a pediatrician and helping people. Or would he go to seminary? Another time, he had deliberated about whether marrying Layla at such a young age was wise.

During these quandaries, John Mark had sought counsel from wise men and women. He was inclined to think that there was safety in such counsel. The more, the better. Trusted mentors were hard to come by, but he was fortunate to have had a handful of such souls in his life.

During this inner conflict, now, it struck John Mark that he should call the mentor that had started all of this—Bishop Johnson. He vowed to call first thing in the morning and hoped for a good night's sleep. He slept better than anticipated and stuck with his plan to call the wise elder.

"Bishop Johnson's office," announced Mary, the bubbly secretary, over the phone.

"Hi. This is John Mark Wright from St. Mark's. Is the bishop available?"

"Good to hear from you. Let me check, Pastor Wright. I'm sure that he would love to talk to you."

Bishop Johnson's booming voice greeted John Mark in no time. "My man! You've done it again." John Mark squirmed a little in discomfort.

"Well, I may have really done it." He nervously laughed.

"Do tell, John Mark," said the bishop.

John Mark continued, "I thought things were going great. . . ."

Bishop interrupted. "That's the word I get here. All of the ways to measure effectiveness are tracking in the right direction. All of the numbers are exceeding my biggest hopes."

"Well, Bishop, that's the confusing part. I got blindsided in the last meeting by the church board."

"I want to know all of the details, John Mark—and don't be cute about it. I mean, don't be a nice guy. Tell me exactly what is going on." The energetic old man was genuinely concerned. He had navigated troubled church waters many times. He had seen firsthand what could happen if trouble was handled incorrectly or in an untimely fashion. He had too much riding on his rising star to let him fight alone.

"I feel like I got ambushed. We've been having great meetings. The board seemed enthusiastic—especially Chuck and Jim. But in the last meeting, well, the train didn't skid off the tracks—it exploded, seemingly out of nowhere."

Bishop Johnson urged him to go on.

"The main three—Stan, Bill, and Larry—said they didn't like the direction the church was going. Said it was unsafe. Losing identity. Said I was a charismatic charlatan, basically. Even called my wife a trollop."

Bishop Johnson sighed. "Stan, Bill, and Larry. Sounds like The Three Stooges. I've always said that 'quality is meeting expectations'—that's not original with me, John Mark. What exactly did they expect from you?"

"That's just it. I don't know. I told them exactly what I was and what my ministry philosophy was in the interview," John Mark expressed. "There was no bait-and-switch."

"You're doggone right there wasn't! I told them too, John Mark. Told them exactly what the formula seemed to be with you regarding the other turnarounds."

"Bishop, it just seems to me like they wanted to hire a chaplain. Marry, bury, dedicate babies, and give short speeches that aren't too boring. They didn't expect to hire a leader that has an evangelistic heart."

The bishop boomed, "Exactly right! That is an astute way of putting it. A chaplain! I suspect that what you just had the guts to describe to me is what has been happening to all of the other preachers we send there that have been put into that wood grinder." He continued, "Let me get one thing straight. The 'interview' you described wasn't really an interview. It was a courtesy. It was a confirming conference. I don't wish to flex my muscles, but I am the one charged with the awesome responsibility of placing ministers in these cities, towns, and hamlets."

John Mark said, "Well, that's what I've always understood. These guys say they've lost their identity. That the growth we're experiencing is some kind of mystical, weird, charismatic happening."

"Well, this isn't my first rodeo. I've cleaned up a lot of horse manure in rodeos. I know the constitution and bylaws of that church. I am intimately acquainted with them. There is a clause specifically outlining how the Bishop of the Conference can remove obstinate members of the board."

John Mark groaned. "I wouldn't want to do anything that would damage the church body. So much good momentum has occurred."

The bishop was long in the tooth, and the wisdom that accompanied his age kicked in now. There was a reason John Mark looked at him as a mentor. This special wisdom gear had helped guide the young pastor on more than one occasion.

"John Mark, you know what I read today in my quiet time?" Before there was an awkward response from the young preacher, he continued.

"I read about Peter facing down the religious thugs in the Book of Acts, chapter five. I'm sure you're familiar with that chapter—you may have even preached it before."

John Mark grunted in acknowledgment.

Bishop Johnson continued. "The bullies were busting Peter's balloons for preaching about Jesus, and his answer to the jerks is our answer as well. Remember what it was?"

"Yes sir. We ought to obey God rather than men."

John Mark could hear the bishop pound the table. "Bingo! Obey God and not men. We submit to authority even when the authority is not submitted to God. But when the authority circumvents the express plan of God—especially related to the Gospel and the Bride (referring to the church)—then we obey God instead of these—these—these circumventors."

John Mark processed the old bishop's advice and honestly allowed himself to begin to feel a modicum of hope, and a gentle—albeit small—bit of peace.

Bishop Johnson continued his coaching session. "John Mark, I have another fire to work on in the conference room, but let me leave you with this. When I take action—and I will take action at the first available opportunity—there will be a little fallout. A little bit of blow-back."

"I understand, Bishop. I don't really want you to fight my battles. . . ."

Softly now, Bishop Johnson said, "John Mark, the battle is the Lord's, but I get paid to lead His charge in these kinds of fights.'

"I defer to your wisdom."

"John Mark," the bishop said, "when you have to remove a tumor from a patient, there often has to be some good tissue that is extracted with it. You would never take good tissue from a person under normal circumstances. However, for the sake of the patient—to give the patient a future—sometimes the good tissue is caught up in the process. Remember that when you start seeing a few good people get swept up in this drama. Got to go just now, but know that I am praying for you, and I am proud of you. I couldn't have hoped for a better job than what you are doing. My love to Layla."

That was that. John Mark had received nuggets of truth from a trusted mentor, and he had a simple plan: keep being John Mark Wright. He believed the key to knowing who you were was to know who you weren't. He'd recently spoken to his ever-swelling congregation about that very subject: "John the Baptist knew who he was because he knew who he wasn't. He said, 'I'm not that prophet. I'm not Elijah. I'm not Jesus. I am just a voice crying in the wilderness.'"

John Mark knew he wasn't a chaplain. He wasn't a mystical faith healer. He was just a simple pastor who had a passion for loading the train bound for heaven with as many people as possible.

For the next few Sundays, he kept being who he was and did not try to be who he wasn't. He suspended the monthly board meetings for two months. The constitution allowed that privilege. Other than the board room, every single thing remained the same. Things kept trending in an upward trajectory.

CHAPTER FIFTEEN

The letter was official and certified. John Mark opened it and became curious—concerned, even. It was from the bishop's office. Rather generic. It wasn't even signed, which struck him as odd in light of the certified mail status. It announced that Bishop Johnson required his presence at the office the following week. It made it seem like it was not optional.

John Mark had been heeding the advice previously given from that office for two months and regularly reported the progress. He'd sent "praise reports" to the office. He could never have had a better supporter than Bishop Johnson.

That's what made this notification so challenging to understand. The tone was different. One might even say it was diametrically opposite of the tone of their most recent conversation.

John Mark told Layla he had a meeting next week at headquarters—probably about regular church stuff. He didn't wish to concern her. He surmised that this was something official Bishop Johnson wanted to have in the record as he became involved in the internal tension at St. Mark's. That momentary logic helped him not go a little bit crazy wondering why such a formal summons had been mailed to him.

The day of the meeting had arrived. The drive was about three hours. John Mark put some jazz on in the car to help him relax and not over-think. He knew Bishop Johnson had John Mark's best interests at heart. Always.

John Mark entered the building and approached Mary cheerfully. Her effervescent personality was always refreshing. Today, she was fresh out of bubbles. She tried to force a smile. "Good morning, Pastor Wright. The acting Bishop will be right with you."

"Acting Bishop?"

Mary bit her upper lip. She didn't respond verbally. Just a non-verbal shaking of her head which communicated, *Don't ask*, as she busied herself with urgent administrative tasks.

John Mark sat on the same leather couch he'd sat on when the St. Mark's project had first been initiated. His head was spinning. He kept repeating to himself, "Acting Bishop?" Mary wouldn't make eye contact. John Mark felt compassion, but for what he didn't even know. "Acting Bishop?" There was a pronounced sadness attached to Mary, like a dryer sheet clinging to a pair of jeans. He fought the awkwardness for about forty-five minutes. The certified letter had stated it was imperative that he not be late. He'd gotten up pretty early to be on that couch ten minutes before nine. It must not have been a priority for the "Acting Bishop" to honor the appointment.

Finally, just before ten, the door opened, and Interim Bishop Anthony Bailey stepped through it. Bailey was forty-eight and nearly bald. He kept his hair long on the sides, but the top of his head looked like an airstrip. His long, pointed nose accentuated an overall odd appearance.

The effect of the man transcended his physical appearance. John Mark's first impression, never having spoken to the man in his life, was that this was a person of deep and devious insecurities. The first words the Acting Bishop uttered confirmed John Mark's instinct.

"Come in, Wright. I will see you now."

John Mark thought, *Wright? Not 'Pastor.' Not 'Reverend Wright.' Not 'John' or 'John Mark.'"* He had never met this person; however, this person felt the license to simply call him by his last name. An hour late at that. No apology. No explanation. No graciousness. John Mark's "spidey senses" were on high alert.

As Reverend Wright walked to the door, he glanced at Mary. She banged at a keyboard and quickly shot a glance back. Tears were in her eyes. *My God, this feels like a wake*, John thought as he entered Bishop Johnson's office.

John Mark was struck at the office décor. All of Bishop Johnson's knickknacks were in a box—stuff he had collected from around the world on various missionary expeditions. Figurines of wood and ivory from Africa. Missing were the various wooden tea containers from the Amazon. Pictures with natives and buttoned-up leaders from Europe. All of it was just . . . gone. Several framed photographs of the Acting Bishop with people who must have been famous had replaced the bishop's objects. John Mark didn't recognize any of them.

The pictures on the walls were in boxes. Nothing had replaced them. Well, maybe the faded paint could be considered a replacement. The whole scene made John Mark's skin crawl.

"I'm Anthony Bailey." The man's eyes were cold.

"Where is Bishop Johnson? Mary was very mysterious about it." Bailey was about business. John Mark could be all business, too.

"She better be cryptic. She gets paid for her discretion and knows she will be unemployed and unemployable if she violates confidentiality," Bailey said matter-of-factly. Business.

"Reverend Bailey, what is going on here? Where is my Bishop?"

"The bishop is unable to be here today. I am working in his stead and also in his authority. Now, take a seat," Bailey ordered.

John Mark knew he was required to love everybody on every list, including his list of enemies. This dude was quickly and firmly establishing himself as someone on that enemy list.

John Mark attempted to get on the high ground. He calmly asked, "How may I be of service to you, Reverend Bailey?"

"Well, I'm glad to hear you phrase the question like that. Let's get right to the point," Bailey said.

John Mark suppressed the thought, *Right to the point after an inexplicable hour-long wait!* He decided on the high ground.

"I do need something from you, Wright," Acting Bishop Bailey continued.

"Oh?" asked John Mark.

"Let me be blunt. I am actually going to need you to be prepared to move in one month. We are reassigning you."

John Mark felt sick. He glanced at the trash can, wondering if he might need to employ it for an unholy assignment. His head was spinning. "Reassign me? We are just now getting our wings in Columbia. St. Mark's is moving in the right direction. It's rolling."

Bailey shuffled some papers behind his desk in an inattentive manner. He refused eye contact. Not so much from intimidation, but instead in a rude, terse manner. "Well, I'm going to need you to roll somewhere else."

Pastor Wright dug in. "I'm going to need to talk to Bishop Johnson about this. He was quite adamant in his vision for St. Mark's when he just recently gave us that assignment."

"That will not be possible," Bailey said. He had a disturbing smile as he spoke. He involuntarily reached into a desk drawer and brought out a pack of long skinny cigarettes. He grabbed a lighter and then remembered he was in a conference. And he was in a building.

"I drove three hours, and I'm happy to wait. Let's just tell Mary to get me on his book. Today would be preferable, since I'm already here."

Bailey shot back, "As I said, that's impossible." He sat back in his chair and fiddled with the smokes. Smiling, he said, "I am not supposed to tell people this news...."

John Mark thought he was acting like a teenager who snuck a look at the homecoming queen vote total before anyone else knew.

Realizing he was smiling a little too much, the Acting Bishop feigned some sympathy to finish the sentence. "Bishop Johnson suffered an aneurysm."

"No! An aneurysm?! Is he alright?" John Mark didn't have to fake sympathy. He genuinely loved the man.

"Only God knows with certainty. I spoke with his neurologist. It doesn't look good for the old fella."

The stifled glee in this skinny little wannabe made John Mark look at the trash can again. "So, you are the . . . ?"

Acting Bishop finished the thought. "I'm the new sheriff in town, as they say. If Johnson . . ." *There the guy goes again with throwing out last names without earning the right.* ". . . is unable to fulfill his term, the national committee has charged me as Interim Bishop, subject to full conference ratification in May. Just a formality."

John Mark wanted to ratify that the titles "Interim" and "Acting" were equally appalling for this guy, but not as much as "Permanent." He asked, "Why the urgency for us to move now? And where do you want us to move?"

"Second question first. We are sending you to Clary. There is a small work there that we think would be perfect for you."

"Clary!" John Mark protested. "Clary? There's nothing in Clary but cows and corn. Do more than ten people actually live there?"

Ignoring John Mark's question, Interim Bishop Bailey continued. "Now for your first question. There's an urgency because of some circumstances that have recently been brought to light at St. Mark's in Columbia."

John Mark retorted, "You've gotta be kidding me. What circumstances?"

"The church is discouraged about the direction your leadership is taking it."

"Reverend Bailey . . ."

"I think you would be safe to call me Bishop Bailey," the Reverend interrupted.

"Interim Bishop Bailey, the push-back comes from a tiny handful of disgruntled men who believe it's their duty to run the church instead of following a duly appointed pastor. That's the source of the discouragement. Everyone seems thrilled, with the exception of three loud voices."

"Be that as it may, you'll be leaving in thirty days," Bailey coolly replied. "Keep perspective, Wright. I have found it is good medicine to experience some humility early in one's ministerial career."

John Mark thought that this dude must have skipped all of his humility classes.

"And if I refuse?" John Mark asked.

"If you refuse? Well, I hadn't considered that." He rubbed his chin. In reality, he had considered it and even rehearsed the line that was coming next. "Well, Wright, there are several other denominations in which you might investigate membership. Some that may fit your style better. However, if you wish to stay in this tribe, I highly recommend that you do not cross me."

"Well, Reverend Bailey, then I guess that's that."

"Again, Bishop Bailey to you."

"Perhaps I will wait until the real Bishop's body is cold before I bequeath the honor of that title to you. Thanks for the coffee." John Mark's voice trailed off. "Oh, that's right, you kept me waiting for an hour and offered me zero hospitality. Enjoy the rest of your day, Bailey.'

With that, John Mark Wright walked out of the office. So much for him taking the high road.

CHAPTER SIXTEEN

When John Mark was a boy, he loved to watch professional wrestling matches. Some of the bouts pitted several wrestlers against one another in a steel cage. One side would prevail and leave one man to fight many men. That was precisely the metaphor for what was happening on the car ride home.

John Mark was wrestling with deep disappointment at the prospect of leaving yet another congregation in which he had developed loving connections. Just when he slammed that into the turnbuckle, another opponent crawled into his emotional ring. He wrestled with having to tell Layla. She had indeed blossomed in this growing and progressive congregation. She was truly coming into her own.

He wrestled with the thing many men wrestle with continually—his identity as a competitor. The thought that Stan, Bill, and Larry would win their little power struggle was nearly more than John Mark could take. They were so vile. So smug. They had so much vitriol. How could that ever be rewarded, in this life or the next one? He imagined their next meeting smoking victory cigars.

John Mark wrestled with his own depth of emotion at what he considered the elephant in the room. Bishop Johnson, a treasured and valued mentor and minister for decades, seemed to have been cast aside and dismissed. It was deeply saddening. Strangers just seemed to step over his body on the way to the bus stop to collect the next person to fill his shoes—to fill his *unfillable* shoes. What committee approves something like that? Who casually decides to keep such an urgent matter away from the constituency? This wasn't the result of just one man. Who was complicit in this injustice? John Mark wondered about these questions.

But the fiercest wrestling opponent on the drive home was "the dog." John Mark continually strove to keep his "dog," his "carnal nature," under control. He had worked on it since high school. In school, he'd had a reputation of being a "good church boy," but with a "take no prisoners" mentality. If he got smacked in the face on the basketball court, he wouldn't respond immediately, like a hothead. He would pick his moment, and at some point, during the remainder of the game, he would aggressively let that opponent know that his smack in the mouth was neither appropriate nor forgotten. This information was administered generally through a reciprocal smack in the mouth—or something even more potent.

This guy. Bailey. He wanted to smack him in the mouth, to say the least. He was wrestling with a big temptation to hate the guy. That was the "carnal dog," as John Mark referred to it. The "Spirit side" of him knew that forgiveness was the high ground. He wasn't in the mood to climb up to the high ground. Being in this hateful valley felt too good at the moment. John Mark preached, "Make sure that your carnal side—the dog—is the size of a Chihuahua so you can snap the leash in the direction you know you should be heading. Control that Chihuahua. If you don't control it, then it will grow to be the size of a Rottweiler." Right now,

John Mark's carnal side was about the size of a Neapolitan Mastiff. He wasn't walking the dog. The dog was walking him.

Pulling into the beautiful parsonage, John Mark knew that there was no protecting Layla from the truth they were about to walk through. Sitting by the fireplace, it took her no time to process the circumstances. She had moved enough during their marriage to know the deal. But this deal stunk, and she received it bitterly. The tears came immediately.

She stood up and ran her hand along the ornate mantle. She had this mantle just like she wanted it—tastefully decorated but not tackily. Appropriately. The stability that was elusive to her as a child was within her grasp right here in this place—or so she had believed. She had imagined their children running around in the spacious backyard. Imagined a house full of friends and neighborhood children. She had just the place for the Christmas tree. Now, it felt like she was trying to catch a waterfall in her hand. Broken dreams and shattered hopes were familiar feelings.

John Mark desperately wanted to comfort her but was savvy enough to give her space. It was much like grieving a loss. In between crying sessions, she managed to ask some questions. "Where again are they shipping us now?"

John Mark answered softly, "Clary."

"Where is that?"

"Between nowhere and no place," John Mark quipped, immediately regretting his answer. It wasn't the quipping time. Nothing was funny about what was being thrust upon them.

"What happened?" Layla asked. "I thought things were going so great."

One of the things Bishop Johnson taught John Mark and many other young ministers was the importance of their pastoral duties regarding the home. For many years, all the way back to high school, John Mark had been discipling Layla. He was the one who'd invited her to church. She was a constant motivation on the basketball court to make sure that he walked "the dog" instead of "the dog" walking him. John Mark didn't want to portray a poor witness of what it meant to walk with God. He tried not to be a hypocrite or contradictory because Layla was watching his life.

That same sense of responsibility landed on him like a rock just now, sitting by the fire. He wanted to tell her everything. Therein lay the rub. Two competing value systems were pulling each other in opposite directions. John Mark wanted to fiercely protect his wife from the awful and disgusting world of church politics. He never wanted one thing to dissuade his precious wife from pursuing a pure and sincere faith.

Competing with this powerful instinct was his passion for authenticity. He was a transparent leader. John Mark didn't mind telling his congregation things that painted him in a poor light. He loved the celebration side of his profession, but only if it was genuine. There was a time to rejoice and a time to weep, and he embraced both times. This value pushed him to be transparent with the church that met in his home—namely, Layla.

"Layla, I have tried to protect you from the ugly side of the church for years. I know you're smart enough to pick up on a lot of the negative junk. Still, I tried hard not to drag the smell of church politics into our home. But I need to tell you the bad and the ugly. Not just the good."

Layla wiped a tear from her eye with a tissue. "Of course. We always tell each other the truth."

John Mark leaned in closer. "Layla, I have never lied to you. At least, never knowingly. I just tried not to vomit all the junk and pressure. . . ."

"Just spit it out, John Mark," Layla insisted. "Someone is turning our lives upside down, and I deserve to know why."

So John Mark just puked it out. The good—all the incredible momentum and favor that they were enjoying. The bad—the horrible board meeting a couple of months earlier. The ugly—the backroom deal that had to have happened between the disgruntled board members and the newly-appointed denominational leadership. John Mark told her the horrific timing of it all as it related to Bishop Johnson's aneurysm. He told her about Mary, the receptionist, and her depressed countenance. He told her about his impression of the bully that had taken over the bishop's office, about the impulse to smack the guy and the suppression of said impulse.

John Mark had been to Clary a couple of times, so he knew something of it. He knew enough about it. The hardest thing to tell Layla wasn't that they had to give up the beautiful parsonage and healthy salary. The hardest thing was to tell her the ugly truth about Clary. It was country. *Really* country. As the old joke goes, it was so far in the country that people traveled toward town to go hunting.

Clary had no beautiful subdivisions. No theater. No athletic teams. No cinemas. No coffee shops. Probably most disturbing to throw at her was that it had no commerce—no grocery stores or big box stores. He told her that he remembered a gas station with a chicken fryer and a couple of picnic tables.

That particular fact made her cry hard for a few seconds, but then it turned into a laugh. They both needed a moment of levity. John Mark needed it the most. They cried. They talked. They stressed over saying goodbye. They sat quietly until the fire died out, and then they got up and collapsed into bed.

CHAPTER SEVENTEEN

When the Wrights moved from Smithville to Columbia, they benefitted from a paid-for moving company. They barely touched anything. This move... not so much. They loaded a U-Haul truck with their few possessions. They had the assistance of a handful of grieving congregants. It was a grueling process. Not many people enjoy moving. It rarely makes it onto a résumé under "hobbies."

This move was no exception. It was profoundly unenjoyable. Injured knuckles. Sweating buckets. A broken lamp or two. But these two young lovers were pretty tough. There were hugs and tears and promises of keeping in touch. Off they went, pulling the one car they owned.

Rolling into the metropolis of Clary, Layla realized that John Mark was a prophet. There were many trees, a healthy number of weeds growing through the scant sidewalks, modest houses, and, so far, not a single sign of commerce.

The truck turned right, and there it was: commerce. The gas station with a sign out front – the kind of sign that had those two-inch interchangeable letters—"Chicken Fryer." The lights, three-and-a-half of which were burned out, flashed the grand announcement. Layla's reaction was the opposite of what she had experienced when she first heard about the chicken fryer. She burst out laughing. The laugh organically turned into a quiet sob.

There was virtually no one to help them unload the truck—just a couple of older men in overalls who quickly announced their back problems but willingness to help with the light stuff. There was an older lady that spoke with a thick, Southern accent. "Welcome y'all. I'm just here to help you with the decoratin' and such as."

The trio apologized for the smallness of the welcoming committee but explained that their arrival had unfortunate timing. Three things were going against them: something about the crops, something about "slaughter season," and something about the last day to hunt something or another. The Wrights assured them that it was fine and graciously thanked them for their efforts.

The efforts of the trio lasted about half of the truck, or maybe a little less, and then they made their exit. "Reckon we'll have to leave it with y'all." They excused themselves, citing evening medications, relatives that would be worried, and something about chicken vaccinations. That last one made Layla and John Mark shoot a look at each other.

Somehow, the Wrights managed to wrestle the furniture in the front of the truck down the ramp and into the parsonage. Layla was being brave and working hard. Layla just decided to bow her back and do the work in front of her. She surmised, perhaps subconsciously, that if she was busy and productive she would not have time to notice what she was losing.

John Mark was grieving every time he took a trip into their new home. He wasn't grieving for himself. He could sleep in a shed. He was simply wired that way. He was grieving for Layla. Their new home was not so much a house but a single-wide trailer. Layla seemed okay, but John Mark was a mess. He kept thinking about the beautiful parsonage they had just vacated. That home was so big that there were literally empty rooms because they didn't have furniture or anything else to put into them. Although the Wrights did not possess much at all, what little they had did not fit into this new abode.

John Mark was also grieving the loss of connection. He mused that it felt, at times, like someone built a home only to have people come by and pull the framing down with a chain and a big truck. He imagined planting a beautiful garden only to have derelicts drive their four-wheelers through it halfway through development. John Mark had built. He had planted. He was beginning to see the budding harvest of his seeds. He grieved the people, the connections that were torn down and ripped apart.

It took a couple of days to unpack and organize their belongings. Once the pictures were on the walls, they set about to do what they always did: the ministry. They had to get out of the trailer. As much as Layla tried to beautify it, there was still a little pall of depression about the place. There was also a slight, indiscernible odor. They launched an investigation, but it turned into a cold case. The harder they tried to mask it, the harder it fought.

So they set about to get a lay of the land. They drove around the trailer parks and tiny housing developments. They found nothing that compared with Columbia. There were a few apartment complexes that looked more like third-world housing than urban rental spaces. Still not one sign of commerce beyond the chicken fryer. No real sign of progress, for that matter. People in Clary referred to going "to town" to get some groceries. The closest town was about a thirty-minute drive one way.

They pulled into their new church lot. It was paved with the best quality dirt you could find anywhere: Georgia clay with a few ruts here and there. Avoiding the grooves, John Mark parked their car and opened Layla's door. They walked by a crumbling church sign. John Mark looked down at one of the ruts and mused that it was a metaphor for where his ministerial career had arrived. *"First Church"? More like only church.* John Mark couldn't imagine a "Second Church" trying to compete for the handful of farmers in this area.

John Mark had a ring of keys. There were many, but no indication of what they opened. After several attempts, he finally found the magic key and unlocked the old door of the church. The door made a suctioning sound as the rubber weather stripping released from the wood. John Mark wondered if they even used the front door. They walked into a musty-smelling, tiny foyer typical of churches built during this era. If eight people occupied this narthex, people struggling with claustrophobia would have been highly uncomfortable.

John Mark and Layla took a self-directed "tour." It took about eleven minutes. Moving into the sanctuary, they found two rows of pews covered in orange material. The floors underneath were actually lovely wood. The maroon center aisle carpet did not match the coverings of the pews. Not so lovely. At the back of the sanctuary, behind the pews on the left side, an oddly-constructed area didn't quite seem to fit. They surmised from the two rocking chairs and few toys strewn about that it was some kind of makeshift nursery.

They walked up the three steps to the stage—a tiny space even smaller than the narthex. There were two smaller pews toward the back of the stage against the wall. They were underneath a baptistery that looked like it hadn't been used in a generation or two.

At the front of the sanctuary was a side door on the left that opened to the outside and more clay dirt. The right side had a door that led to "the new building." It was an adjacent add-on from the original building. It was "new," as in, "built fifty-three years earlier." That building featured a large room covered with a stained linoleum floor which could accommodate about forty people if seated at tables. In the corners were stacks of metal chairs and some old tables leaning against the wall.

A hallway led to three classrooms. Two of these rooms were currently being utilized for storage. There were boxes of old Christmas decorations, plastic garland, and tacky wreaths. The third room had a round table and eight metal chairs around it, apparently serving as an actual classroom.

There was no conference room to be found. There were no offices, even for the pastor of the congregation. There were no storage rooms beyond the ones being misappropriated. No fun-filled and sanitized children's areas. No elaborate sign-in mechanisms for nurseries. No cool youth rooms with couches and slick video games. Just this. Clay. Linoleum. Metal. Dirt. Must.

John Mark had seen plenty of action movies. There is often the obligatory flash-bang grenade scene. Someone yells a command. A window breaks. Someone else throws the object. Bang! Smoke. Confusion. Dazed combatants. Aggressive assault. John Mark had often wondered what it might be like to be on the receiving end of that experience. He stood in the parking lot of an ancient and irrelevant church in Clary, GA, and thought he was much closer to understanding what that experience must be like.

CHAPTER EIGHTEEN

John Mark Wright stood straight as an arrow. He had on a crisp shirt, clergy collar, and nice jeans. Layla looked like a stylish magazine cover. She had on the latest in pantsuit fashion. Perfect accessories. Her makeup was flawless. Both looked woefully out of place. The small sanctuary had a smattering of people, and none of them looked like they had come off the cover of a magazine. Well, maybe *Farmer's Quarterly*. Most were wearing work clothes. Tattered. Stained. Flannel. Steel-toed shoes. A couple people had name tags on their shirts.

In the conversational tone that had helped build two churches into powerful community influencers, Pastor Wright said, "That is the offer. Peace, joy, and confidence. I believe that is what we all desire. As we sing this hymn, if your desire is for more, come to this sacred place we call an altar. Ask God for it. Come now as Delores plays the piano softly."

Playing an old piano for so many years must have given Delores a mild hearing problem. "Softly" didn't register with her somehow. She banged an ancient hymn so loudly that John Mark actually flinched. But he stood ready to minister to the saints, as was his custom year after year during his young career. Not one soul moved, and poor Delores continued to bang the out-of-tune Baldwin dinosaur.

Undaunted, John Mark continued. "Remember the words of our Lord Jesus. In several places in the New Testament, He asked, 'What do you want Me to do for you?' So, what do you want? Why don't you come and let's tell Him?" The audience just looked at one another, a little baffled.

Finally, Billy Lawrence, a plain-speaking worshipper in his finest bib overalls, broke the awkward silence. "Preacher, are you a askin' that we come up 'ere and sign up for somepin'?"

John Mark just kindly smiled and answered, "Billy. Right, your name is Billy?"

"Yessir," Billy confirmed.

"Billy, I am inviting all of us to the Lord's feet for more of Him. More of His love and power."

That little epiphany, revelation, instruction, encouragement, note, or whatever one would call it did not move the needle one bit. People just stared straight ahead. They did not do it in defiance. It was more like disorientation.

"Oh well. That is okay. We will just learn together as we go. Bob Earl, would you dismiss the service in prayer from right back there where you are?" John Mark asked. The pastor wanted to be crystal clear about this new request.

Bob Earl obliged with a rural Georgia accent that John Mark and Layla had to strain to interpret. "Hebleny Father, we thank thee for thine many blessings and for affording us the opportunity to once again gather in thine house, and now we beseech thee that thou wouldest guide thine people as we undertake the responsibilities of our hands this week." Finally, a breath. He prayed a run-on prayer with the speed of an auctioneer. "Grant unto thine servants . . ." John Mark couldn't make out the last part of it. "Amen."

Bob Earl's prayer seemed like it was simply part of the fabric of his life, sort of like the denim he was wearing. John Mark did not feel superior to him or to any of them. He felt strangely moved with compassion. His initial assessment: *These folks are the salt of the earth.*

After the service, the pastor and his wife walked to the back of the shotgun sanctuary to greet the parishioners—another ministry custom. The tiny "lobby" was decked out with a big picture of Jesus, a box of Kleenex on a faded doily, and a small stack of bulletins. The bulletins were simple pieces of typing paper folded in half with pitiful artwork inside announcing nothing much going on. There was a funeral happening for Sister Grindle a couple of towns away. A potluck was coming up in a couple of months and a deer drive, which didn't mean anything to a city boy like Pastor Wright.

A few people mulled around the back and some in the little narthex. Billy Lawrence approached him. This simple farmer vigorously shook the pastor's hand. "Preacher, I'ssa sorry I got up in the middle of your preachin'. I promise ya that I weren't mad or nothin'."

John Mark graciously offered, "Billy, don't worry a thing about it. I barely noticed it and thought nothing of it."

Billy pushed back, "No sir. I gots to apologize. See, it hit all of a sudden like I had to go number two real bad, and I couldn't wait." John Mark had no response other than to stand there looking astonished.

Near the door, Layla called out, "Pastor Wright." It always seemed a little weird to hear his wife call him by a title. In her mind, it was a way for her to be dutiful. He excused himself from this penitent worshipper and stepped to the first lady of their new congregation. Smiling, Layla said, "Pastor Wright, I would like you to meet someone. This is Loraine. She just visited today for the first time and wanted to meet the new pastor. She enjoyed the service, and she wants to invite you to something special. I'll let her tell you about it."

Loraine was forty-two years old, but she had high mileage. She didn't look a day under sixty-one. She was life-hardened—a tough lady who stood all of five feet two inches high. She wore no makeup on a face lined with the evidence of her hard work. She had on thick denim jeans, worn-in Chukka boots, and a reasonably new brown Carhartt jacket.

Petite though she was, she grabbed the pastor's hand with a strength that would rival any man's handshake he'd ever received. "You done a good talk, Preacher. Nice to make your acquaintance."

"The pleasure is mine," John Mark responded. "Thank you and thank you for coming."

"Like the missus said, I'd like to invite you'ns, if ya ain't too busy, to my little business. I'd like that you'd dedicate it and speak a good vibe or blessing on it, or whatever the religious thing is."

"Well, we'd be honored to do that. What kind of business do you have?" John Mark asked.

"Oh, it's just a simple little slaughterhouse. We can't compete with the big boys in Douglas, but we do okay. I think it could be better, so that's why we want you to give us some of your lucky words," Loraine requested.

"I'm sorry, did you say *slaughterhouse*?"

Layla smirked and nodded her head.

John Mark continued, "Well, if you could email me the particulars, I'll be happy to oblige this invitation."

"Oh, we ain't got the emails yet." Loraine said. She assured him that they were hoping to acquire the email technology in the next few months.

"No problem, Loraine. If you could just write down the information on the back of this bulletin, I will put it on my calendar. Thanks again for the opportunity to be part of this."

Gleefully, Loraine said, "On your calendar. My, my. Sounds so official-like. Purty cool."

John Mark stepped out onto the small steps that led up to the front door. His thoughts drifted to St. Mark's Church. He remembered the building. The state-of-the-art facilities. The streamlined systems. The gorgeous organ and talented singers. St. Mark's was so deep in talent that they had to be creative and deliberate about scheduling in order to utilize everyone. He had first-, second-, and third-string participants in the worship arts. He couldn't summon a first-string team here at First Church. A first-string here wouldn't make his third-string at St. Mark's.

He reminisced about the services—about the electricity. The excitement. The anticipation for gatherings. The influence of the church, which had been growing throughout the entire region. John Mark preached to his people that they should strive to be "unoffendable." He knew all too well the poison of unforgiveness and the malignancy of bitterness. He had exhorted his people over the years to fight against them. On that little, broken, bricked step in the middle of nowhere, he caught himself fighting mightily not to be offended.

John Mark felt like he was in some sort of cruel time warp. Who on earth hasn't gotten the email machines? Even homeless people back in Columbia had smartphones.

At the exact moment that Pastor John Mark Wright was wrestling with forgiving the Judas (and all the assistant Judases) that had exiled him to this backward patch of Earth, Bill Nella and Bishop Anthony Bailey walked out of the doors of St. Mark's. They strolled down the beautiful, new brick steps and were, as the old saying goes, thick as thieves. These men collaborated to build an alliance that did indeed steal from John Mark Wright and St. Mark's.

This little cabal stole a bright ministry gift that was effectively operating in the church. They stole a shepherd that held the collective and individual interests of the sheep close to his heart. The thievery extended to John Mark's career and his future vocation, to which he felt a divine call. This plunder would prove to be even more severe.

"Now, we're not looking for a stallion, Bishop," Bill said. "Right now, we could use a steady pack mule."

"Clarify," answered Bishop Bailey.

"The other fellow you sent us was a little too fast for us. He was a racehorse that seemed a little out of control. We couldn't keep up and, frankly, didn't like the direction he was running."

"Gotcha."

Bill continued, "We want somebody who will just plow the ground. Steady. Nothing flashy. Just get the job done."

Bishop Bailey offered, "Duly noted, Mr. Nella. This congregation requires overturned dirt but not blue ribbons."

"I suppose you could put it like that."

"Well, I think I might have a half dozen that fit that bill. My conference has plenty of mules and very few stallions," the new bishop smarmily assessed.

They had a hearty laugh. Bill draped his arm over the bishop's shoulders and said, "Let's get a beer and kick it around a little more. Say, have you ever been sailing, Bishop Bailey?"

CHAPTER NINETEEN

Back in Clary, Layla was washing dishes in her new domicile. She had never lived in a trailer before, even in her most challenging days growing up. It was not a nice trailer. There were rust areas around the bottom of the thing. It was nestled in the middle of a pine thicket on about a half-acre. The landscaping consisted of pine straw—lots and lots of pine straw—scattered in every direction. If a good storm blew through the area, these trees were known to snap like twigs.

There she was, washing the dishes and singing sarcastically. The longer she sang, the more abuse she placed upon the items she was cleaning.

"Fish don't fry in the kitchen." She slammed the cup down hard. "Beans don't burn on the grill." *Slam.* "Took a whole lotta tryin', just to get up the hill. Now we're up in the big leagues." A pot slammed down. "Getting our turn at bat. As long as we live, it's you and me, baby." A plate slammed down and the edge chipped a little. "There ain't nothin wrong with that."

Layla's husband walked in after the last lyric of the song. He'd heard the singing, but the percussion section hadn't particularly resonated with him from the other room.

"I'm proud of your positive perspective, Layla."

"I'm being sarcastic, John Mark. We are not moving on up. We are sprinting on down. Hurtling headlong."

"It's not that bad," John Mark replied. "Come on." His assessment of the situation was realistic but, apparently, had not become as bleak as his bride's.

Layla responded, "Oh no?" *Slam*. "So what if I don't have a dishwasher, or a closet, or a store within eighteen miles? We do have a slaughterhouse and a chicken ranch. So there's that. And don't forget the chicken fryer. John Mark, where are we?!"

Now defensive, John Mark answered, "Do you think that I signed up for this? I was sabotaged. But this is where we are. This. Here. Now, not forever. Let's make the most of it." There was an uncomfortable silence. "Isn't home where the heart is?"

"I don't know, John Mark. I've had so many homes and moved my heart so many times. I can't answer that question with any objectivity."

Softly now, John Mark responded. "Look, I don't want to fight. Can't we just try to make the most of right now and figure out the rest?"

Sighing, Layla said, "I'm trying. But I am tired of all of this moving. I'm tired of saying goodbye. I'm tired of unpacking. I'm already tired of this. I am just tired." She gave her husband a half-hearted hug. John Mark never really appreciated the "side hug" but would take it today over no hug at all.

"Take a nap, honey. Things will look different when you wake up."

"Will we still be in this trailer when I wake up?" Layla asked.

All John Mark could offer was a sympathetic half-smile.

CHAPTER TWENTY

As a rule, John Mark was determined to practice what he preached. John Mark also applied this policy to what he preached at home. He desperately tried to make the most of this situation. If a documentary crew followed "a day in the life" of John Mark Wright, they would have a nice variety of material to choose from—not that it would be exhilarating.

Some mornings, John Mark could be found visiting a "shut-in" couple like the Ammons on their front porch. One positive thing about living in a time warp was that there were never traffic jams. There were no clogged lines at registers, as there simply weren't many registers to clog. No one seemed to be in a hurry.

The Ammons were undoubtedly not in a hurry, but they were hungry for human interaction. John Mark had eight couples and six single people on his list that fit this description. These people had been formerly involved in the tiny community and the little church, but age and circumstances had forced them inside. He tried to make at least one pastoral visit to these people each week. It was how ministry used to be done before the days of hundred-thousand-dollar LED screens, conference tables, and fashionista pulpiteers.

John Mark entered these visits void of any agenda. He had a "let's just sit and talk" mentality. "How are the Ammons today?" he asked.

"Oh Pastor, we are better now that you dropped by," Carol said. "I have a fresh blueberry pie, just out of the oven. When it came out, I was a hopin' you might be a droppin' by." She could barely contain her enthusiasm.

The Ammons were unique in that there was still a level of functionality in their circle. They didn't "get to the meetin's" anymore because they could not navigate the steps, and somehow the American Disability Act hadn't yet fully penetrated these deep woods. John Mark had that on his to-do list of future improvements: make the church disability-friendly.

"Oh dear lady, thank you; but I have already gained six pounds since I moved here," John Mark said with a laugh.

"Huh?"

John Mark remembered that he needed to speak up. He repeated himself in a louder voice, adding, "But how can I say no to fresh blueberry pie and your sweet face? Thank you." He enjoyed the pie and enjoyed listening to the same stories he had heard a few times before. He responded as if these stories were breaking news.

That was how it went during these visits. People were hungry to be heard. People repeated the events that shaped their existence. Some had perfect recall of events from fifty years ago but couldn't remember who the current president was.

It was during these visits that Pastor Wright somehow felt the smile of God. This ministry was not statistically measurable other than that it was done. It was nothing dramatic enough to write a magazine article about or to garner admiration from his peers. But to John Mark, slowing down enough to sit on a porch, eat pie, and listen to these "seasoned saints" brought him a newfound sense of joy.

He ended each visit essentially the same way. On special days, he would serve communion. But mostly, he just provided a word of gratitude, a Bible verse, and a prayer for protection and provision. Three or four people on his list always made sure the preacher had their tithes and offerings, meager as they were. John Mark always handled them with the care he would use with any holy thing.

If the documentary crew continued to follow this country preacher, it might find him taking some donuts to the volunteer firehouse. If Layla drove by the mom-and-pop grocery store in the closest city, she would pick up a box of donuts from their make-shift bakery. John Mark enjoyed passing out the donuts as an expression of the church's care. Sometimes the budget could handle it, but the Wrights paid for the donuts out of their meager salary more than half the time.

John Mark knew all of these firefighters by name and came to know some of their family dynamics. He loved the smile that donut day brought to them. They were a rag-tag crew of half-trained men and boys using hand-me-down equipment from wherever they could find it. They took their jobs as seriously as if they were in downtown Atlanta with state-of-the-art appliances. Pastor John Mark felt proud of them while simultaneously hoping that he never needed their services.

A day-in-the-life might find the minister ankle-deep in turned-over clay talking to a peanut farmer. Those were always short visits. "Hello, Mr. Pritchard. I want you to know we miss seeing you at church, but I know it is your busy season and totally understand. Do you need anything?"

People have an impression that ministers work an hour on Sundays and play golf the rest of the week. Of course, the nearest golf course to Clary was nearly a plane ride away. John Mark believed in work. He always had. He loved the visits with the farmers, even if he had to keep his head on a swivel to and from his old truck in order to look for snakes.

The documentary might end behind the county high school. There was actually a pretty decent baseball field there, and it was maintained with pride. Most of the churches fielded softball teams. Unfortunately, only two of his players were connected to First Church. That's just the way it was in the south. Outsiders supplied most of the teams. If a preacher tried to change that policy, the church simply would be left in softball oblivion. So many of the churches in the region were filled with older tax and tithe-payers, and softball competition would be a physical hazard to them. So grandsons, cousins, and neighbors were recruited in order to supply athletes.

John Mark was never bored. He found work. He created work. On the other hand, Layla had a profoundly difficult time finding spaces and places to utilize her many gifts and talents. The opportunities did not as readily present themselves to her. She tried. She looked. She offered. But more and more, she just stayed at the trailer and tried her best to make it feel like home. Unlike previous moves, she couldn't seem to capture the essence of hominess. Mostly, life continued to feel awkward to her.

John Mark sensed this tension and became more and more concerned. It was a prayerful matter to him. He'd surmised that his beautiful wife had always found her way and established her rhythm, and this season would be no different. However, the tension between them was evident, and it was building. John Mark remained determined to simply serve his God, serve his wife, and serve the people entrusted to him.

CHAPTER TWENTY-ONE

"Layla! This is my fifth voicemail. Why do we even pay for cell phones if we don't utilize them?" John Mark stood by the cab of his modest, old truck in Grady Page's peanut field, barking into his phone.

"Listen," he continued. "I have to go to Springfield to visit Betty Grimes. She's having major surgery in the morning. I won't be home for dinner. I'll call you later, and please pick up when I do." He almost wished that he had a flip phone so he could dramatically hang it up. Hard to be aggressive when you're just pushing a little button.

There were some positives to living in the time warp. Of course, there were some negatives, as well. Cell coverage was sketchy in several places in the county. That didn't necessarily explain Layla's unresponsiveness to so many calls. The trailer was close enough to the tower to get a signal. Some people had to drive to the water tower to make a call. It's just the way it was in these parts.

One absolute negative to living in Clary was the quality of health care. A little clinic was located seventeen-and-a-half miles from Clary. It was helpful for rashes, ear infections, and simple triage. If a physical ailment presented in a Clary citizen exceeded those boundaries, they would have to take a trip to the real hospital. That hospital was far enough away that a person would take a packed bag in case the ailment turned into an admission. John Mark had made a few of these runs, and they chewed up most of his day—especially if the diagnosis was serious.

When he ended his call, he utilized the voice application to reinforce his message to her. "Text Layla. Layla, hey, check your voicemail. I'm on the ninety-minute drive to Springfield. No dinner for me. I'll try to call again when the visit is over."

John Mark took advantage of the drive to think. He played some old seventies music and let his mind enter autopilot. He passed a large number of pine trees and swampy forests intermingled with cows, old farms, and silos. As the miles passed, so did the vistas. Swamps turned into trailer parks, which switched to industrial parks. Eventually he reached civilization, equipped with commerce and subdivisions. Finally, he rolled the old truck into the heart of the city. There were chic restaurants, bars, and coffee shops scattered all around. There were also some charming little boutiques.

Changing churches changed John Mark's disposable income, in the sense that there now wasn't any to dispose of on frivolous items. As he locked the old truck manually with an old-fashioned key (the new truck had to be turned back into his previous employer upon his transfer), he noticed something. Reflected in the window was a store he had not previously seen on his hospital runs.

He spun around to look at the fabulous new boutique and its signage. "Sally Sister's Boutique." He smiled as he thought about what Layla's reaction would be if she were with him. She loved little niche stores like this. The merchandise was always overpriced, but the items were almost never cookie-cutter pieces that chain stores offered. *I'll bring her to Springfield on the next run and surprise her with a trip over there and a new outfit.* He smirked at the thought and then imagined having to save for two months to pull it off.

John Mark pulled out his phone to take a photo of the sign. He expanded the image five times greater to make sure he got a good picture. As he pulled the camera away to check his work, he saw a woman on the sidewalk talking to a man. She looked like the doppelganger of his wife. John Mark took five steps toward the store and stopped in his tracks.

It *was* his wife. Layla was standing there.

His mind was foggy, retracing all of the calls and texts. Like a swarm of bugs hitting his windshield, thoughts were pinging in rapid succession. Maybe she'd heard of the store and was on a clandestine reconnaissance mission. Had he misunderstood? Was she making a hospital call today? The fog didn't last long. He looked at the man Layla was talking to and began to tremble mildly. It was Bill Nella, his actual nemesis. A flash of rage burned away the fog in his mind.

It was one thing to sabotage his ministry, but to harass his wife on a sidewalk in public? Fight or flight kicked in. Flight was immediately dismissed as an option, leaving only one. John Mark reflexively pulled his jacket off and threw it in the back of the truck. Before he could even take a step toward this vile man who had blown up his finances, dreams, and ministry, something happened that precluded any movement whatsoever.

John Mark Wright had completely misread the nature of the conversation between Layla Wright and Bill Nella. It was not conflict. It was not tension. John Mark wished to God that it had been. Layla fidgeted, looked left, and then right. She leaned in and kissed Mr. Nella on the lips. It was not a "greet your brother with a holy kiss" either. It lingered. It looked like it felt familiar to her. John Mark froze. At that moment, fight exited to follow after flight. There was nothing left but complete shock. The "couple" walked off shoulder to shoulder.

John Mark had never backed down from a fight. A wave of nausea swept over him. Even if his fight response hadn't exited his mind and body, he wasn't sure what exactly he would have been fighting. He was essentially paralyzed. Nothing worked. He couldn't move his mouth, his feet, or even his head. Looking straight ahead, he simply reeled.

Tears filled his eyes. Grief, predictably, brought about denial and anger. John Mark tried to rationalize—he hadn't really seen that. There had to be an explanation. They'd laugh about this later.

Time was irrelevant. To-do lists were irrelevant. He didn't know precisely how long he stood there, gob smacked. He knew that considerable time had passed because of the shadows. The evaporating light from the sun indicated the progression of the evening.

Exhausted people testify of driving home and not remembering one minute of the drive. That was John Mark's experience. He stood there, reeling, for an indeterminate amount of time. Older people often go into a room and stand there, wondering why they walked in. Before too long, it usually occurs to them, and they grab whatever they were after in the first place. That was John Mark's experience, as well.

Why am I even here? It came to him. He had a hospital call to make. As his life was spiraling out of control, he tried to gather himself enough to offer hope to a family enduring the daunting trial of a major surgery.

Offer hope? If he found hope to offer, it would have to be borrowed somewhere between the parked truck and the hospital elevator. He understood his assignment intuitively. He was there because someone needed a pastor to encourage them during a scary season. In this new, scary season, each heavy step felt like he was rearranging deck chairs on the Titanic.

CHAPTER TWENTY-TWO

John Mark stood at the door marked 1121 in the west wing of the medical center. He smoothed his crumpled jacket and attempted to gather himself. He gently knocked.

"Come in." John Mark slowly entered the room and greeted the man who had given permission to enter. Jonah, fifty-two, was sitting beside the bed of his eighty-year-old mother, Betty. She had her eyes closed.

"I'm Pastor Wright, and I'm here to pray with Miss Betty," John Mark said softly.

"Thank you, sir. This here is a biggun', Preacher. Doc says she's got to have the surgery, or she won't make it. But heck, she may not make it through the surgery."

Betty opened her eyes.

The pastor dutifully asked his congregant, "How are you feeling tonight, Miss Betty?" He sat stoically. His head spun. The windshield of his mind was one giant splatter of bug guts. He couldn't see. Couldn't think. Could barely breathe. Apparently, he couldn't hear, either.

"Pastor. Pastor." Louder now. "Pastor."

John Mark finally reacted. "I'm so sorry, Betty. You were answering my question. How are you feeling?"

"Pastor, are you alright? You look worse than I do."

"Miss Betty, I am so sorry. I just . . . "

John Mark abruptly jumped up and raced the three steps to the patient bathroom, a no-no in hospital visitation etiquette. The etiquette was banished because there was no other option. He didn't even have time to shut the door.

The people paying for the hospital room just looked at each other, embarrassed for the minister as they heard him heaving. And heaving.

Now it was John Mark's turn to be embarrassed. He walked out of the bathroom, accompanied by the sound of a flushing toilet. He wiped his face with a paper towel.

"Preacher, you okay? You look a little green," Jonah diagnosed.

"Yes, thank you. That was embarrassing. Never done that. Wow. I apologize."

"Oh, honey," offered the patient.

"Dear lady, it has nothing to do with you or with visiting the hospital. I am not sick or contagious—of that I am certain. Something just didn't agree with me. Anyway . . . "

Betty consoled the professional consoler. "Honey, go home and get some rest. You don't want to wind up in here beside me. I know you are praying for me, dear."

"I am, Betty. I will check back on you tomorrow. Depending on the situation, it may be one of the deacons who will check in with you . . . if that would be okay." John Mark wanted out of that room before another debacle occurred.

Betty bravely attempted to minister to the minister. "I'm confident in the Lord. We've been through worse. However it goes, everything will be okay. I promise."

CHAPTER TWENTY-THREE

Betty's words held the flavor of the prophetic. They had the aroma of the pathetic. John Mark walked to the car hoping for the flavor of prophetic. He desperately wanted everything to be normal. He wanted Betty to be right. "Everything will be okay. I promise." *How does that work? How can any of this be okay?*

John Mark fumbled with the keys and managed to unlock his truck and sit in it. Everything inside him wanted to turn back the clock—not to yesterday, but to when they lived in Smithville. Things were simple there. Life was rich. Marriage was magic. Ministry was rolling. Why had he listened to the old bishop and gone to the place that had brought him to *this* place?

The dam began cracking. Nothing was making sense. Nausea and numbness gave way to a stifled cry which turned into a hard sob. That's all he could do—put his head on his steering wheel and wail.

John Mark's hour-and-a-half drive expanded to two hours and five minutes. He was on serious autopilot—no seventies music. No podcasts. More than one horn honked, passing John Mark as he went well below the speed limit posted on the two-lane roads. He was oblivious. Of all the challenges he had faced in life, this one had him stumped. He didn't know how to even begin to approach it.

It was about 9:30 p.m. when John Mark pulled into the dirt driveway. He opened the door slowly and dropped his briefcase in the old armchair. Layla was sitting on the couch with her legs tucked under her, covered by a black-and-white throw blanket. She flipped through a fashion magazine.

She barely looked up when he entered. "Where have you been?"

The words stung and disgusted John Mark. "You have *got* to be kidding me! Did you lose your phone in a storm drain?"

Layla looked up. "What are you talking about? It's right there on the table."

"I called you like six times. I sent texts. I have been driving for four hours today, making a hospital visit. In Springfield." John Mark intensely studied her face. "What have you been doing all day?"

His wife continued to flip through the pages casually. "Same ol', same ol'. Trying to find things in these sticks to occupy my time. Just livin' my best life." She looked up. "Living the dream."

"I could have sworn that I saw you today in Springfield."

Layla's gaze sprang up. "You drove to Springfield today?"

"Yes. As my multiple messages on the phone indicated—and my answer to your question ninety seconds ago." John Mark walked to the kitchen and poured a glass of water. No one spoke for a couple of minutes.

"I could have sworn I saw your twin in Springfield," John Mark said, breaking the silence.

"Oh, really?" she said, unconcerned.

John Mark responded, "I think it was you."

"Hmmm? Nope. Not me."

"Really? It looked just like you. And I think I saw Bill Nella with you. Is that possible?"

"You have quite the imagination, John Mark," Layla responded. She played off the question, but her face flushed.

John Mark was tired of playing this game. He pulled his phone out of his pocket. He hit the photos button and enlarged the latest picture. Holding his arm towards his wife, he said, "So are you denying that this is you?"

As soon as Layla saw the photo, she jumped to her feet, shocked and angry. "My God, John Mark! Are you stalking me? Spying on me?"

"Are you kidding me? It has never occurred to me that spying on you would ever be needed for one second of our relationship. Until today, that is."

"Then what is that, John Mark?"

"That is the question you should be answering, not me. What. The. Heck. Is. This?!"

Silence. The formerly wildly-in-love couple just glared at each other.

"I'll go first. Layla, I was taking a picture of the boutique sign where you were standing. I noticed it and thought I would show it to you and maybe plan a trip. You happened to be standing right in front of the store. What timing, huh?"

Layla looked down at her feet. Now *her* mind was reeling. This little revelation had not been on her agenda for the day.

"Your turn, wife. What is this?"

Now defensively, Layla answered, "Well, you got me, John Mark. What do you expect?"

"I expect you to keep our wedding vows!" John Mark shouted. He never shouted. This startled Layla. It even surprised John Mark.

"How long has this been going on? Are you sleeping with that jackass? Were you sleeping with him while we were in Columbia?" John peppered her with crass questions, emotionally spiraling.

Now it was Layla's turn to scream. "Absolutely not!" She paused for a couple of beats and under her breath, added, "Maybe I should have."

"What did you just say?"

"Look at what you've done to us. You took me out of my beautiful home and put me in this tin can in the middle of nowhere. I can't take it anymore. What do you want from me?"

"What do I want? I want you to be my wife!" John Mark answered. "And I don't want you to cheat on me. You're a bright girl, Layla. It's pretty simple."

Layla sighed. "It's not that simple. I have tried as hard as I can for a few years. John Mark, you are just so passive. You turn all the cheeks. I've run out of cheeks to turn. You let people run all over you. Why do you have to be that way?"

John Mark thought he might lose his mind. "You mean people like Bill Nella? That piece of crap you were making out with in the middle of the street? Do you know that he called you a trollop in that ambush of a board meeting?"

Layla said nothing.

John Mark continued, "Do you know what a trollop is, Layla? It means a prostitute." He thrust his finger in her direction and yelled, "That is what your new boyfriend called you! He called you a whore!"

This whole thing felt out of control for Layla. Ironically, one of her pastor's sermons came to her at this precise moment. Pastor Wright had spoken about how gentle answers turn away wrath.

"John Mark," she said softly.

The gentle answer wasn't working as advertised—at least not quite yet.

John Mark continued, "Maybe your boyfriend had a little prophetic insight. That horrible little man is the reason you're in this tin box that you keep complaining about. And you just . . ."

Continuing the soft approach, she interjected again. "John Mark, I want to have a family. I don't want to raise children in this trailer. It doesn't matter how we got here."

Now John Mark looked at his feet. Looking up, he responded, "I had no idea just how shallow you are. Maybe I've just been ignoring it."

In truth, Layla was not shallow. She was open to all of the work that her husband had been called to do. She felt just as called to the ministry as he was. She hadn't been well-versed in their work at first, but she was a fast learner. She sincerely enjoyed helping people, and she was her husband's biggest cheerleader.

There was something about this isolation that created a disconnect—like a train car disconnected from its train, she'd kept going for a while until, some time back, she'd stopped. John Mark had been too busy making the most of the situation to notice that she wasn't going with him. The distance between them had grown. Lack of maintenance in their marriage had created this explosive night.

"So you think I'm a passive man, huh? A real docile sort of fellow? A pushover? Nice to finally know what my wife really thinks."

"John Mark."

"No, I gotcha. I get it."

John Mark walked over to the small coat closet by the front door. He pulled out a shotgun.

Layla took two steps toward the back door. *Forget gentle answers now.* She screamed, "What are you doing, John Mark?"

Now John Mark had the soft answer—and its calmness was creepy. "Oh, leave your apathetic husband alone. I'm just going to go passively end this affair. I'll be back in a few hours." The trailer door slammed—an odd juxtaposition to his soft voice. Layla jumped at the sound.

CHAPTER TWENTY-FOUR

Driving can be a draining experience. John Mark had been driving all day, it seemed. Almost four hours of driving earlier to make a hospital call, and now a couple more driving back to Columbia.

Rather than feeling exhausted, he felt freakishly energized. Adrenaline carried him along the drive. He was not on autopilot. In fact, he was driving a considerable number of miles over the speed limit. He was engaged in all manner of thoughts, possibilities, memories, and visualizations. He stopped only once, and that was for fuel. He made the complete transaction at the pump and spoke to no one.

He had no real plan. John Mark was a man who liked to make plans. He generally didn't go to bed until he had a written "vision" for the following day. But now, he was spit-balling. In his entire life, he had never written the sentence, "Tomorrow, I have a vision to inflict physical violence upon my enemy."

He pulled his truck up quietly to the home of Bill Nella. He had dropped off documents to him in a previous life, so he knew exactly where he lived. John Mark turned off his headlights two houses away because he had seen enough action movies to see how these kinds of things are done . . . whatever *this kind of thing* was.

Because it was now 10:30 p.m., he half expected to see no lights on in the house. Instead, it was lit up like a trophy case. It was an impressive home indeed. The architecture was Mediterranean and gorgeous. However, it seemed out of place in this suburban Georgia neighborhood. There were no other Spanish Colonial or Italian Renaissance homes within a hundred miles. John Mark mused that this was quintessential Bill Nella—he wanted what no one else had. That is, until he wished to have what someone else had.

Not only was the outside brightly illuminated, but it also seemed like every light inside was switched on. Instead of retiring for the night, it looked to John Mark as if the family had a full-blown board game taking place. As John Mark sat in his truck across the street, the irony of the scene was not lost on him. This family seemed happy. Bill was laughing and enjoying himself.

Teenagers are typically peculiar creatures. They are often moody and sullen. Many are complete narcissists. Add to this generalization the dynamic of a driven father who rarely has time for his kids, and the stage is set for lots of future therapy.

That generalization, though, was not the picture John Mark was observing through the window of Bill's beautiful home. This seemed like a happy home. Bill's wife, Tina, seemed equally happy. The kids passed bowls of snacks around and gleefully spun the wheel or whatever the game's machinations required. Their teenage daughter made a move, and the two male family members put their heads in their hands while the two ladies threw their hands up in celebration. Back and forth it went.

Are you having a good time, Bill? I sure hope you're enjoying your family. You have blown mine up. In the throes of their weekly game night, the family was oblivious to the minister of the gospel outside their home in possession of a deadly weapon. *You know, it's one thing to sabotage my ministry, but this is on another level altogether.*

John Mark got out of the car with his gun in tow. He always kept a sports coat in the truck for pastoral calls. Now, he wrapped it around the shotgun, readying himself for this particular call. This visit was patently different. Typically, John Mark had command of their general direction. The seminary's pastoral theology classes had never instructed him about this kind of call. In fact, *that* curriculum might be better suited to prison rec yards.

The street was quiet, and so was John Mark. But he was sweating. It wasn't particularly hot outside, but he was steaming inside. He nonchalantly tucked himself in between a giant oak tree and a row of shrubs in the front yard. Anyone walking their dog would have immediately detected that a man crouched on one knee behind a tree with a sports coat oddly folded in his hands was out of place. There would be a 911 call, a little suburban drama, and that would be that.

But this night, there happened to be no one walking their dog. All was quiet except John Mark's mind. John Mark did not have a plan, but he did have motivation. He was determined to prove to his wife that he was not passive. He was motivated to give a little retribution to Mr. Nella. He wanted to prove to him that he was nobody's pushover. John Mark was convinced that Bill had the devil in him, and he hoped tonight to scare a little of that hell out of him.

CHAPTER TWENTY-FIVE

John Mark crouched between that tree and shrubbery so long that his legs began to cramp. He had to adjust a couple of times as he continued to stare at the little party behind the glass. His eyes lingered on the kids. John Mark was drawn to a curious scar on the teenage boy's face. He remembered that he liked the boy. He didn't recognize that scar. As he studied the kids, his fire began to cool. The previous motivation started to evaporate. He caught himself in the pastoral mode of wondering what happened to the child. That ministerial inkling kicked in, and it irritated him. This visit wasn't the ministry kind, but he really didn't know what kind of visit it was.

Back at the trailer, Layla paced anxiously. With such a small space, she did multiple laps. Some laps had her stopping at the table and staring down at the phone. A couple of times, she picked it up and brought up the number for Bill Nella. It was an alias. She hadn't wanted to get caught, and even now she kept the false name in her phone. Each time she picked it up, she put it down again.

Layla worked out scenarios in her mind. *If I call and Tina answers, what then? If I call and the alias Bill has for me pops up, will he be furious when answering? After all, we had an agreement. If he isn't mad—or even if he is—what would I say to him?* "Hey Bill, watch your six. Your old pastor is coming to your house with a shotgun." Preposterous.

She couldn't imagine that John Mark would use a gun for violence. To her knowledge, he had never even shot one. He had the shotgun in the closet to "scare off the boogeyman." Layla wasn't even sure that the thing worked.

Should she call her husband? *"Pastor John Mark, I feel prompted to tell you that you probably shouldn't kill anybody. It might make your precious little church look bad."* She almost laughed at the thought. *This place is so remote; it might never make the news because no one would be able to find the murderer.* Humor immediately disappeared. She was mad at her husband. She was mad at Bill. She was mad at churches. She was angry at herself. She knew better than to do what she'd done, but she didn't care. She had sown the wind, and tonight she was reaping the whirlwind.

Not knowing what to do, she did what a lot of people do in baffling situations. She prayed. She pleaded aloud, "I know I don't deserve to be listened to and that I've made this mess. But if You would help John Mark not to do anything stupid. . . ."

She picked up a framed picture from the coffee table. It was a photo of their honeymoon. They were enjoying the water with smiles as big as Texas. Happier times. The picture wasn't from that long ago, but somehow it felt a hundred years old. She began to cry. She didn't often cry. She was not crying for herself but for the people she had hurt.

Rage had turned into steady anger for John Mark. His anger morphed into nebulous determination. Determination, oddly, changed into compassion for this family, the Nella family. But compassion quickly jumped back over the fence, giving way again to routine anger as he played memories in his mind. He could not unsee the kiss. It was on a replay loop.

Then, he allowed something to happen that he had preached against over the years. Here in the bushes, he did not practice what he had often preached. He had cautioned his churches to avoid "vain imaginations." These imaginations are the horrible "what ifs" of life. The fantasies now played in his mind like an IMAX movie, huge and brightly-colored. The imaginations were not memories. The kiss? The kiss was burned into his bank of memories. The imagination movies were the nagging questions about what she might have done.

He imagined the First Lady of the churches he had pastored, his dear bride, in intimate settings with Bill Nella. Then, he did an inventory of every conversation he could remember between his wife and a member of the opposite sex. *Is she having an affair with Rex? She seemed friendly with Alberto. She told me one time that Sean was such a handsome guy. She even wondered if perhaps she could fix him up with a friend.* On and on it went. That pushed him back into a rage.

Enough! The constant back and forth in his mind had completely exhausted him. One cannot live enraged for very long. It is simply too draining.

He fixated on the boy again. That scar reeled in his mind. There he went again. He was leaping to compassion. Before long, John Mark settled into full-blown embarrassment.

He slipped away from the tree, trying to be as nonchalant as a clergyman with murderous thoughts could be. He hadn't really planned to kill anyone. At least, he didn't think so; but he did have a gun. Maybe he'd been about to present the weapon dramatically and scream, "Back off!" Perhaps he would have shot a mailbox for dramatic effect. Now, the entire act just felt ridiculous.

When he got back to the truck, he opened the door and threw the jacket and gun in the front passenger's seat. He sat down but jumped right back out. He hurled for the second time on this horrible day. There was nothing more to spew. Still, he continued to dry-heave, praying in his mind that no one would hear him.

He fell back into the driver's seat. He didn't know if he had the physical strength to drive one more mile, let alone almost one hundred miles. His emotions were like a scene from a famous movie about tornadoes. Instead of cows, barns, plows, roofs, and the like, he had other things flying about in his head. Embarrassment. Regret. Shame. Retribution. Self-righteousness. Anger. Repentance. Disillusionment. Despair. Hate. Love. Confusion. Hopelessness.

When John Mark tossed the jacket, the shotgun barrel slipped out into view. He looked at it a long time. Then, his eyes moved down the barrel to the book beside it. The book was a large brown leather study Bible that Layla had given him upon his graduation from seminary. That had been such a proud day. He'd graduated in the top one percent of the class. So much promise. So much vision. So much love.

So much for all of that. John Mark's thoughts now focused, and they burned. *What am I doing? I am supposed to be a man of God.* He let out an exasperated sigh that sounded like a flattening tire. *I am supposed to be a leader of people—leading them to God. What a joke. I am as wicked as my enemy. No! More wicked. I am more wicked. I am supposed to be a minister, for God's sake.*

For God's sake, indeed. From the rage to the compassion, he'd been pushed to the edge of the abyss of self-loathing. John Mark had always had holy self-esteem. Any trace of that self-esteem was now gone. He despised himself for being oblivious to the deep dissatisfaction in his own home. He was a failure at leading the most important follower of all, his own wife. He sat there hating himself to his core. He felt stupid, and somehow dirty.

With one more glance at the little party behind the window—with the entire family standing and laughing—he put the vehicle in drive and slowly crept away from the curb with full headlights. He didn't care if anyone caught him. At this point, he didn't have the energy to care about anything. He was completely numb, and he was numb every mile to his tiny, rusted trailer. What an evil day this had been.

CHAPTER TWENTY-SIX

A few minutes before midnight, John Mark pulled into the dirt driveway of the church's parsonage. He stepped out of the truck holding the barrel of the shotgun haphazardly in his hand, almost dragging it behind him. John Mark liked to put things back where they belonged. It was reflexive. The gun didn't belong in the truck. It didn't belong in his hand. The weapon belonged in the closet. He planned on putting it back inside the closet.

He hadn't thought much about the gun he kept for protection. He hadn't thought about it in months. That is, until tonight. He so wished he had forgotten entirely about owning a gun. Walking up the metal steps to his home, he knew that he had made matters worse.

He didn't want to wake Layla. Maybe they could sleep on the matter, and the sun would rise on a fresh, hopeful perspective. He didn't have the emotional reserve to even grasp at straws of hope. He just wanted to sleep.

Quietly, John Mark opened the trailer door. It was odd that Layla hadn't locked it. People in these parts bragged about not having to lock their doors. The Wrights did no such bragging. They had lived in the city too long. But the door being unlocked tonight alarmed John Mark. He gripped the barrel a little more tightly.

The lights were off except for one dim bulb over the kitchen sink. John Mark quietly slipped down the narrow hallway of the trailer. He poked his head into the guest room. It was bare except for a few boxes of stored odds and ends—exactly as he'd left it.

He turned the light on in the bathroom. Empty. He padded down the hall to their bedroom. Heart now pounding, he pulled out his phone for light. He entered the bedroom and shone the light toward the bed. It was still made. No one was in it. Turning on the light, he examined the closet and the floor on the other side of the bed. Nothing.

John Mark walked back to the kitchen, turning all the lights on along the way. He noticed something out of place: the table was usually clear. John Mark and Layla were both a little OCD about the house, including the table. On it sat a white legal pad and pen. John Mark walked over to the table. There was a note written on the pad in the lovely handwriting of his beautiful wife:

> *I loved you very much. I will probably love you until the day I die. Our lives are going in the wrong direction. You know it as well as I do. It's not just about this trailer, and you know that in your heart. I can't do this anymore.*
>
> *A friend—a GIRL—picked me up. Don't look for me.*
>
> *If you are not in jail, I hope you have a good life. You deserve it.*
>
> *I know it may not be worth much, but I am sorry.*
>
> *L*

John Mark shuffled over to the crummy couch and collapsed onto it. That morning, he had awoken as a pastor in a tiny community doing God's work, trying his best to make a difference. He'd had a beautiful wife. He'd had an impressive resume for such a young minister. He'd had a bright future. He'd had a relatively good attitude and an optimistic worldview. He'd had the growing respect of his community. That's what he had had. Now, he had a legal pad with ninety words written on it.

He needed to cry. However, John Mark Wright had cried himself nearly dry. He let the gun fall onto the floor and put his head back. He gave in to his exhaustion and fell asleep. But sleep didn't last long. The brightly-colored, amplified images jerked him awake. The IMAX movie played again. The harassing imaginations roused him the same way a stomachache would.

At about 3:45 a.m., he crawled off the couch and made his way down the hallway. When he went into the bedroom, the emptiness of it sucked at his very soul. When he saw the closet that was three-fourths empty now, his anger rallied again. He threw the legal pad he was still holding against the wall. At the top of his lungs, Pastor John Mark Wright screamed a curse word. He hadn't cursed since college when an elbow had caught his nose going up for a rebound. It has been said that a well-timed curse word makes one feel better. Ten thousand curse words would not have brought him any relief on this night.

John Mark fell into bed and hoped for sleep. He did not pray for sleep. He hoped for it. But sleep never came.

CHAPTER TWENTY-SEVEN

There was a different mood at First Church on this particular Lord's Day. Sundays were generally a comfortable time of gathering for the parishioners. John Mark had long ago given up on the notion that he would experience the phenomenal growth that had happened at his other two churches. He had given up even on making a significant community impact here.

He'd once told a good seminary friend who shared an affinity for college football that he was stuck in a no-win program. They had both shared a favorite football coach who had won national championships at two universities. John Mark attributed the coach's success to one word. It wasn't "process," "effort," "determination," or anything like that. It was the word "talent." The coach didn't consider the talent his own—it lay on the field, in the players he'd recruited.

Continuing with his friend along that line of logic, John Mark shared that a great coach in a rotten recruiting location would not have the same success. Period. Take the coach from a great program like Alabama or Ohio State, stick them in New Mexico, and see how many national championships they could win. Stick them up in Buffalo and see how many five-star recruits they could talk into coming.

John Mark had lots of metaphors for the work to which he had been exiled. He felt sabotaged with a one-word job description: mediocrity. His job was to maintain. He wasn't a "maintainer" sort of man—never had been.

Today's atmosphere was, simply, nervousness. The sheep of First Church were acting more like cows watching a coyote approach. Uneasy. Herding together. The anxiety stemmed from the fact that their shepherd was nowhere to be found. People were chatting, and many were looking at their watches. A teenager preoccupied with her smartphone answered an older saint when asked what time it was. "Ten after. Hey, I thought this show started at ten?" She went right back to tweeting or texting or whatever.

"Well, where is he? Does he ever come in late?" asked Loraine to no one in particular.

Bob Earl answered, "Naw. He's always early. I been calling, but he ain't picking up." He looked around and asked a couple of groups clumped up together, "Anybody heard from the preacher?"

Both groups simultaneously shook their heads.

The preacher was not at his post. He was six miles away from his appointed post in a pine grove. He had never missed a Sunday. John Mark's sense of duty and responsibility was keen. He was disciplined. He did strength exercises on Monday, Wednesday, and Friday. He did aerobic or cardio on Tuesday, Thursday, and Saturday. His habits and disciplines had both impressed and annoyed his wife.

John Mark sat on a tree stump. He had lost all track of duty, discipline, and time. If asked, he wouldn't have been able to tell anyone how long he had been sitting on the stump. He was officially having what the mental health professionals call an existential crisis.

Sundays were always "game days" for him. But this Sunday, John Mark had woken up and driven down a dirt road that led to a prime deer stand. A fellow in the church had given him the green light to hunt there. He had been here a few times, but never to hunt. He liked to pray here.

He didn't make it to the stand. He didn't have the energy. He parked his truck, grabbed the brown Bible, and sat down on the first stump he saw. He kicked around it to make sure that there were no slithering attendees to his existential crisis. Satisfied that he was alone, he sat down.

His mind was a blur. His memories were in a blender. Seminary. Smithville. Loving Layla. Bishop Johnson. First sermon. His first date. Justice League. Columbia. High School. Springfield. Bill Nella. Chicken fryer. Beautiful parsonage. Slaughterhouse. Childhood. Shotgun.

As his recollections kept blending, he caught himself muttering incoherent phrases and words. He momentarily thought he might be having a nervous breakdown. At that thought, another memory popped up like a half-shredded banana against the blender glass. He remembered a joke he'd told in a sermon: "I went to the doctor the other day, and he asked me if anyone in my family suffered from mental illness. I thought about it a minute and said, 'No, Doc, we all enjoy it.'"

He might have allowed himself a chuckle on this tree stump, but what was happening inside him was no joke. This crisis was deadly serious. In these woods, he found himself in a Robert Frost poem. Instead of two roads diverging in a yellow wood, he couldn't manage to find even one road. Everything that had ever given him framework and boundaries was now overgrown. There simply wasn't a visible path to navigate. On the stump, the preacher sat stumped.

John Mark's muttering managed to find a different gear. It turned into actual prayer, out loud and outdone. "What did I do to you?" He was half-expecting an answer. The only response was from a red-headed woodpecker. *Rat a tat tat. Rat a tat. Rat a tat tat tat.*

John Mark would have preferred a response from the One he had dedicated his life to as a little boy. Honestly, he wondered what he could have done to cause the Creator to banish him to this very stump. So he continued asking questions.

"Is this my payoff?"

Silence.

"Really? Sabotage?"

No answer.

He stopped there as emotion caught in his throat. The whir of the movie projector kicked up in his mind, but he pushed it away. He couldn't emotionally handle the vain imaginations right now. He had a celestial business meeting to conduct, and he needed to finish.

"Hustling sixty hours a week working for you, and this is it? Back-stabbing? Betrayal?"

At the word "betrayal," John Mark abruptly paused his business meeting. He had to stop this conversation. It seemed one-sided anyway. He remained in the middle of the pine thicket and put his face in his hands. He let out a deep, moaning cry. He truly missed Layla. Today, he wasn't even mad at her. He just missed her. He especially missed the old days, when the banter had been hilarious and the nights had been warm. Through his shoulder-shaking weeping, he uttered one word. "Layla."

Eventually, it was time to resume business. "You know I have never been lazy, right? Did I do something wrong? Is this really my reward?" He wanted to allow the other participant to respond, so he sat in silence for a long time. John Mark had asked ten questions. He would have been happy with just one answer.

He didn't expect an audible voice. There were so many things he hadn't expected that had impacted him. He'd never expected a trailer and a country church after two successful pastorates. It had never presented itself as an option during his professional training. "Do good, and go up the ladder. Do wrong, and go down the ladder." That was implied strongly as standard operating procedure. John Mark, by all measurable scales, had done good deeds.

He'd never expected an evil man to sabotage his calling with seemingly no consequences. He'd never expected to not receive any assistance from above. He hadn't expected his friend to get a brain aneurysm. He hadn't expected a wormy replacement to fill that friend's post.

He hadn't expected the evil little man who sabotaged his career to decimate his soul by trying to steal his helpmate.

I am a fool.

The pastor had mentally outlined so many unexpected things. He just hoped for one more—an unprecedented, audible answer from heaven. After all, audible voices happened in the brown book he was holding in his hand. So John Mark Wright sat on a stump giving ample time for some two-way conversation. That is what prayer was supposed to be, after all. As he understood it, prayer was not designed to be a monologue.

Plenty of time had passed, and John Mark had given God plenty of opportunities to speak. The wrens, woodpeckers, and finches gave their thoughts. A few squirrels replied by kicking up some pine straw. Other than that, there was abject silence.

Resolved to the obvious, John Mark stood up. He looked up and softly and measuredly said, "Okay. I get it. Well then, please find somebody else. Find a better man. I didn't sign up for this."

He gently put the brown Bible on the stump where he sat. Then the pastor prayed the last prayer he ever intended to pray in his life. "Please pick someone else. Find a better person."

CHAPTER TWENTY-EIGHT

One week later, John Mark Wright walked onto the tiny stage at First Church. He stood behind the little old wooden pulpit. He was wearing jeans and a dress shirt. What he was not wearing was a collar. The small flock immediately noticed that he was out of uniform. They also noticed that his pretty wife was not in the morning worship service.

There was something else missing beyond the collar. John Mark didn't have his Bible. He always had his Bible. He had nothing to put on the pulpit. No Bible. No electronic device. He didn't even have a piece of paper. He didn't get too close to the wooden desk. That was a symbol of his calling. It was a symbol of the divine communication between heaven and earth. It might as well have been one of the electric fences that the farmers utilized to control their livestock. He wouldn't even touch it. In fact, he decided to remove his physical presence from the pulpit altogether.

A pin could have been heard if it had dropped as John Mark slowly walked down the steps and stood on the floor to address the congregation. "Good morning. Let me begin this morning by apologizing for last Sunday. It was rude of me to be absent without communicating. That has never been my style, and you deserve better."

Fifty-year-old Gladys said, "It's okay, Pastor. We love you."

"Thank you, Gladys. I love you too. I love all of you. I went AWOL, and it isn't okay, and I am not okay."

John Mark looked over his shoulder at the pulpit. "There will not be a sermon today. There will not be one from me again."

There was a stir in the pews. This announcement was upsetting to those in attendance. A gasp or two could be heard, while others gestured with their hands, palms turned upward as if to say, "What's going on?"

John Mark decided to rip off the bandage and not remove it in stages. "I am not your pastor anymore."

Now no one tried to conceal their confused worry. Before anyone could ask a question, John Mark continued his little speech.

"Please believe me when I tell you that this development is not your fault. You are such good people. I am going through something personally, and it has totally rocked me. It caught me off guard, and it has taken all the wind out of my sails. I wouldn't hurt you for anything in this world. I am hurting too badly to be of any help to any of you, so. . . ."

Bob Earl interrupted, "We'll a help ya Payster." His offer was real, raw, and precious. When these people committed to something, they nearly always saw it through.

John Mark answered, "Thank you, Bob Earl. The decision is final. The tree has fallen, so to speak, and it is not going back up."

He paused and quickly smiled with his lips together, expressing sincere gratitude to Bob Earl.

"So with that, I'll ask Miles Denton, our board chair, to please come and take over the service. Lead us in a creed, hymn, a reading; share a testimony, or do anything that you feel like doing, friend."

Miles Denton looked a little shell-shocked but quickly recovered. He was a veteran in these parts. He was only sixty-one years old, but he had successfully retired as a peanut farmer. He had an impeccable reputation for the kindness he extended to his employees. In many respects, he was a perfect board member. John Mark had often secretly wished that Miles had been on board with him during his last post.

Miles certainly hadn't expected to be part of the order of service on this Sunday morning. He slipped out of the pew and made his way to the stage. While he was approaching, John Mark scanned the assembly and concluded his talk. "Goodbye. Thank you for your understanding and your love. I love you."

John Mark nodded slightly to Miles as he went to the front pew, but Miles wouldn't let him pass by. He lovingly but firmly grabbed his pastor's arm as he tried to pass.

"Pastor John Mark, you do not have to do this," Miles said softly enough that not another soul could hear.

"Yes, I do, Miles."

Miles didn't let that go nor his arm. "Whatever it is, you can get through it. I'm with you. *We* are with you."

"Thank you, Miles, but. . . ."

"We can get through this. Don't go alone, man. Let us help you. Let God help you."

John Mark's eyes filled with tears. He embraced Miles and held on long enough to maintain his composure for the sake of his shocked parishioners. Finally able to step back, John Mark looked at the farmer and said, "You're a good man, Miles." He then stepped to the front pew as Mr. Denton climbed up to the pulpit.

"Well, I am no preacher. An excellent preacher is standing right there," Miles began. At least three worshipers said "amen" as if on cue. "I ain't much of a singer either. I reckon when someone doesn't know what to do, they just ought to pray. That's what the good book says, and I believe it."

Miles instructed the gathering to bow their heads in prayer. Slowly, the good man began to pray. "Dear God, I pray for the comfort and wisdom of the Holy Ghost. We now pray for our pastor. He has been there for us over and over, and now we stand with him. Touch your servant John Mark Wright. . . ."

He stopped and looked up towards the back pews and spoke to the crowd. "Hey, I think it would be a good idea for a few of us to gather around the pastor."

Bob Earl enlightened the deacon with these three words: "He gone, Miles."

Mr. Denton looked, and John Mark was indeed gone. As soon as Miles had asked for heads to be bowed, John Mark took his head, feet, and ministry future—or lack thereof—out the side door that led to nothing but clay and despair.

The service was over. So was John Mark's career. So was John Mark's marriage. Reverend John Mark Wright walked out and never intended to enter a house of worship again.

CHAPTER TWENTY-NINE

J ohn Wright kept his plan alive for the next ten years. It was the only real plan he had. He intended not to darken the door of a church again. So far, he had been successful. In reality, it had been relatively easy. The only time the plan had gotten sticky was when someone invited him to a special event held at a place of worship.

The first few years of his ministry, John had developed creativity for engaging people in meetings. He now used some of that creativity to avoid gatherings such as christenings, weddings, funerals, and the like. Drifting around the country made it easier still. No close relationships meant fewer invitations to intimate religious settings.

John—he'd dropped the "Mark" when he'd walked out the side door ten years earlier—was a drifter. But he wasn't a grifter. He didn't swindle anybody or work for a circus. He had odd jobs here and there. Honest work. Fair pay. He would work until he got bored or until people seemed to be getting too close to him. Then he would pull up the stakes—stakes that were always loosely pushed into the earth—and he'd be off to find another gig.

When you work with people, they give you invitations to their weddings and such things. John was never rude, but he always managed to be busy for the ceremonial parts of these events. However, he was often able to make it to the soirees afterward. He would miss the ceremonies but arrive at the reception halls for the dancing. Not wanting to have a reputation as antisocial, John would arrive at homes for the grieving, or whatever the occasion might be. He was always an in-and-out sort of fellow. He came a little late and left a little early. He had a heart for those he worked with, but he had lost all heart for sanctuaries or other trappings of religion.

John had left First Church that Sunday ten years earlier, climbed in his truck, and started driving. He had already packed a large duffle that day with clothes and essentials. He included $300 that he had hidden in a sock drawer. He'd been saving it for a future anniversary weekend in Atlanta.

John would have sold his few possessions, except for two problems. First, he did not want to stay in Clary for another minute, and it would take a while to negotiate transactions. And second, he didn't own anything of value. Some items held nostalgic value. Those few items, he brought with him.

The gun was probably worth a few bucks. John certainly did not want it. So he'd made sure it was empty and put the thing in a large plastic yard bag. He'd driven to a neighboring town and thrown it in a green dumpster behind a Pizza Hut. He had watched enough TV to silently muse, "I wonder if the old thing has any murders on it." He scoffed at that foolish notion. The gun had never knowingly been out of his possession and had primarily stayed in closets. It didn't even have a duck murder on it.

During the weeks of John's existential crisis, he didn't eat much. He didn't sleep. He didn't check the mail. He didn't pay the bills. He mostly thought and mostly hurt. When the notion of drifting rose in his mind, so did a practical thought: *I better check my bank accounts.*

He and Layla had exactly two accounts: a checking account for bills and a savings account. He'd built up some savings in hopes of getting out of the parsonage business and giving his wife her own home one day.

Following his abrupt resignation from First Church in Clary, the next item of business was to check his accounts. Layla had handled all of the family business, and he didn't even know how to access the information on the internet. He'd been too busy with the Lord's work to concern himself with mortal business.

That last Sunday, he drove north from Clary until he got to a Days Inn near the Atlanta airport. He checked in. When asked for payment, he pulled out a credit card but quickly put it back into his thin wallet. He opted to pay the $98 in cash. He wasn't sure why. Maybe it was because he had seen it done in movies. Frankly, he didn't want anyone tracking his whereabouts—not that anyone cared enough to do so.

He wasn't a criminal. He was just on the run from something. He threw the duffle on the table and stretched out on the hard motel bed. *On the run.* That made him think of Jonah from the Old Testament. Jonah ran from a divine assignment.

In the adjoining room, an argument was taking place between a couple over something or another. *Great.* Eventually, someone apparently decided to activate the silent treatment, and the room got quiet again. John was relieved. Until he wasn't. Alone with his thoughts, Jonah came back to mind. John surmised that the only thing he had in common with Jonah was that their names started with J.

Jonah ran from an assignment. John had no such assignment. God had actually spoken to Jonah and given him marching orders. John had waited on a stump to receive his marching orders. No such directions had come, and he had waited for an ample amount of time to hear them, by his estimation. He was frustrated. It felt somewhat like the frustration of people who do not return a phone call or a reply to their text message, except that this was the most crucial return call John had ever hoped to receive, and it hadn't come.

So here he was, in a dumpy little motel next to the busiest airport in the world, with nowhere to go and almost nothing to do. The only thing on his plate for the foreseeable future was to see if Layla had cleaned out their accounts—to confirm how broke he was.

The trash truck was his wake-up call at 7:03 a.m. *Who picks up garbage at the crack of dawn?* He was initially irritated, but he felt accomplished when he realized he'd get an early start on the day's business.

He availed himself of the complimentary breakfast buffet. The "buffet" was profoundly disappointing. There were no hot offerings whatsoever. However, there was a large inventory of stale muffins and crumbly danishes. He passed on the carbs and grabbed an overripe banana, a peanut butter packet, and some plain oatmeal.

At 9:00 a.m. sharp, he showed up at an Atlanta branch of First Southern Savings and Loan to determine the status of his empire. A polite teller named Jasmine asked how she could be of service.

"I'd like to see the balance on my accounts, and possibly close my accounts."

"We certainly can accommodate you, Mr. Wright, and may I say we will hate to lose your business. A personal banker will assist you momentarily if you would like to have a seat in the lobby."

He looked around the bank. Three other customers were waiting for something or someone. They were completely engaged with whatever was happening on their phone screens. They seemed oblivious to each other and totally content.

The bank was clean. The carpet looked and even smelled new. John thought, *This place is decorated in modern obsessive-compulsive disorder.* Nothing was out of place. Neat stacks of withdrawal and deposit slips lined the customer desk. The staff was professional and polite. For an industry that was required to be exact, the place felt perfect.

Finally, a handsome, six-foot-five African American man named Robert Anderson strode across the lobby, shook his hand, and beckoned John into his office.

"Thank you, Mr. Anderson, for making time to meet with you and handle an important matter." John didn't have time for pleasantries, only business.

However, he did not tell Mr. Anderson *all* of his business. He left the marriage trouble out of the deliberations.

After a few investigative clicks and clacks on the keyboard, the revelation came. There had been two withdrawals at a branch in Albany, Georgia, ten days earlier. John held his breath a little. Each withdrawal was for exactly half of what that day's balance was.

John leaned back in his chair, processing the facts. Layla had traveled northeast and stopped in Albany to get some money. She could have gotten all of it. Withdrawing half of the funds demonstrated a characteristic that had appealed to John from the beginning. Layla was a person with an innate sense of fairness. She was also tough enough to stand up for herself. John worked hard for the money, and she wouldn't leave him high and dry. She worked hard, too—especially in the beginning. She put up with an enormous amount of the angst associated with his vocation.

She deserved her share of the spoils, what little there were. Mr. Anderson's data was just so Layla-esque. He smiled and felt grateful. Yes, she'd destroyed his heart by stepping outside of their marriage. But she hadn't compounded her indiscretion by decimating his finances. He thought he might even like to thank her, but he had no idea where she was. He wasn't about to go hunting her down by digging around. He had the phone number of her stepfather but quickly dismissed the whole notion of giving the man a call.

Why bother with any of that? Layla had made her choice when she'd walked out of that trailer. He did not intend to chase her. Nor did John want to judge her life by her worst moment, any more than he wanted to be judged for sitting outside a man's house with a shotgun. Today, he felt grateful, and he would try to walk out of the bank with the remaining money in the account.

"Thank you, Mr. Anderson. Would you mind closing those accounts?"

"Be happy to. Is Mrs. Wright with you in your vehicle?"

"What?" John was stung by the banker's question.

"Mrs. Wright is a signatory on the account. Is she here?" Mr. Anderson asked pleasantly.

"Um, no."

The banker smiled and said, "Well, take this form and have her sign it. Bring it back to any of our branches, and we can officially close your accounts."

John became slightly flushed. He hoped it wasn't a "tell" to the banker that his world was falling apart. He regained his composure quickly.

"Mrs. Wright is out of town. I'll be happy to take this with me. Meanwhile, please withdraw the money in the accounts and leave $10 in each. We need to utilize this cash and will officially close the accounts sometime later."

"No problem. Wait right here, and I will get you the money."

For a fleeting moment, John thought that Mr. Anderson saw through the whole deal and was going to get security. He knew it was a ridiculous thought. John wasn't robbing a bank. He was withdrawing his money. Within five minutes, Mr. Anderson walked back in with an envelope. Handing it to John, he said, "Here you are, Mr. Wright. Can we do anything else for you?"

"That will do. I appreciate your help." They shook hands, and with that, John walked out of the bank with $2,857.63, which was significantly more than he thought he would have for himself. He walked out and got into his truck, then placed his head onto the wheel for just a minute before popping up. "Where to now?" he offered to no one in particular. And no one, in particular, answered a word in response.

CHAPTER THIRTY

John's entire estate was in a duffle bag, a cardboard box, an old truck, a bank envelope, and a little nostalgia. He turned the old truck onto the interstate. He traveled north on I-85 to I-20 West. He had no deadlines and no agendas. His parents were aging. Dad had dementia and didn't recognize his son any longer. He was spending his last years in a home that could care for his needs. John didn't have the heart to tell his mom how things had unraveled in his own life.

At least once a week, and often more, John checked in on them and made sure they had everything they needed. He didn't have many resources to help but would have depleted them to take care of his folks. They were great parents, and they were always very proud of "their Johnny."

When they talked, he consistently steered the conversation away from his life to his father's situation, his parents' friends, and their needs.

It was getting more difficult to talk because Mom was asking too many questions about Layla. "I haven't talked to her in so long. Did I make her mad, Johnny?"

His default answers rotated from, "She must be so busy helping folks," to, "She has always loved you, Mom," to, "She gets in seasons, Mom. How are they treating Dad?"

He knew that he would have to break the news to her soon. There was no way he would do that over the phone. He'd have to drive to Tallahassee, where they had retired. Or, if he hit it big sometime, he could splurge and fly down there.

That decision was for another day. Today, he had to get somewhere called nowhere in particular. He'd spent a fair amount of his childhood traveling through the Southeast with his dad, who had worked for a medical equipment company. Dad had been pretty successful at it, right up until the time he got sick.

His dad hated waking up in a different hotel every couple of nights. There was no glamour in it for him. John sort of loved it. To him, it had been highly glamorous. During the summer travel season, he'd felt like a VIP at the breakfasts. He'd always been proud that his dad was a "Gold Member" at a couple of motel chains.

Motivated by a newfound wanderlust, John decided to drive until something hit him. He didn't plan on driving until "the Spirit hit him." He preferred not to be hit by Him anymore. Hopefully, their breakup would be amicable. Something else would have to hit him—not a presence but some intangible preference.

Loosely, he planned to go to Birmingham. He'd been impressed as a fourteen-year-old by the "Steel City," fascinated by the Statue of Liberty replica at an insurance building that had later moved to a commercial development park near I-459. Birmingham it would be. Why not?

At a stop for fuel between Six Flags over Georgia and the Alabama state line, he saw a brochure for the city of Guntersville, AL. The brochure touted the virtues of the city: The State Park, the fishing, the theater, the legendary fish houses, and, of course, the beautiful lake. John decided to take the scenic route up to Cedartown and then continue up 411 Northwest.

He'd thought something might hit him, and he was glad it had been a compelling travel brochure.

People always seemed to be in a hurry on the road. Ten miles per hour over the speed limit was the minimum expected flow of traffic protocol. Since John had nowhere to be and no time to be there, he found himself going ten miles per hour under the speed limit.

He enjoyed the drive. He hadn't enjoyed anything in a while. He smiled at the makeshift boiled peanut stands and the fresh tomato pop-up tents. The trees were spectacular and, several times, the highway was completely shadowed on both sides by trees that met high above. The canopies looked like some kind of horticultural hug.

Even though it was a short drive, fatigue jumped on him. Unbelievable weariness cascaded over him. He needed to crash.

John was well-aware of his budgetary limitations. However, he decided to splurge on something a little nicer than a hard bed at the Days Inn. He drove until he saw the sign for Wyndham Garden Lake. It was right on the water. The lakeside rooms looked like they were ten feet from the waterline.

He parked and walked in with his duffle bag, hoping for vacancies. There were plenty. To his pleasant surprise, the rooms cost less than the Atlanta dump he'd checked out of that morning. Unfortunately, the quoted price was for the non-lake front rooms. *Oh. That figures.* He must have been quoted the cheaper rate because of his demeanor and discount luggage. The prime lakefront rooms ran an even $110. "You know what? Let's splurge for the waterfront," he told the clerk.

The smiling clerk asked for I.D. He accommodated. The method of payment got a little tricky. "Cash," John said. "Mr. Wright, we will need to put a hold on a major credit card for incidentals and any damage. Standard policy." He didn't want to do it. Ultimately, John presumed he wasn't being sought out as an international spy, so he reluctantly submitted the card, but he assured the clerk that he would pay cash at checkout.

He slept, ate, watched television for seventy-two hours, looked at the water, walked downtown, and then rotated the order. It was rather glorious. He had been hard-charging for many years. He hadn't realized how tired he actually was. He felt exhausted beyond his years.

He had heard some of his colleagues talk about taking sabbaticals. They would unplug for thirty or even forty days. Frankly, he'd thought they must be weak-minded or having trouble with some kind of life-controlling, sinful issues in order to do something that erratic. His two days spent looking at the lake gave John an entirely different perspective on the concept of sabbaticals.

In denominational conferences, he'd heard the statistic that 1,500 ministers left the ministry each month, and that seventy percent were looking for a way out of it. Those stats had been disputed, but he knew many did depart for many various reasons. People didn't feel supported by the denomination they served. He could check that box. Low pay. Check that box. Expectations that were too high. Stress. Feeling alone. Check. Burn-out. No vision in the church. Low self-esteem. Check. Lack of motivation.

John had determined never to become one of these reported numbers. However, sitting on a picnic table looking at fish jump out of the water at sunset, he realized that he was now officially a statistic. He'd thought he would care about that. Time and circumstances change how people feel. He was a fish out of water.

Unfortunately, he didn't know how to get back to whatever body of water he was supposed to be in at that moment.

PART 2

10 YEARS LATER

CHAPTER THIRTY-ONE

John was sweeping up the floor of Hank's Hardware Store on an ordinary Tuesday. Hank's had been a fixture in Guntersville, AL, for generations. It started when soldiers returned from World War II, and took off as people began remodeling their homes or building new ones.

John looked about the same as he had the day he'd arrived in Guntersville ten years earlier. He ran five days a week. He kept his weight down and was conscious of his diet. His hair had receded just a little. He'd expected that. It had happened to his father and his father before him.

Ten years ago, he'd planned to drive and keep on driving. He'd stopped to sleep in Guntersville, and he had been sleeping there for ten years. The day he checked out of his "room with a view," he'd had breakfast at the Huddle House across the street.

That day, he'd been standing in line to pay his bill, and the man in front of him had been chatting with the cashier. He'd told her he was desperate for some help and asked her to inquire if she came across anyone willing to lend a hand. As he'd turned, the man had collected his change and looked at John, who was a total stranger to him. Matter-of-factly, the man said, "Hey, buddy—don't suppose you need a job, do ya?"

John had barely spoken to anyone for three days, and the question caught him off guard. It kind of stunned him. He didn't even take the time to think before he said, "Yeah." He said it because it was the truth. He didn't have a source of income, and his three-day sabbatical had cut into his cash. The job would be a good thing.

On receiving that unexpected answer, the man, named Louis Hank Sullivan, grabbed his chin and said, "Seriously?"

"Yeah," John answered again.

Louis looked at the cashier and said, "Tell her not to clean my booth. I have an interview to conduct."

Looking at John, he said, "If you need a job, I assume you have time for a sit-down, right?"

John nodded, and the two men walked over to the booth that Louis had previously occupied. *Serendipity*, John thought.

In the present day, John had worked himself up to the assistant manager's position. He employed the same strengths he had utilized in his previous vocation. He was good with the people. The customers loved John. He hustled. He had never shied away from work.

The pay wasn't great, but he kept his personal expenses low. He was a minimalist before minimalism was cool. The store owner had a connection with Inez Brandon, a widow with a farmhouse near the lake. It was more than she could manage. She had a functional apartment above the separate garage that she'd built for her grandson, who later moved to California.

The arrangement was simple: John would keep an eye on Inez and assist her with minor chores such as carrying in groceries and mowing the grass. He could live in the garage rent-free. There wasn't even a charge for utilities, although John insisted on paying a couple of hundred dollars a month and was willing to pay more. He could sit and look at the lake from an awkwardly-built deck on the southeast corner of the apartment. It was soothing to his soul, especially in the summers when daylight stretched a few hours past his quitting time at the store. Over the years, he had made a few relationships with customers. They had casual conversations about football and local politics. These relationships never became too deep.

One advantage that developed from a couple of his relationships was boat access. They had boats. John did not. So a couple of times a month, John would get in a bass boat and forget the world while he cast spinner-baits and pulled in a large-mouth bass or two.

On this particular Tuesday, John was joyfully going about his sweeping and other tasks, dreaming of his next fight with a fish. Carrie Long, a forty-five-year-old first-time customer, bounced up to the counter. John leaned his broom against the wall, wiped his hands on his apron, and walked to the register.

"Good morning," Carrie said, unusually bubbly. Southerners typically seemed to exude that joyful hospitality, but this lady seemed to be baptized in it.

"Good morning," John reciprocated. "Will this be all, ma'am?"

"I believe so," Carrie said. "It's refreshing to see a small hardware store that still exists. I love it."

John appreciated her enthusiasm. "I'm afraid these old hardware stores are becoming dinosaurs these days. They're nearly extinct." He cupped his hand over his mouth and whispered, "Don't tell the owner I said it."

They both laughed. Carrie vowed to keep the secret and added, "This is Quintessential Americana. Norman Rockwell."

"Well, I'm glad you think so, ma'am. Here is your bag, and thanks for your business." It was precisely that kind of customer service that had endeared John to old Louis Hank Sullivan. "Have a good day."

Carrie thanked the assistant manager of Hank's Hardware and walked to the door. John resumed his sweeping and heard the white noise of the bell as it tinkled a goodbye. Immediately afterward, it tinkled another hello. John looked up, and the bubbly patron was back.

"You have a pleasant way about you, sir. My husband just got transferred to Guntersville. We moved from Chillicothe, Missouri, and don't know anything about this town or state, for that matter. May I ask you a couple of questions?"

Ah, there it was. Carrie wasn't a "true Southerner" according to Alabama's unwritten rules, regulations, and mores. She was overcompensating. But John was glad for the diversion and, frankly, was proud of the knowledge he had acquired about the area over the course of ten years.

"Absolutely!" he answered. "Fire away."

Carrie held up the bag. "We can fix minor things like this. But not the tough stuff. We need a plumber for this old lake house we just moved into. Could you recommend a good one? An honest one?"

"Mike Brown," John answered without a moment's hesitation. "He's as good as there is in this town. If he gives you a price, it will absolutely be a fair one. Here's one of his cards."

"Thank you so much," Carrie said.

"By the way, I don't get any kickbacks from Mike. I just believe in what he does." They shared a quick chuckle.

"This is so great. Thanks again." She leaned in a little to see John's name badge. "John. Thank you, John."

"You're welcome. I have lived here for a few years. If there's anything else I can do for you, just let me know."

She said, "We're squared away on schools. We have one son. For years, we didn't think we could have any. Later in life, our little miracle came. Jonah."

"Jonah, huh? Strong name. How old is he?"

"He'll be ten in November. I hate to ask you for another favor, but maybe you could help me with something else?"

John genuinely liked this lady. He imagined that she must be a terrific mother. One could discern the depth of gratitude she possessed to even have a child. She reminded him of his own mom. She had the same demeanor. She even dressed like her. Carrie wore a knee-length dress with sunflowers on it and a powder blue sweater that perfectly complimented the dress. Her perfectly-coiffed hair even reminded him of the way his mother wore it, especially at Carrie's age.

"I'll try," said John. There were no other customers this mid-morning, and the job could get a little monotonous. After ten years, he didn't have to put a whole lot of thought into stocking screws and shelving hammers.

"I wonder if you could recommend a good church. We're traditional folk, but we'd like to find something with a little life, you know. Not too far out there, but definitely lively."

John's countenance completely changed—an involuntary reflex. His customer service had its limitations. This lady was suddenly "tearing up his nerves," as they said in these parts of Alabama. He thought of eleven things that he needed to do around the store right this minute. He looked down at his shoes and contemplated her request.

John pulled himself together enough to offer a response. "That's a little tougher. Plumbers, painters, and electricians are more in my wheelhouse. I'm just not too churchy these days, so I can't give you any good reviews."

Carrie looked a little disappointed as John continued. "Now, Barbara across the street is pretty dialed in on the religious landscape, I think. You may want to pop into her beauty shop and ask her."

"Perfect! I am trying her out tomorrow at three p.m. That was a good tip."

John offered a smile. She thanked him yet again and walked to the door. She turned halfway back and said over her left shoulder, "You know, when we find a great church—and I know there are great churches out there—my husband and I just might come back in here and invite you to go with us. And we'll buy your lunch! Jonah loves to meet new people."

John offered a courteous half-nod. The bell said goodbye again, and he just stared at the door. Under his breath, he muttered, "Yeah, go ahead and do that, lady."

At that moment, a switch went off inside John. This customer made him uncomfortable, and he was not used to this level of discomfort. Her bubbly nature. Her religiosity. She dared to name her "miracle" kid after a run-away preacher. Something about this encounter turned his life stale. It may have been coincidence or cause and effect.

After that encounter, even the view from his porch didn't appeal to him. When he locked the door to the hardware store that night, he felt like he'd set a timer. His shelf life at the hardware store dramatically shortened that day.

CHAPTER THIRTY-TWO

Louis Hank Sullivan did not enjoy receiving a two-week notice from his star employee. He tried mightily to sweeten the pot to make John stay. Ultimately, though, he counted himself fortunate to have had ten years with John. He completely trusted him and counted his service as a true gift. As unexpectedly as he arrived, he left.

John had not accumulated much of anything in ten years. He had the same duffle bag as before, and his empire had expanded from two boxes to three. His worldly possessions filled only half of the back seat of an old Nissan Titan pickup with 213,000 miles on it. John headed south and west.

In ten years, he had saved over $50,000 because he had no hobbies and virtually no expenses. Minimalism had its advantages. John was generous to his landlord. He bought an occasional wedding or birthday gift and socked away all the rest.

To John, his savings seemed both huge and inconsequential. He was savvy enough to know how quickly that amount of money, like water, could slip through a hand—especially for people with life-controlling problems like drugs and gambling.

Fortunately for John, the only life-controlling issue he had was fishing. In fact, the only regret he had as he pulled away from his little corner of paradise was Lake Guntersville. He would miss that lake. He had scouted out all the best honey holes during his fishing tenure there.

On occasion, a Bible character, story, or principle would insert itself into John's consciousness. He rarely appreciated those intrusions. They were painful and reminded him of a bygone era in his personal history—one he longed to move past. On the occasion of his departure from Guntersville, a passage from a poetry book in the Old Testament hit him in such a random way: "And if a tree falls to the south or the north, in the place where the tree falls, there it shall lie." These words seemed entirely appropriate to him, so he didn't immediately dismiss them as he had done with other intrusions.

Over the last ten years, other people had invited John to church pot-lucks, revivals, programs, and the like. Mostly, they had been half-hearted invitations. However, when Carrie Long had asked him to attend a church she hadn't even picked yet, the "tree had fallen." Her enthusiasm exuded into his world, and it was troublesome to him. A tree had fallen—he hardly knew what it was—and it was not going to spring back up. He'd decided at that moment that the spaces he was currently occupying felt crowded. The walls were moving in on him, and John refused to be trapped by anything or anyone, including himself.

He pulled the old truck into a cheap motel parking lot in Columbus, MS. Although he had more money than he'd had ten years earlier, he didn't have the urge to splurge. He didn't see any lakeside hotels. Thus, Motel 6 was enough for him. He spent a couple of days walking the streets of downtown Columbus.

The town felt like Guntersville in some respects. He did enjoy visiting the first home of Tennessee Williams and walking past the Mississippi

University for Women Campus. He walked historic Main Street and wandered into some specialty shops. St. Paul's Church, lit up at night, was particularly impressive.

He went to a local print shop and made a flyer offering handyman services. He had developed some skills in Clary. It seemed like everything in that church had been falling apart, and he'd learned some things by trial and error. Working for ten years in a hardware store had also increased his abilities.

He hung fourteen flyers in some local greasy spoons and a few Mexican restaurants. He even got permission to hang one in the window of the local hardware store. The store didn't particularly impress John. When juxtaposed with Hank's Hardware, this one was sorely wanting.

To John's astonishment, his phone began to ring almost immediately. He had a few things going for him in this new entrepreneurial effort. First, all of the contractors in the area were "covered over." They didn't have time to fix leaks, rehang shutters, and the like. John was happy to provide those services to a sometimes-desperate clientele.

Another thing he had going for him was his first customer. Larry Brennan was a sixty-five-year-old professional who lived alone. John was delighted to get this gig so quickly. He hit it off right away with Larry. He was an easygoing widower who had grown up in the Northeast. He told John that he'd moved about twenty-five years earlier and was delighted with Mississippi's slow pace and rhythm. Metropolitan Boston had become far too hectic for him.

The project Larry needed help with was a pool house. It was a simple bathhouse at one end of the swimming pool—well-constructed but in its original, worn-out frame. It contained two bathrooms and a quaint common area with outdated indoor and outdoor furniture and even a wall-mounted television. The doors opened wide so that guests had a clear view of the large, modern screen from the outdoor seating. The pool house needed a couple new fixtures, new flooring, and the doors had warped a bit, making them extremely difficult to close. John confidently quoted Larry a price and said he thought he could do it in one week or less, if the weather cooperated. Larry didn't blink and stuck out his hand—a gentlemen's agreement.

Monday morning, John showed up as promised, at exactly 8:00 a.m. The materials he'd requested were all there, piled up neatly by the doors. John carried his brand-new tool bag from the hardware store, the tools he had purchased the day before inside of it. He didn't notice the sales tag hanging from his bag until he was on the property. Then, embarrassed, he quickly snatched it off, desperately hoping no one had seen. John could have gotten all of his new equipment more cheaply at some big box store, but he'd wanted to patronize the local business as a matter of principle.

After this recent trip, however, he realized he didn't like going into the hardware store. He decided it was because he kept making mental lists of work that needed to be done immediately. The shelving needed to be repaired. Inventory needed rearranging. Dirt in the corners needed to be dealt with, as well as the attitudes of the clerks. Rather than making him feel good about his patronage, his visit had stressed him out. If he stayed in Columbus, he would have to decide on where to make future purchases.

John put his headphones in and listened to an eclectic mix of music. He enjoyed everything from rap to classical. He listened to funk, jazz, eighties rock, and even bluegrass. His selections depended on his mood and his activity.

John quite enjoyed the first two days of the project. No one bothered him, and the parameters were clear. On the third day, Larry came home from work and surprised his worker with some delicious Southern BBQ. It was a beautiful, clear day in Mississippi, and John welcomed the break. He accepted the chopped pork platter, fried sides, and sweet tea as well. He even appreciated a little human interaction.

Usually, there was an initial conversation in every relationship that unearthed the ordinary mysteries of life. John didn't really want to dig into the "where you from" and "what do you do" conundrum. He didn't particularly want people excavating his life, so he maintained that position towards others as a matter of policy.

Between bites, Larry broke this invisible protocol by peppering John with questions.

"Where are you staying?"

"Do you have a family?"

"Where are you from?"

"How long have you been doing handyman work?"

"Where did you learn to do this kind of thing?"

John deflected every question like a baseball player leaning away from wild pitches. Quick answers. Comments about the food. Shallow questions. "Do they have this kind of food in Massachusetts?"

John finally deftly moved the discussion completely. "Larry, tell me about yourself. What brought you to Mississippi? I assume your work did."

Bingo. Larry took the bait—and did so happily. John would quickly regret his question. "It was indeed my work. I am a pastor." The sentence smacked John in the face, and a wave of nausea hit him hard. He had in no way expected or suspected this revelation. "I had a sweet little setup in the suburbs. Nice salary and benefits package. But I got bored. My denomination posted about this opening in Mississippi, and the change appealed to me."

Larry went on to tell John all about his new position. All of the problems and possibilities. Larry said he was the pastor of the local "high-brow" church. He didn't realize when he came to Mississippi that, sometimes, folks in certain pockets of the deep south looked down on that sort of religion. He had even been called "Pastor Fancy Pants" by some older citizens.

John had never wanted to get back to work more than he did at the end of that lunch break. He was nervous that Ol' Larry might just want to convert him at worst or get him to come to a service at best.

What happened next stunned John. It stopped him in his tracks as he was collecting his lunch trash. Larry said, "I stopped believing in God about ten years ago."

Granted, John Wright hadn't attended a church service in ten years, but this felt like alternate-universe territory. What were the odds? Two existential crises, precisely ten years ago, and two vastly different responses. John thought about it and almost said, *Since when have ministers continued their employment as atheists?*

Larry saw that his handyman was a bit dazed, and he relished it. Larry loved to shock people with these disclosures. Before John could even verbally respond—though he doubted that he could even form a response—Larry continued his faithless homily.

"Oh, I did believe in God like a good little minister, like all of my colleagues. I was in lockstep. But then I began to look at the facts. The headlines. The injustices. If God was real and all-loving, why would He allow so many catastrophic calamities? Ultimately, it boiled down to that old question, 'Can God create a rock so big that He cannot move it?'"

John was downright bewildered. The only thing he could manage to utter was, "What on earth do you tell your congregation every week? I mean, what do you preach?"

Larry let out a hearty laugh. "Oh, my handyman friend, there is so much richness from the old book. I don't have to sell them on the fables and the fantasies. If they need that, plenty of televangelists can feed it to them. I concentrate on the bedrock of human principles and offer a hearty menu of potent philosophers as well."

There was something about this guy that now mildly disgusted John. It was not so much what he was saying but his demeanor. There was a peculiar cockiness about him. John wanted to be responsible, keep his word, and have integrity in his work. He also wanted to replenish his account with some income. But as much as John wanted all of that, he couldn't help himself. "Are you just in this for the paycheck?" he asked.

Rather than being offended, Larry leaned his head back and roared. John would have preferred if he'd felt insulted and clapped back. Instead, his response made John feel creepy.

"My friend, I have a calling. Just not a 'divine' one.'" On the word "divine," he made an exaggerated quotation marks gesture. "It is an earthly calling. I beat the drum for justice issues on the earth. Oppressive systems.

Empires. Inequalities. My life's work is to tip the balance on the scales to equality."

The irony was not lost on John, but it seemed lost on Larry. Here they were beside a crystal-clear swimming pool in an affluent Southern neighborhood. The pool house may have been outdated, but as far as John could tell, everything else on the property was premium quality. Larry had a Cadillac sedan with traces of the sticker still on the window. His garage was full of all kinds of "big boy toys." This faithless preacher was on a soapbox about injustice and poverty, projecting himself as some religious guru and living in affluence. John was, after all, remodeling a secondary home that billions in the third world would be thrilled to have as their primary domicile. John quietly wondered how many years of his old "Justice League" budget could be funded from just half of this charlatan's salary.

CHAPTER THIRTY-THREE

John didn't fancy himself a man who ran away from problems, per se. After all, he had plugged away in Guntersville for ten years. On the surface, an uncomfortable invitation from a town newcomer seemed to have flipped a switch for John in Alabama. He would later realize that there must have been something deeper at play—some subconscious wanderlust, an inherent dissatisfaction with the status quo, and a need for change. It was too much for him to get his head around, really.

The one thing he did know was that Columbus, MS, was not the place for him. The pool house job was done on time. Larry was satisfied. Expectations were met, and John had even exceeded a few. Larry promptly paid John and even gave him a $20 tip. "Get yourself a six-pack," Larry said as he handed it to him. Larry pledged that he would keep John's number because there were some other minor things he needed to address in the months to come before they became major things. John smiled and thanked him, but silently vowed in his heart to never work for this guy again and to do everything he could to not see him again in this life or in any life to come.

The entire encounter had been profoundly unpleasant. There was a bitter taste in the handyman's mouth. It was time to launch the sail and see where the wind might blow him. Again, he rationalized to himself that he wasn't running. There was nothing to run from. No, moving on was merely a matter of personal taste and style, he opined. Like the wrong cut of jeans, Columbus didn't fit him the right way. He had merely scratched the surface of the city's culture and what it had to offer, but alas, he did not enjoy what he'd discovered.

So off he went. He turned his truck onto SR-14 and headed south, deciding to try his luck in Florida. He wanted to change his vista from lakes and tributaries to ocean views. Preferably, he'd land in the Panhandle on the sandy beaches near Destin—perhaps Navarre Beach. There were faster ways to Florida, but he liked the backroads. So he took US-80 E to US-43 S and then US-84 E to SR-41 S.

John's dear father had passed a few years earlier, when he still lived in Guntersville. At that time, Louis Sullivan had given John two paid weeks to help his mother with all of the details and administrative duties concerning the funeral service. The boss was glad to do it, as John rarely asked for anything particular, let alone time off. It was a mentality that departed from that of his other staff. Louis even gave John a little gas money.

John called his mom on the way to Florida. One reason he wanted to land in this part of the world was to be closer to his mother. The distance between them had been challenging over the last decade, but with the passing of his father, he knew that Mom might lose her reason to live. She was a doting and full-time caregiver, even after having placed her husband in a care facility. She'd punched an imaginary clock every day and attended to the many needs that the care facility staff didn't have time to handle. Her husband had been her reason for existing. John didn't want his mother to give up on life after her reason had passed away.

John drove slowly and sipped coffee from his Stanley mug. Why be in a hurry when there were no deadlines and not even an exact target location? He drove and listened to some movie soundtracks and a little bluegrass. He listened to *The Mission*, *Jurassic Park*, *Titanic*, and *Goldfinger* soundtracks but broke them up with a bit of *Nine Pound Hammer*, *John Henry*, *Whitehouse Blues*, and *Bringing Mary Home*.

John had a pocketful of money. Literally. He had cashed Larry's check right away and checked out of the dumpy little motel, leaving the twenty-dollar bill he'd received from Larry on the bedside table for housekeeping. He was in good spirits and in the mood to upgrade his vagabond living situation, albeit temporarily.

On his call to his mother, John gave her the good news. "I'm moving somewhere closer to you, Mom."

She nearly giggled with excitement and then became quiet. About a year before the funeral, John had shared some quite sad news, in person, about Layla. He was concerned, even that night, that his mom might lose some of her motivation to live. He'd been genuinely worried about her. She'd had to lie down and hadn't been herself for days.

Mrs. Wright had so hoped for grandchildren from John and Layla. John's saving grace in that situation was that his sister, Michelle, had given their mother three healthy, beautiful grandchildren.

But this call was indeed a happy one. John promised to get to Tallahassee soon after he got settled and spend a few days with her. He would do some work on the yard and on any other projects she hadn't been able to tackle. By now, he was somewhat proficient in the fixing-things-up department.

John drove to Navarre, the third-largest community in the Panhandle of Florida. It hadn't always been this big. In 1970, there hadn't been even two thousand people there. In fifty years, it had increased in population thirty times over. The town was made up of federal workers, military personnel, and people in the defense industry.

This little spot twenty-five miles east of Pensacola had become popular with people for various reasons, not the least of which was its miles of white, sandy beaches. Nature enthusiasts were drawn to visit and move to the area for the stunning topographical variety that brought joy to that ilk.

When John got to the corner of US Route 98 and State Road 87, he began looking for a place to throw his duffle bag for a few days. There were a few hotels along the way. Some were national chains, and some were local outfits. He preferred chain motels as a rule when he traveled because he knew that there were basic expectations for all of them. Some even exceeded these expectations. Other chain motels had occasionally disappointed him.

When it came to restaurants, he loved local spots, those hole-in-the-wall joints that a traveler could only experience in that particular location. Restaurant chains bored his palate. He'd wondered if that was what had happened to his marriage. Had Layla simply become bored with the mundane menu?

Realizing that he was hungry, John rolled his truck into one of those establishments with a local feel. "Bo-Samson" was the name of the hole located in a wall. It would be the *soup du jour* today. The special of the day wasn't soup, but a huge fish sandwich, which John discovered to be thoroughly outstanding. When he walked to the register to pay, he saw the "Help Wanted" flyer. John jotted down the phone number on his receipt and tucked it into his wallet, doubting he would do anything with it. However, he was on an information-gathering mission, and this was simply a piece of information. Bo-Samson needed a cook. He was undoubtedly not a cook, but he did meet one important criterion: the need for a job.

CHAPTER THIRTY-FOUR

The trio was in rare form on this day. There was a short, portly woman. There was a gentleman in his mid-fifties with zero patience. He had several spider veins on his face. There were many potential causes for these broken blood vessels. John didn't think that genes, sun, or injury had caused them. His best guess was alcohol. The third member of the trio was an attractive woman in her early thirties named Sharon. They were all "singing," but they sang different songs and had a complete lack of harmony.

"Where's the patty melt?" screamed the portly waitress. She yelled it two more times for good measure, in case the first primal howl hadn't registered.

Spider Vein Guy gave a deep and authoritative directive. "Drop some onion rings and start a top sirloin! Medium!" While the alto and the bass were simultaneously bellowing, Sharon the soprano added, "Table three says the lasagna is cold."

John interrupted their dissonance, "It wasn't cold until it sat there for ten minutes. Pick up your food, people!" He was not enjoying their performance in the least.

John had been on the job as the short-order cook at Bo-Samson for four months. He'd taken the job for several reasons. At the top of the list was his practical need for employment. Second, the only jobs available in Navarre were largely comprised of military or tourist positions. He met no qualifications for military employment. He'd interviewed well for an assistant maintenance position at a new apartment complex.

Finally, he decided to take the cooking gig because it might stretch him. He did not qualify for the job because of his experience, per se. Instead, he met several of the primary requirements. He walked upright, breathed, and he was not currently incarcerated. Having reliable transportation also put him at the very top of the heap of candidates.

"How hard could it be?" He thought to himself. He had experience eating food and a working knowledge about how poorly-prepared food tasted. John was right about one thing: it did stretch him. He was pretty good when the restaurant wasn't busy. He took pride in his work, just like when he'd worked at the hardware store. His meticulous nature tended to slow him down a bit.

The busy days, like this particular one, were challenging to him. Timing was everything in this job. The toast had to pop up when the eggs were finishing, and so on. It was always helpful when the wait staff cooperated in the process. He took it as a personal affront when someone complained about the food he prepared.

Even in the chaos that accompanied high-traffic days, John tried to maintain an inner calm. He didn't have the first instinct to quit this job because it was hard. Inherently, he knew that cooking wasn't the final stop on his life tour. However, he loved a challenge and would not even think of moving on until he had mastered this simple job, which had proved to be not that simple after all.

For three months, John lived at a local motel. It was located across the busy highway from the ocean. There were some glimpses of the water between other high-rise condos. He negotiated a decent rate with management because he was willing to live on the backside with a less-than-picturesque view of a marshy area. The view didn't have to be postcard-worthy.

Most people in the service industry lived several miles away because they couldn't afford to live near those they served. John felt fortunate to live near the restaurant. He would take his UGA Bulldog canvas chair across the road and watch the tides roll in or out when he wanted an ocean view between shifts.

After three months, he got tired of the crummy little motel. It was musty. He developed a mild cough and surmised that he must be inhaling mold coming from the wall air conditioning unit. Mold wasn't the only irritant. Pillows were, too. It proved impossible to find pillows that were thinner than the ones offered by the motel. The "personal bathmats" were glorified paper placemats similar to those used on the tables at his restaurant.

Although John wanted to master this job, he no longer needed to master living in a dump. He had graduated to bigger and better things. So he went back to the new apartment complex where he had previously interviewed. He'd saved enough money to put down the first month, last month, and a security deposit. The apartment he rented was practically new. One person had lived in it just six months before being transferred to another military installation. It still had a slightly fresh construction smell, which was a vast improvement over sniffing mildew.

John didn't consider himself to be materialistic. He wasn't exactly a minimalist. To him, a minimalist was a person that used the moniker not only as identity but almost like an obsessive hobby. Some people boat. Others play disc golf. Minimalists simply did *minimal*. In contrast, John just didn't need much. Existing without much was not as much purposefully intentional as it was organic. However, he did have to admit to himself that the older he got, the more he appreciated comfortable, clean space.

John tossed his apron and clocked out of his shift on this particular day. He didn't immediately leave the restaurant, but parked his truck in a familiar spot near a large oak tree with moss hanging off it. From that vantage, he could see beautiful, exotic birds fly into and out of a canal nearby. He sat in his old truck listening to a language app on his phone.

He repeated phrases—first in Spanish and then in English.

"*Estoy escuchando música hermosa.*" "I am listening to beautiful music."

"Where is the cathedral?" "*¿Dónde está la catedral?*"

He was lost in the lessons when an abrupt banging sounded on his driver's side window.

John nearly jumped out of his skin. He rolled his window down. "You scared the life out of me!"

Sharon was chomping on her gum. "Yeah, sorry about that. Didn't mean for my ring to bang the glass that hard."

"I thought something cracked my window. May I help you, Sharon?" he said, subtly irritated.

"Um, yeah—what the heck are you doing? It looks like you're talking to yourself, and doing it in French or something. I've been standing here for like five minutes. It's creepy."

John replied, "Yes, that is kind of creepy. Watching me for five minutes like a stalker is the definition of creepy."

"Stalker? You wish. Nobody is stalking you except the Slow Cook Police."

"Funny." John was not amused. "I ask again—may I help you?"

"Seriously, John, what are you doing?" Sharon answered.

John smiled. "What does it look like I'm doing?"

"Having a nervous breakdown."

John smiled again. "If y'all don't pick up your food quicker, I might have to be institutionalized." They both laughed.

Then, he continued. "Sharon, I'm not sure I owe you an explanation for my activities unrelated to our professional arrangement. But if you must know, I am trying to improve the quality of my life by learning something new."

Continuing to stand at the window, Sharon pushed, "Learning what? How to mumble to yourself more skillfully?"

"No ma'am. I am trying to learn Spanish. *Español. Pequeño.* You know? A little Spanish."

More seriously now, Sharon asked, "Why? I mean, all kidding aside. Why would you kill yourself in there putting up with us just to come out here and do something like this?"

All John could muster in response was, "I don't really know."

"Come on. Seriously, why?"

"I just felt like it, I guess. There are some people in my apartment complex who speak Spanish. They live here in some kind of special work program, and their kids mostly speak it. I'd like to know how to say hello and interact with them. You know, with some level of competency."

"That makes sense," Sharon said.

"*Competencia.*"

"... What?"

"*Competencia* means competent. Want another lesson, Sharon?"

"Maybe not a lesson, but how about some company? Want some company, John? I have some learning enhancements. How do you say 'learning enhancements' in Spanish?"

As she said this, Sharon pulled something from her Bo-Samson waitress apron. She held them in her open palms, showing them to John. At first, he thought they were pancake syrup bottles, and it confused him momentarily. How would syrup enhance his learning?

At this point in his life, John was still somewhat naïve. He didn't realize exactly what he was looking at. He leaned in and read the labels on the bottles. Sharon was inviting him to enhance his Spanish lesson with tiny airline whiskey bottles. She had quite a variety. One J&B, a Bacardi, and two different flavors of Jack Daniels—a sour mash and something else he couldn't quite read.

"*¿De donde de esto?*" John said.

"Is that how you say 'learning enhancements?'"

"No, Sharon. That means, 'Where did you get these?'"

"Wouldn't you like to know." She brushed her hair back in a flirty manner.

John just stared at her.

"Fine," she said. "My girlfriend is a flight attendant in Pensacola, and she keeps me stocked up." Now speaking softly, she added, "Do you want company or not? It is getting chilly out here."

John tried not to miss opportunities to be chivalrous. This invitation presented two challenges: one minor and one major. The minor one was the fact that Sharon was standing in Florida at four o'clock in the afternoon. Granted, it was the Florida Panhandle, which tended to be a little cooler than the Peninsula, but she was wrapped in an apron—which should have been tossed in a bin inside, by the way—on a sunny day. John disliked dishonesty to his core. That was an inconsequential issue.

The dominant problem was that up to this moment, John had been a teetotaler. As he'd told that dreadful contingent of board members in Columbia many lifetimes ago, he was not a "religious objector" to alcohol. Generations before him, 'his father had wrestled with the bottle. John carried suspicions that his father fought bottle battles in John's early life, as well. John had set a course to space himself far away from any addiction in his adolescence. He had stuck with that course up to this very moment.

Standing at his window was an extremely attractive coworker offering company and escape. She also said she was cold, and who's to judge a person's predisposition to cold? Timing was critical here. Just like the toast has to be done at the same time the omelet is finishing. He had to make a decision. *Timing!* The quicker, the better. He stared at the bottles for an uncomfortably long time. He was doing an internal investigation regarding the rationale of his adolescent decisions. He was wondering about the wisdom of their long-term implementation.

While his introspection was in full throttle, Sharon continued to feign being nearly frost-bitten by the Florida breeze. "That is very tempting, Sharon." He wasn't lying. "Really. It is very kind of you, but I was just on my way over to the community college to see if they have any classes. The language app doesn't explain stuff the same way as having a teacher does. Thank you for the offer."

Sharon did not have a poker face. She tended to wear her emotions very plainly. The disappointment on her face made John feel a sense of sadness. He did not like disappointing anyone; not a congregant, a customer, an acquaintance, or a coworker. She was lovely, lively, and funny. A woman had once crushed him, and he'd never actually recovered. He wasn't anxious to open himself up to that torture again. He also wasn't prepared to enter the onramp to any addiction that he had fearfully avoided for decades.

When weighed on the scales, the sad countenance of a coworker was more tolerable by far than the possibility of romantic anguish. It was more tolerable than dependence—the proverbial monkey on the back.

That day was a win for John, although he didn't feel like a winner. However, he did feel like he had a modicum of integrity as he rolled into the local community college and signed up for Spanish 1 for the upcoming quarter. He kept his word to the waitress. He had this errand. He had no idea why he wanted to audit classes. It was just something to do, and it certainly couldn't hurt him.

CHAPTER THIRTY-FIVE

And so it went in beautiful Navarre Beach, FL. John kept to himself. He minded his business and existed. He wasn't trying to change the world anymore. That proved to be too dangerous. By the same token, he wasn't interested in the world changing him either.

He worked. He dabbled with learning another language. He visited with his mother as often as possible. He sat by the ocean alone. He was often alone. Alone had a feeling, and he felt it to his bones. Patients with chronic pain often find that neither medicine nor therapy can help them. They just learn to live with pain. John just learned to live with the loneliness.

When his mother fretted over him being alone, he told her that the right "fish" had not "presented in the net yet." That phrase amused her. He tried to set her at ease. She asked, "Johnny, you have so much to offer a woman. How can you bear the loneliness?"

He knew the question was motivated by her own numbing aloneness. His answer to those questions was inspired partly to assuage her maternal instincts and partly to subtly "coach her up," as they say in the sports world.

"Mom, it's like ringing in your ears. You can let it drive you crazy or learn to accept it and thrive despite it."

She would ponder this and then press a little. As his answer sank in, she would take hold of something else to fret about, as mothers do. "Johnny, you are such a talented man. You're an eloquent speaker and have such a winning way with people. I can't stand to see you bury your talents."

Assuage her interests. Coach her up.

"Mom, it's a different kind of help I am offering now. It is a market-place ministry." He recoiled a little at the word. The word "ministry" was often accompanied by a feeling that he thought must be PTSD.

"Mother, it is incarnational." She liked it when he used his fancy theological words around her. "I am positioning myself among the people— the irreligious people." This statement was true; however, it was only a partial truth. He didn't bother to tell her that positioning himself among the people was *all* he was doing. Sure, he was kind to them. He most assuredly was not trying to point them to any light. Instead, he was just living. He was not thriving, as he'd implied in previous analogous answers. He was in the marketplace, but he was definitely not engaging in marketplace ministry.

When John felt that he'd learned everything he needed to know about being a short-order cook, he made a lateral move to the world of a coffee barista. He did love a good cup, but he didn't know much about making them. One day, on a whim, he asked the local coffee shop manager how their staffing situation was going. The manager informed John that one of his best employees was about to move with his spouse, who was being transferred to an important base job out west.

Just like that, John had a new career: barista. The learning curve was fast. During his two weeks' notice at Bo-Samson, he crammed like a seminary student during finals. Between restaurant shifts and his Spanish

2 homework, he tried to learn everything he could about the world of fine coffees. Ellie's Coffee had those fine coffees and a fine reputation in the area. Although relatively new to the community, the café had quickly built up a fiercely loyal clientele. People loved the folksy charm, the extraordinary flavors, and the skilled employees. An employee wasn't hired unless and until they convinced the owners of their strong work ethic and consistent, friendly nature.

It was no time at all before John was promoted to shift supervisor. He excelled in that position and was made manager within six months. The owner recognized what other bosses in his life had recognized: John Wright was trustworthy and likable. He had an innate likeability that could not be taught in a classroom or perfected in a seminar. One either possessed that "it" quality or they did not.

John also had an advantage that most of the other employees did not have, which wasn't exactly fair. He was ten to twelve years older than the youngsters the coffee shop employed. Ellie's provided premier job opportunities for people discovering themselves and their abilities on their way up life's ladder. One might argue that John found Ellie's Coffee Shop on the way down that same ladder.

He didn't try to look at it that way, though. He didn't waste time with such morbid introspection. He just tried to keep his head down and be a productive member of society. He did not want to cause trouble nor receive any. He wasn't trying to discover himself nor his abilities. He was trying to learn a few new things to occupy the void in his mind. There was so much in the world that interested him and that he didn't know.

An old expression says, "Jack of all trades and master of none." This phrase is a derogatory expression for those who do not focus on excelling at just one worthy thing. John had worked in his twenties on the "master of one" track but now considered the "jack of all trades" track much more enjoyable.

Another advantage John had over employees of every age demographic was his absolute lack of commitment elsewhere. He did not have to report to a spouse. There were no children's games to attend. He was not part of any civic organization. He did not participate in religious services or service projects.

John worked. He slept. He sat by the water. He regularly exercised. He read. He pored over his Spanish lessons. Sometimes, he tossed around a football or shot some basketball in the park that adjoined the apartment with the kids from the same complex. The single moms often looked on with smiling appreciation—sometimes even with interested attraction. John was always courteous and polite, but never flirtatious. Then he repeated the activities the next day, often in different orders.

John definitely enjoyed the vibe at Ellie's more than the restaurant. The day could get busy at times, but his outstanding staff never allowed it to feel out of control like Bo-Samson had. Stuff got done, and it was handled courteously and excellently. The music was at the perfect volume and the genres rotated in a nearly-perfect eclectic variety.

The place just seemed to fit John. People came in and read alone. They held mini-conferences or one-on-one meetings. They bought merchandise. Some bright students would hole up in a corner and cram for exams while drinking four hours' worth of coffee. John had no greasy aprons to wear nor oily skin and hair at the end of the day. He could see himself riding this wave of employment as long as he'd ridden the hardware store wave. That was, until one particular Thursday.

On this day, John had his back turned toward the door. He was stacking some new inventory on the shelves near the register. Maggie, one of John's star employees, was waiting on a customer. She was an energetic and effervescent ginger. Everyone loved Maggie.

The shop was comfortably full, and the counter was void of customers, but two were coming in the door. Maggie said out loud to no one in particular—although she was aware of her boss's proximity—"Wow, I haven't seen anyone dressed like that in here in a year or two."

John had seen various uniforms, clothing styles, and even costumes during his tenure at Ellie's. He'd seen clowns grabbing a cup on their way to birthday party gigs. He'd once seen a United States Air Force General. He had done business with mimes, ghosts, and witches. Zombies had come by before Halloween spirit week at school.

He stacked the last bag of Maple Pecan coffee beans on the top shelf and started smiling, anticipating the surprise awaiting him when he turned around. When he did, he saw two customers that were not in costume. They were in uniform, and their uniforms disturbed John more than any zombie or warlock.

Two young ministers walked into the coffee shop in full clerical regalia. The man had a head of stunning gray hair. He was in his fifties, but his hair was cut in a very modern style. He wore black slacks, some attractive yet practical Samuel Hubbard dress shoes, and a clergy shirt. It was one of the shirts with the sewn-in collar and no tabs. In a past life, John had preferred this style. The shirt was generously cut for comfort, and the sleeves were short, perfect for Southern weather. John had always loved the single breast pocket with the black zipper. John always thought the outfit looked a little stuffy but felt immensely comfortable.

A young Hispanic female accompanied the older minister, wearing attire a bit more modern. She had on lovely dark jeans and a clergy shirt with designer buttons and a premium clergy tab collar. The two were laughing about something as they came in and appeared to be perfectly content. The young lady recognized one of John's customers close to the window—close enough for John to eavesdrop. They carried on a conversation in Spanish, and John understood about ninety percent. It actually gave him a mild sense of accomplishment that his Spanish lessons were paying off. He understood them as they talked about the goodness of God.

John's initial instinct was to run. The sight was too painful for him. His secondary instinct was to warn these two ministers about the assured pain awaiting them in their future. John immediately brushed off this notion as at least half ridiculous. Obviously, the gray-haired clergy had encountered some amount of pain and betrayal by now, but he hadn't laid his Bible on a stump in the woods and walked into the sunset.

When John had initially sized up the clergy as they stared at the menu on the board behind the register, he looked at Maggie. She looked back, but not with her customary smile and warmth. Maggie looked confused as she tried to read the expression on the face of her boss. She had never seen this countenance before and didn't understand it. The only thing John could muster up to say to his star worker was, "I'm overdue for a little break. You got this?"

Maggie replied, "I got it, Boss."

CHAPTER THIRTY-SIX

He recognized it on his own. John Wright did not need an intervention team to detect his issues. Besides, there were no relationships in his life that were close enough to pull off an intervention successfully, anyway. He acknowledged that he had a problem. Certain things triggered him: a lady expressing a desire to recommend a moderately charismatic church to her family, their son whom he had never met, named Jonah; an agnostic shepherd drawing a nice paycheck; most recently, a couple of clergy members doing nothing more offensive than wearing their clerical garb.

He knew he had a problem, but he had no desire to solve it. To solve this problem, he surmised that his one-person intervention was simply too painful. It would require digging up stuff long buried. Digging up stuff often unearthed a stench. He had an aversion to smelling the tidy graves located in the depths of his soul.

His current, triggered dilemma provided limited options:

Toughen up and get over the triggers.

Find some help to get un-triggered, or at least to function when triggered.

Get a therapist.

Find a psychologist or psychiatrist.

Maybe a priest or other counselor could help.

Or he could stay on the run.

Running was always an option. John didn't even try to justify or make excuses for it. He didn't try to convince himself that he wasn't a runner. Running appealed to him the most, as it seemed to hold the path of least resistance. It also presented the most worn-down path. He had a long experience with running away. The trails were tamped down and well-worn. Like they say about drugs, once that bridge gets crossed the first time, every subsequent trip gets easier.

John Wright was on the run again. Usually a very responsible employee and citizen, John resigned from his job via text to the owners of Ellie's Coffee. He made up an excuse that had just enough truth to make the lie seem authentic: "Mom needs me." Mom always needed him. The actual truth was that two perfectly happy people who happened to be wearing clerical garments made him too uncomfortable to work as a coffee shop manager.

What did John expect? Did he expect that he could run off to a geographical location completely void of ministers or religious leaders drinking coffee or functioning in society? None of his behavior or reactions made a bit of sense to him. He knew it wouldn't make sense to rational people either. So, "Mom needs me" was the story he told. The lack of two weeks' notice stung the owners. What stung John about it was that it didn't even sting him at all. For a man who prided himself on being a do-the-right-thing employee, it bothered him that he didn't care about leaving Ellie in the lurch.

It was simply time to go. His lease would be up at the end of the month, so there was no foul there. John gifted the apartment management company an extra two weeks and three days to get it ready for the next tenant. The apartment was furnished, so all he had to do was throw the duffle, the boxes—which had grown by two—and a suitcase in the back of his truck. John added the suitcase to accommodate a wardrobe that had grown a bit due to the expectations of being a hip barista.

Where to now? That was the question. He drove north on Highway 87 and then East on I-10, away from Navarre Beach for two hours. He got hungry, and one of the waffle joints that littered every other exit in the South appealed to him. He had waffles and sausage on his mind.

As he exited, he saw a billboard for Cavern Car Sales. His old truck had almost 300,000 miles on it, and he was in the mood for something a little more reliable. If he purchased a vehicle, he knew he would have to pay cash, as businesses tended not to finance people without permanent addresses.

He had two questions for the waitress. "Where am I?"

She informed the hungry traveler that he was in Marianna, FL. "Some people love it here, and some of us hate it," she elaborated while chomping her Juicy Fruit gum.

He asked the second question. "Where is Cavern Car Sales located?"

"Two miles south of this upscale dining establishment," she said. She further educated him that it was called "Cavern" because of the Florida Caverns State Park just north of town.

She continued her mini-lecture, informing John that there was a diving cave in Blue Springs. The water in the Springs was freezing even in the middle of a Florida July. She spoke so glowingly that he realized his original assumption might have been wrong. His first impression had been that she was part of the "hate Marianna" group.

After a good waffle, over-easy eggs, grits, hash browns, and sausage patties, he drove around the sleepy little town. Like so many Southern towns, Marianna had a complicated past. The town was founded in 1828 by Scottish businessman Scott Beverage. He named it after his two daughters, Mary and Anna.

Nearly two centuries earlier, North Carolina citizens had relocated to the Marianna area to farm the rich, fertile soil. In September of 1864, there was a mighty battle in Marianna during the Civil War. Federal troops crushed the secessionists and militia. Slavery had been the norm during the preceding years, and the town had housed many plantation owners. Radical racists were no longer openly walking the streets. John was confident that there were closeted racists, however, because he had encountered them in many other cities and towns.

This town did have a certain warmth to it. The downtown area was charming, and walking the sidewalks was like stepping back in time. This downtown Historic District included many beautiful antebellum homes.

The citizens of Marianna seemed exceedingly friendly and helpful. He had only been in town for a few hours and had heard about the beautiful Chipola River three times, as well as the other attractions the waitress had mentioned.

John walked onto the lot of Cavern Car Sales at three o'clock on a Thursday afternoon. Cavern was officially a Toyota Dealership, but the store prided itself on moving a fleet of various high-quality brands. His initial observation was that the most extensive inventory on the property was the quality used car lot. For a small town, this lot was massive. He noticed a couple of folks looking at the new cars, but about a dozen people walked along the rows of used cars.

"Bob Barfeld!" A man seemed to appear from nowhere, thrusting out his hand. It was alarming yet oddly charming, and John reciprocated.

"John Wright."

"Whatcha in the mood for, John?" he asked during a vigorous handshake. Before John could even answer, ol' Bob offered some suggestions. Bob would have made a good waiter. He knew the menu and had solid opinions.

But these were motorized vehicles, and the stakes were higher than a twenty-percent gratuity on a surf-and-turf. Bob was highly motivated. "We got a beautiful cherry red Corvette two days ago. Just got her out of detail. Wanna be the first to drive it?"

John tried to answer, "Well, I was just . . ."

"No! You look like a four-by-four man! How about a low-mileage F150? It is primo, man."

Bob threw out about three more options, and when he took a breath, John saw his chance. "Truck! I'm looking to trade in my old faithful for a new faithful."

They both laughed as Bob realized he might be a little too caffeinated and over-motivated with this prospective customer. "My bad, dude. It's just that I'm a little new, and this place is like a shark tank."

"What do you mean?" John inquired.

"Well, the guys kinda circle up and swap stories until a fish—um, *you*, the customer—comes by. Then the fastest guy there gets to pitch the beautiful product."

As Bob said this, he made a broad, dramatic gesture towards the motor carriages around them. "I've got a bum knee. Blew it out playing tackle at FSU. Let's just say my forty-yard dash ain't what it used to be. . . . and it used to be pretty slow."

They laughed again. John liked this guy. Bob's next zinger enhanced that feeling. "John, I got deceptive speed." He paused for the perfect beat. "I'm slower than I look."

John laughed hard. "You know, Bob, that doesn't seem fair. I don't know much about this industry, but shouldn't there be a rotation system of some kind?"

When that question tumbled out of John's mouth, he had an immediate flashback of a sermon he had preached in Springfield and also in Clary—albeit refined a bit the second time. It was about a man in the New Testament laying with a multitude of sick folks. As the story goes, an angel would occasionally stir the water, and the first one in was healed of whatever ailment they had. The guy from the story could never beat the others into the water. That account is what Bob's predicament felt like. As John recalled, he'd even titled the message: "Stuck in the Shark Tank" or something along those lines.

There was nothing like a dredged-up ministry flashback to wipe a perfectly good smile off of John's face. So he pivoted and got down to the matter at hand. "Bob Barfeld, I would like to give you some business, bum knee and all. That is, if we can come to terms on a good, low-mileage reliable truck."

For a second, there was a possibility that boisterous Bob Barfeld might just start crying. He needed to make a sale. The very thought that he might not have to haggle, wrangle, and use his gimmicky tricks to catch this fish was perfectly refreshing.

CHAPTER THIRTY-SEVEN

John drove his Nissan Titan with low mileage to his job at the Cavern Car Sales. In just two years since his conversation with Bob Barfeld, a few interesting things had happened. First, Bob had become a good friend—and John hadn't had a friend in a long time. He even cracked the door open for the first time and shared with another human being a glimpse of the angst of his past. Bob was a good listener and always seemed interested in John's journey.

Then there was the job. John felt tremendous satisfaction in selling cars. It surprised him, and he couldn't explain it. For his friend Bob, the job was more of a necessity. He had a wife and two small children. Another child was on the way. He was a motivated "shark."

To John, the job was a game. It was a contest. He liked the competitive nature of the thing. He didn't so much compete with others, but rather against himself. He wanted to improve his performance from month to month.

John did well. Very well. He moved a lot of vehicles. The franchise owners even talked about his future after the first year. Inquiries were made regarding any desire he might have to be the sales manager for the fleet of twenty-six elite "stallion salesmen." When presented with the offer, he thought, "Pick a metaphor and stick with it." He liked the shark metaphor better.

He was flattered, but John had had his fill of bossing people around back at the coffee shop. He would stick to sales. He didn't want to be the boss, but he did enjoy offering input and suggestions. During his second sales staff meeting, he recommended a simple rotating sales force when a potential customer came on the lot. He wrote on the whiteboard an uncomplicated system. *Eureka!* They implemented the plan immediately, and eighty-five percent of the team was thrilled. The dissatisfied fifteen percent happened to be those that were the fastest stallions/sharks. But the company implemented the system, and it stuck.

On this morning's drive to work, John was in a good mood. Sales were good. The weather was perfect. The money was good. His friendship with Bob was good. Life seemed as good to John as it had in a long time.

He turned on the radio and started scanning some stations. He flipped through morning talk radio comedians that were not funny, a country song that was too twangy, and a country song that was too "un-country." Hard rock. Punk rock. Stock report. Weather report. He just let the stations automatically scan. Classical. Jazz. Something that sounded like Japanese.

The next station was a preacher. He wasn't a country preacher pounding the wooden pulpit with the typical Southern preacher radio scream. This voice was measured and articulate. "When Peter said he was going to go fishing, it was about the same thing as saying, 'I'm going to go get drunk tonight.' He wasn't supposed to fish for fish anymore. He had a higher assignment. He was to fish for men. After a night of failure, a man was standing on the shore."

John kept waiting on the station to scan to the next R&B or Pop station automatically. It did not, and John's hands had not moved from the steering wheel. He did nothing to stop the station rotation. The voice continued even as John continued to wait.

"The fishermen thought it was just a man standing there, but it was, in fact, the Lord. The man on shore recommended that they change their vocational approach. 'Cast your net on the other side.' Peter wasn't the compliant sort by nature. I imagine he didn't receive that suggestion as a wonderful coaching tip. Rather, Peter probably thought, 'We've been doing this all night. He thinks he knows everything. Do it, boys! We'll show this man to mind his own business.'"

John had had enough. He started pushing buttons to rotate out of this blather. The voice continued. Suddenly, John's good day turned a little sour. How frustrating. The Titan truck had never given him this kind of trouble before.

"So God is making breakfast for a boat full of backslidden followers. Can you believe it?" John couldn't believe that his radio was broken. "If that were not enough, he allowed them—no, he instigated for them—incredible success. One hundred fifty-three fish. Peter went from zero to one hundred fifty-three in zero point nine seconds, and even blustery Simon knew he wasn't that good."

John liked this preacher and hated him at the same time. He wasn't in the mood for music or news anymore. John turned off the radio. At least, he tried to. But the radio wouldn't go off. The voice didn't go away. "The Lord might actually make you successful in your rebellion. He might even make you breakfast over an open charcoal fire. You know there are only two places in the New Testament where there are charcoal fires, right? One was when Peter denied the Lord while warming his hands, and the other is here on the beach as God circles him back to his purpose."

John didn't know whether to pound the dash in anger or shed a tear. Laughing was not an option because this situation was simply too weird to laugh. A professor of evangelism had lectured about stuff like this in an old Presbyterian training manual from the 1970s during his seminary days. John had been interested and even entertained by the stories, but he had never put a lot of stock in that sort of thing.

He recollected that the manual warned the trainees to beware of and even to expect supernatural and evil interference right at the moment of commitment. The television might come on by itself to distract penitents. The evangelistic team could be unaware of a pet that might come tearing out from under the couch where they were seated. The sleeping baby in the back might just start screaming.

This radio problem seemed to be the reverse philosophy of that ancient seminary warning. John highly doubted that, even if what was happening could be attributed to the supernatural, it was of the evil variety. Why would a devil want anyone to hear Bible stories? He doubted it was supernatural at all. There had to be a natural explanation. There must be a short in the wiring, a problem with frequencies, or just something besides a metaphysical explanation.

Not only did the radio refuse to be turned off, but when he tried to turn it down it got progressively louder. He stepped on the accelerator. He could not get to work soon enough. When he pulled into the dealership, all of his windows were down due to the volume. This attracted looks from the sales force and several customers. He couldn't wait to turn off the engine and silence this radio stranger. When he turned off the ignition, he did not turn off the voice.

The radio blared loudly. "What did Peter think as he swam up on that shore, and there was Jesus? He dripped his way up to a prepared breakfast and remembered a similar scene from years earlier. It was a beach like this where his Lord called him to fish. He had restored him privately earlier, but since his betrayal was so public, it was here he initiated a public restoration."

John could not abide this bizarre scene in the presence of so many onlookers. He popped the hood and disconnected the battery as fast as possible. It did not disconnect the voice. It continued. "Who is pulling themselves up on the shore tonight, dripping with rebellion and dreaming of reconciliation? Where are you? Return to the scene of your divine assignment."

He quickly reconnected the battery cable, started the truck, and parked in the farthest spot at the dealership away from the showroom. He slammed the door and muttered, "Preach away, loudmouth."

He wasn't about to engage anyone in conversation about his ludicrous morning. The entire thing rattled him. He wanted to forget about it. Forgetting was a difficult assignment. He could not forget that it happened, and he could not ignore the spoken words. He had no intention of taking them to heart.

He went to the truck at lunch to see if the man was still blaring from his radio and giving his stump speech about backsliders. There was no voice. "Thank God," John said. Even as he said it, he realized the irony of the utterance. "Thank God that no one is talking about God." He half-expected that the radio had drained his battery from whatever anomaly had caused the malfunction. The truck started right up. "Huh," he said with a shrug. He drove off to get a sandwich but made a very calculated decision that he did not need any music or entertainment on the drive.

CHAPTER THIRTY-EIGHT

The former pastor and minister of the Gospel of Christ sat alone at a bar. He felt completely out of place, like a BBQ grill master attending a vegan convention. He found himself on this night at the Purple Parrot Saloon. Customers and employees of Cavern Car Sales had often invited John for drinks from the beginning of his employment. They'd asked him to join them at "The Parrot" and many other similar joints. People had long since quit inviting him after a plethora of polite "nos."

No person had invited him on this night. He had driven by "The Parrot" many times on his way home from work, depending on which route he'd chosen. Tonight's invitation came courtesy of a bizarre day. The day beckoned him. Even after twelve hours in the shark tank and closing the deal on two outstanding sales, the circumstances of the day rattled him. How does a radio work when not connected to a power source? Of all things to get stuck on, why did it have to get stuck on some Bible lesson? Rarely had he wished to hear more political commercials, but he would have preferred mud-slinging blaring on a loop to what had jammed his truck radio.

So there he sat, staring at a glass of whiskey. He was twisting it back and forth with his thumb and index finger. He was a complete neophyte in the world of alcohol. He had never touched the stuff. Never. There was that one and only time he'd attended an ecumenical service where they had served communion. He'd been used to the customary sweet grape juice during communion, but that juice had been of the fermented variety. His entire career in alcoholic beverages was comprised of that single communion experience.

He was such a novice that, when the bartender asked what he wanted, John pointed to the wall behind him and asked, "Is that whiskey?"

The barkeep said, "Not really, but this is."

The former Reverend said, "Just give me that."

So he got it. Now, the questions before him were what to do with it and how to do it. Of course, drinking it was the objective. But was one supposed to mix it with peanuts or sandwiches? Was it to be chased with something? He remembered someone in one of his addiction outreaches had talked about chasers. What exactly was a "chaser"?

There he was, contemplating the day, the glass, the future, the chase.

He honestly didn't want to enter the on-ramp of addiction, as he had previously referred to it. However, at this point, he felt that he might be wired strongly enough to imbibe some spirits. He'd left *the* Spirit near a stump back in the woods in Clary, GA. Maybe *these* spirits would lift his own. Twist. Think. Contemplate. He was knocking on the door of fifty, but he suddenly felt like a twelve-year-old staring at an uncle's liquor cabinet.

The sweet, Southern, feminine voice stopped his futile introspection. "Are you going to stare at that drink all night, or are you going to show it who the boss is?" The question startled John back into the moment. He looked to his right and saw a beautiful, auburn-haired woman who looked to be in her early forties. Her stark beauty made her look as out of place as he felt. Mark answered the question with, "I haven't decided yet. Time will tell."

The woman slipped off of her barstool, located exactly three stools over on John's right. She slowly approached him and said, "Hi. I'm Mary Simpson." John politely extended his hand and introduced himself, "I'm John Wright."

She sat down on the empty stool beside him and said, "What brings you to this elegant establishment?"

John caught his heart beating a little faster. Layla had been his life's great romance—and his life's last one. He had become an irreligious monk since she walked out of that dumpy trailer in South Georgia. But John was a man, after all. He was a man with all of the manly inclinations that accompany that reality.

It wasn't that John hadn't had his moments of flirtations and even overtures. He was a better-than-average-looking man. He was still athletically built and strove to keep a professionally-appealing appearance. Over the years, he'd dabbled in innocent dalliances here and there. There had been flirtations along the way, and the occasional entertainment of overtures. But nothing had ever morphed into a full-blown tryst. It had never even gotten close to that.

But now, a gorgeous ginger had gotten very close to John and all of his inclinations. He consciously told himself to breathe a little more slowly and play it cool. He was already off-balance, being in an environment where he was altogether uncomfortable.

He took a deep breath, smiled, and answered. "Well, you know."

Mary smiled back and said, "Not really, John Wright. That's why I asked you what brought you to this elegant establishment."

"Well, I've never been in here, and I'm trying something new."

"New?"

"Yeah. I haven't been in a bar in a long, long time. The last time I was in a bar—the only time—was many years ago when, of all things, I dedicated one for a..." John's voice trailed off.

Laughing, Mary responded, "Dedicated? How does one even dedicate a bar? Like to the gods or something?"

John had dedicated the space that a bar was occupying. The owner had become a newly-baptized convert and wanted to utilize the bar for God's purposes. John subconsciously added that to the list of painful memories and moved on.

Embarrassed, John said dismissively, "Another life ago. Boring. Enough about me. What brings Mary Simpson to this exclusive club?"

"Well, speaking of boring, I have a boring ol' sales rep job, and this slice of paradise is part of my territory," she said, waving with her lovely hand. "I'm here tonight nursing my wounds, I suppose."

"Wounds?" John inquired with genuine interest.

Mary sipped on her watermelon vodka and sized him up. "This is kind of weird..." she started, but he interrupted her.

"If it's weird, tag it onto the bibliography of a very weird day. Oh, sorry—I cut you off."

She took another sip, dabbed her lip with a small napkin, and continued. "That's quite all right. You have a kind way about you. What's weird is that I usually don't open up to anyone. Hardly ever. I play everything close to the vest. But I feel very tempted to open up to someone I met about six minutes ago."

Her smile could stop traffic, John thought.

She continued. "My company promised me a promotion this year, and yesterday that promotion went to a good ol' boy who plays golf with the boss. The guy is such a clunker, too. I guess I couldn't compete with the locker-room banter. That was just the cherry on top of a rotten year."

She measured John's response, seeing if it was safe to continue.

Concluding it was, she did. "About six months ago, my fiancé decided he would preemptively trade me in for a younger model."

"Yikes."

"Yeah. Big yikes. I guess I am boring too, huh?" she asked.

"Not at all. It is thoroughly interesting and completely troubling. Really brutal stuff. Both things sound brutal. Kudos to you for powering through it. I'm sorry that these things happened to you, Mary."

John meant it, and Mary knew that he did. "Don't know how much powering is happening." She paused again. "I knew you were a kind soul. I'm a pretty good judge about these kinds of things, with a few notable exceptions."

"Not too sure about that, but thanks."

"Since I'm breaking my own rules on privacy, l might as well walk a little further out on a limb."

"Walk on," John encouraged.

"I am not in the habit of asking a stranger for anything, usually, but. . . ."

"We aren't strangers, Mary. We've been friends for over eight minutes," John said as he became a little more comfortable in these environs. They let a little laughter break some of the severe tension in which they suddenly found themselves. "How can I help you?"

Sheepishly, she answered, "I came here with a client. She got queasy right after we walked in. She thinks it was something she ate. I told her I would get a car service back to my 'five-star' motel. If it wouldn't be too far out of the way, would you mind dropping me off?"

The question paralyzed John. He looked into her blue eyes for a long time. When it reached the point of embarrassment, he looked down at his untouched whiskey.

Now Mary was embarrassed. "I shouldn't have asked. That's too much, and I've made you uncomfortable. I am so stupid."

John interrupted her. "Not stupid at all."

She tried to explain the request. "I had a bad experience in a taxi in Atlanta once. *Frightening* is more like it. The creep took me down some side streets, and I had to jump out at a stop sign and run. Anyway, I'll get a ride from one of the phone apps. I need to get over my fear."

"No way. I get it," John said. "Truly, I do. Normally, I would love to help a damsel in distress. A gorgeous one at that. Not that you're in distress." His awkwardness was back and vexed him, but he decided to keep plowing. "I'm sorry. I have work early, and I just got out of a relationship. I am all thumbs socially."

John hated lies and liars. He found justification in this one because, in his mind, time was relative. After all, God supposedly created the world and everything else in six days. So "just getting out of" could easily mean decades ago. Using God's math, it all worked out in his mind—at least for the moment.

So John purposed at this moment to do two things: maintain his personal boundaries and help this beautiful woman in the Purple Parrot Saloon. "My mother tells all of her friends at the weekly bridge game in

Tallahassee that her Johnny is very chivalrous. I am determined to make my mamma proud."

Mary offered a disingenuous chuckle.

"I have a friend at work that I would trust with my children's eyesight—if I had children. His name is Bob Barfeld." His awkwardness wouldn't go away. "But Bob has children! Like three of them. He drives a couple of days a week for one of those internet companies. He needs the side hustle with all of those mouths to feed. Drives a black Camry with one of those light deals on the dash. He lives close to here. Let me get him up here."

She tried to object, but he was already ordering the ride on his phone as he talked with her.

"There, Mary—it's done. And I put it on my credit card, because I am honored to meet you and happy to try and do a good deed at the end of a long, bizarre day. You have been a bright spot to the day. I mean, I probably should have bought you a drink or whatever the bar-life protocol requires."

"Well, okay . . . and thank you very much," Mary said disappointedly.

Sensing some sadness, he asked, "Hey sales rep, do you have a business card? I might need whatever it is that you sell. I guess we didn't get around to that conversation, did we?" The offer made her smile. She handed him a card.

"Here you go. Whatever elder care needs you might have, I'm your woman. Whether it's a toilet seat riser, a bathtub transfer bench, or adult pads."

John took the card and said, "You didn't tell me you peddled such sexy products."

"You failed to tell me what product or service you peddle," she said.

His phone vibrated. "Look here. Saved by the buzz. Next time, Mary. Bob Barfeld is already here. I told you he was close. And motivated!"

"Do you have a card?" she asked.

"Let's keep it mysterious. I'll contact you."

"What a brush-off," she said, half-playfully. "John Wright. Well, I can finally tell my mother that I met Mr. Wright." She looked him in the eye and winked. "You are a kind soul, Mr. Wright. I hope you get it all worked out."

He looked confused. Mary pointed to his whiskey. "Work it out. Find out who the boss is." As she walked by him, she gently touched his shoulder. The touch gave him an involuntary reaction, a sort of shudder, that he hoped was unnoticeable.

"I'll walk you out to Bob. You know, chivalry and all." He did just that and thanked Bob, who profusely thanked him back while cutting his eyes at the beautiful woman. He gave his buddy John a "wowzah" look with a slight head tilt in her direction. John shook his head "no" and sort of rolled his eyes. "See you tomorrow, Bob, and thanks again. Good night, Mary. I'll be in touch for all of those elder needs on the horizon. Bob, don't tell her what we do. Keep the mystery alive. Let her think we're in the CIA."

He watched Bob and the beauty drive off to her lodging. When they were out of sight, he walked back into the Purple Parrot Saloon and assumed his prior position on the stool. He picked up the glass again, looked at the saloon door, and threw the whiskey to the back of his throat just like an old pro.

He was hit with an immediate wave of regret. He didn't regret breaking his perfect record. He was terrified that he had done drinking wrong. John could not imagine his throat burning worse if he had downed twelve ounces of Texas Pete Hot Sauce. *Is this normal?* John thought. For ten full seconds, he contemplated calling the nearest poison control center.

After reacting like a person who had never experienced potent alcohol, he said, "Hit me again, barkeep." It sounded like something one might say in the world of bars and saloons.

CHAPTER THIRTY-NINE

"Johnny, Johnny, Johnny! You are well on your way to becoming salesman of the month. Again! Now, don't get the big head." This morning motivation was brought courtesy of Adam Vans, boisterous Sales Manager. He was a couple of years older than John but looked to be fifteen years his senior. He liked to say that he had "high mileage." He was big, bombastic, and perfectly likable.

Adam fit the mold of the quintessential used car salesman. He was good with people and had just a touch of smarm in his personality. He liked to consider himself more of a sales coach, not a sales manager. He constantly used football metaphors and analogies.

Of course, Bob Barfeld loved to be "coached up" by Adam because it took him right back to his days of blocking and tackling at Florida State. Salesman of the Month rotated between John and Bob, who had now hit his stride on this new gridiron, the sales lot. They maintained a good friendship and enjoyed the friendly and healthy sales competition.

A newbie, Sam—short for Samantha—had won the prestigious honor three times last year and was coming on strong this month, too. Sam was a vibrant, energetic daughter of a car dealer from Portland, OR. She had come to Florida on a volleyball scholarship but 'hadn't been able to find a job in her major: psychology. Sam lost interest in that line of work, so she got a sales job—it was her default setting. Having grown up in the industry, she thoroughly understood it. She loved to psychoanalyze the boys at Cavern Car Sales, and it drove them a little crazy.

Adam walked off from his little coaching moment with John, offering him a sturdy and literal slap on the back. John usually enjoyed those affirmations, but this particular morning, the voice and the smack did not bless him. In fact, it worked in the opposite direction. He was working through something of a hangover on this particular day.

His lifetime of caution about "the devil's brew," "the poison scourge," and "the bloody monster" had been proven justified. Four months after his chance meeting with Mary Simpson in a watering hole named after a hooked-billed, brilliantly-colored bird, he found himself squarely on the ramp of addiction he had feared.

He'd cavalierly thought that he was mature enough not to fall into the patterns he grew up witnessing in his relatives. His current headache made it painfully apparent that he'd underestimated the quickness with which a monkey can jump on someone's back.

To make matters worse, the long shift did not help. He was scheduled to work until closing. The pain relievers he had consumed an hour earlier had finally started to kick in.

At dusk, a fish entered the little bay they called Cavern Cars. John looked over at the other sharks to determine which one was next in line to pursue. The salesmen were clumped together in one little school, laughing at jokes and swapping stories. No one was paying attention when Willis Taylor drove his twenty-year-old Honda Accord onto the lot. John decided to violate the exact rule he had recommended be implemented. He pursued the Honda out of order.

Willis parked at the endcap of a row of beautiful and expensive sports cars. Sizing up a fish's parking decision was part of the salesforce training process.

"Sir, what are you driving home today?" John asked with a smile.

"I like your confidence. What are you gonna do to make me a great deal?"

John liked the confidence Willis exhibited. He was six feet tall and had the frame of an athlete. He was a thirty-year-old African American and might just as well have been an All-American athlete, judging from first impressions. His car was a beater, but the rest of his effect and demeanor was anything but lacking. "I'm John. John Wright."

"Willis Taylor."

The two men shook hands, but Willis was rotating his head towards the gorgeous cars before he even loosened his grip. "Beautiful cars you have here, John."

"Oh, yeah. I know that I'm biased, but this is the best lot in the entire region."

"I believe it," Willis agreed.

The two men spent an hour together. They studied stickers and sat inside several vehicles. Lots of questions were asked and answered. If the others in the sales force were irritated at John for breaking protocol, no one seemed to express it. They may not have even noticed—John wasn't the only one nursing a pounding headache from the night before.

John had his elbows on the passenger's side door of a beautiful blue Corvette with the windows rolled down. This Vette was a used one, but barely. It had less than five thousand miles on it. Willis liked it when John pointed out that the owners had driven the depreciation off the car.

The previous owner had wanted a new toy that could go through the swampy mud in that part of Florida, so he'd traded it in. The condition was pristine, and the price was okay—not great, but fair. In his mind, John could already see the ink drying on a contract.

"Willis, of all the cars we've looked at tonight, this one seems to make you light up the most. What's going through your mind right now?"

Willis answered, "'Two roads diverged in a yellow wood.'"

John softly chuckled. "That's a new one. You're behind the most beautiful sports car in the county, and Robert Frost is on your mind. Okay. That checks out, because this car is poetry in motion."

"Smooth, John. Fast too. I like it."

John deadpanned. "Well, I do what I can."

"I'm standing—or seated—at a crossroads. If I go down the left road, I can definitely afford this one and maybe even keep my junker for those dirty errands. If I go down the right road, not so much. Probably have to cruise the low, low, low end of your used car lot."

John responded, "Not sure that I follow."

Willis explained, "I have a big life decision to make. My uncle has just offered me the VP position at his textile company. There's a pocket of a resurgence in some places down south. He bought two or three mills in Alabama, and they're starting to catch fire. If I work for him, this car— even a brand new model of this car—would not be a problem."

"That sounds great. But I detect that there could be a problem somewhere. Is it down the right road?"

Willis considered the question and looked for a couple of beats into the salesman's eyes. He exhaled and answered. "I am a minister. I pastor

New Horizons over in Okaloosa County. Let's just say that my current profession has not left me very liquid right now."

"Do you like what you do?" John asked.

The question surprised the prospect. "I wasn't expecting that response." He thought about it a second and said, "Man, I love it. I love helping people. But I don't like being broke. It's one thing to say, 'I walk by faith.' But it's a whole other thing to like it."

John now talked to him like a friend instead of a customer. "Okay. Put yourself in the corner office for your uncle. How does that feel? Can you see yourself being in the executive chair and enjoying that?"

"I can see enjoying the perks. The retirement. The expense accounts. I have to admit that I like the idea of being the boss of a few hundred employees." Then Willis let out a sigh and said, "When my mind wanders past that lineup of fringe benefits, the rest of it makes me a little queasy.'

John leaned in closer. "Willis, sometimes the truth leaks out in a sigh. I heard yours. There aren't enough bells and whistles to compensate for being miserable."

Willis squinted his eyes and pivoted his body slightly to the right, leaning against the driver's door. "Man, does this dealership offer psychotherapy with their products? I thought you were supposed to sell me an expensive car. The most expensive car possible."

"Friend, I do want you to buy our most expensive car. And from me! But you seem like a good man. I bet you help a lot of people. I would hate to see you give all of that up for something that ultimately doesn't matter to you." John lightly tapped his fist on the door as he said it.

Willis turned his body back to the steering wheel. He felt the exquisite pinewood under his hands. Willis moved his right hand to the beautiful wood on the gear shift. He rubbed the fine leather seats. He smiled a big smile. Turning to the salesman, he said, "Okay, shrink—take me to the lemons in the lot . . . and hold the lemon."

One hour later, Willis Taylor, Pastor of New Horizons Church over in Okaloosa County, drove off of the Cavern Car Lot in a 43,000-mile Toyota Forerunner with a practically-indiscernible dent in the back-passenger panel. Practical. Reliable. Not too flashy. Willis smiled, tapped the horn, and gave a sincere wave to his new friend, John, the salesman/shrink.

Adam Vans startled John with another aggressive back slap. "Stiff upper lip, Johnny Boy. I thought you had a fat commission coming on the Vette. So close! You can't win them all, Johnny. Glad to see that you're a human like the rest of us mortals." When his little coaching session was over, Adam walked off whistling.

John stood there for a long time. He thought about the two roads presented to him on this particular evening. One led to a fat commission that, for the most part, would have gone directly into his savings account. The other led to a much smaller commission. It would be big enough for a nice dinner and a couple of drinks in the bar. Willis took the road less traveled and left smiling all the way.

Three of the sales sharks rolled their demo vehicle up to a contemplative and smiling John and said, "Heading to the Parrot. You in?"

Without a moment's hesitation, he said, "I'm in. Save a stool." His smile left, and then the rest of him left his workplace for the day.

CHAPTER FORTY

Fifty-five-year-old John Wright was sitting in a dimly-lit room drinking cheap bourbon from a glass with soap spots on it. The sights and sounds of Bogota, Colombia, assaulted the senses even at two o'clock in the morning. This Colombia was nothing like his American city with the similar name. Car horns were as natural to the urban jungle as the cries of wildlife were in an actual jungle. There were so many honks per second that they'd virtually lost the purpose for which the horn was invented. To add variety to the symphony, about every five minutes, a high-pitched siren would blast sound waves that bounced off the tall buildings.

The light pollution in this city of almost eight million rivaled Las Vegas, Nevada. There were no star-gazing tourists in this city, because the stars couldn't compete with the flashing lights. Everything screamed for attention from the human eye. The Hotel Azteca was an extremely nice hotel for the price, although the glasses sometimes had soap spots. It was $42 U.S. per night, and John had the reserves to stay a long time. Because he stayed a long time and liked to pay ahead in cash, the management was happy to land on $32 per night in a quick negotiation. There were plenty of amenities, and he could live like a king compared to what that money would get him in the States.

John had made it almost ten years at Cavern back in the United States. He had made a lot of money for the company, and a lot for himself. Then, one month shy of his employment record, he unceremoniously resigned. No fanfare. No problems or issues had inspired it. No cake. No real goodbyes. He just left.

The car sales industry is not necessarily known for longevity. Instead, it is a place where older employees land who have been "furloughed" by their companies. The loyalty of these older employees was often rewarded with a "temporary leave of absence." However, the *temporary* part was often forgotten about. These employees still had enough working years left that they had to scramble for something to pay the bills.

The twenty-somethings often utilized the "temporary" part. Selling cars was a profession in which many younger people worked, as well. They were trying to find themselves and their place in life, and they sometimes found themselves in car sales until the honest answer to the life question presented itself—if it ever did.

John was reliable, until he wasn't. He had always been punctual. But unfortunately, the monkey on his back over the last few years had attacked that positive trait. The addiction complicated other positives in his life. John had no obligations, no real responsibilities, no debt, and no real ties to the community other than his buddy Bob and his dear mother over in Florida's capital city.

Mom was doing well enough in Tallahassee. She was now in one of those retirement communities that offered assisted living services. For the most part, she could afford it, but John would occasionally and anonymously pay her bill ahead for two and even three months. He wanted to give her some margin and breathing room but didn't want his sister to feel bad about it. The siblings were at two very different places in life.

At 2:00 a.m., John had not taken the time to memorize the name of a woman who walked out of room 501 at the Hotel Azteca. She whispered, "Adios," and quietly shut the door. She adjusted her skirt and counted a wad of paper bills. She was busy about her business and off to another appointment. John remained in room 501, busy about nothing aside from some morbid introspection.

Having no obligations, debt, or responsibilities brought certain freedoms that people work all their lives to achieve. It seemed that he had ascertained this freedom early on; in fact, John had been free for the vast majority of his adult life. The other side of this no-obligation coin was that he had no real purpose. He had no compelling reason to wake up or develop any sense of destiny or even structure. His wise father used to tell him too much freedom wasn't always good and brought a confinement all its own. "People need fences, John Mark." He hadn't understood this growing up. Now, sitting in a cracked leather armchair in a South American hotel room, he understood it.

John had no fences, and it was apparent. He could spend his time and his money in practically any legal way he wanted. He wondered why he had saved so much money selling hardware, hamburgers, coffee, and cars if he was never going to spend it. Life was getting shorter and shorter. The money wasn't burning a hole in his pocket yet, but the money was looking for a Zippo cigarette lighter to get the hole started.

Even a drunk can be frugal. Though it may be rare for drunks to exercise moderation, they can be thrifty. John was still selective on where and how he spent his money. He rarely splurged. This was a splurge night, and he already had buyer's remorse. He regretted it. He didn't know why. Was it about wasting money, or was it something else?

The question was too philosophical. John poured another drink. He had no interest in waiting around for some abstract answer from some arbitrary source. So he sat in the dimly-lit room, sipping and looking out the window at the light show that beautiful Bogota was putting on tonight, as she did every night.

As John nursed his whiskey, a song emerged from the cheap hotel clock radio, which had previously played a litany of Latin pop songs. It seemed so out of place. He rarely heard English songs on this particular station. The new music seemed to brighten him a bit as he softly sang along—surprisingly on key—to the Don McLean hit recorded and released in 1971:

"Bye, bye, Miss American Pie. Drove my Chevy to the levee but the levee was dry.

And them good ole boys were drinking whiskey and rye...." [2]

Now he stood and moved his half-inebriated body around as he continued his private concert:

Did you write the book of love? And do you have faith in God above? If the Bible tells you so?..." [3]

He smiled slightly, feeling accomplished that his tired brain could remember this classic. He savored another sip and looked at his watch. As he looked, he made a discovery. His watch was not on his wrist. His father had given him that watch. It was priceless to him. He immediately jumped to his feet and looked around the room. He scrambled over to the bedside table and tossed stuff aside, looking fervently for the timepiece.

2 Don McLean, "American Pie," 1971, *American Pie*, United Artists, 1971.

3 Ibid.

Immediately, he thought that the woman who had just been in his room had taken it with her as some non-negotiated gratuity. He ripped open the drawer and began to rummage through it. Receipts went flying. A few lower-denominational Colombian currencies, tossed inside after several previous nights of drinking, soared with the receipts to the floor. Some medicine bottles, an old John Grisham novel, a few tourist brochures, a small flask he carried around the city for emergencies tumbled to the floor in a fit of fury. Then, at the bottom of all that stuff sat his Timex watch. He stared at it curiously. Although he had been drinking, he was only slightly drunk. He always put his key, phone, and wristwatch on the top of his bedside table. He was habitual and meticulous about his stuff. So how had the watch gotten into the drawer—at the very bottom of the drawer at that? Even at the zenith of his frolic, this had never happened.

Then John noticed the watch had been neatly positioned on a book. The Timex was folded perfectly underneath the book's title, which read *Holy Bible*. It was a Gideon New Testament in both Spanish and English. In the weeks he'd been holed up at the Azteca, John had never noticed this book, perhaps because of "selective viewing." But, he wondered aloud, "Can that be a thing?" Of course, selective hearing was a thing. As he contemplated this mystery, the next song came on the radio, and it was in English:

"Now we're up in the big leagues
Gettin' our turn at bat
As long as we live
It's you and me, baby
There ain't nothin wrong with that."[4]

---

[4] Ja'Net Dubois and Jeff Barry. "The Jeffersons (Movin' on Up)," *Television's Greatest Hits: 70's and 80's*, 1975.

John snatched the bourbon off the cheap hotel table and sat on the side of the bed. He didn't worry about a glass, spot or no spot. He kicked the bottle back and swilled three enormous gulps. John then did something he could not remember doing for many, many years. He wept until he wailed. No one knocked on the door to check on him or to ascertain the reason for such strident cries. It wasn't that unusual in this city—nor in this hotel—for loud laments to join the symphony of horns and sirens.

CHAPTER FORTY-ONE

He was learning to live with a pounding headache that came and went. It was coming more often than going lately. The headaches were similar to the ringing-in-the-ears feeling he'd told his mother about: people either learned to live with it or it drove them insane. John Wright not only learned to live with hangovers, but he learned how to function at a high level. The problem was that he was highly-functioning at things he didn't think mattered that much.

He performed at a high level when exercising in the park, if the pain was dull enough to allow it. He played an occasional pickup soccer game with some athletic men there. He lost a lot but enjoyed it. He ran the beautiful trails. He lifted the few weights—all dumbbells—that his hotel provided. He drank. He was getting proficient at that venture. He also excelled as a tourist.

He enjoyed the culture of the city very much. His command of the language was improving. He enjoyed the attractions Bogota offered. He tried to pick at least one new venture per week. There were museums galore. The National Museum of Colombia was fascinating to him. He tried to find something interesting about each venue. Science museums, art museums, landmarks, elaborate cathedrals—they all held their unique slice of what Colombia offered the world.

For some reason, he liked to return to the Botero Museum. One thousand visitors daily enjoyed the Botero, and he often joined them. Located in a beautiful colonial mansion, the museum exhibited about one hundred twenty-three unique pieces from artist Fernando Botero, as well as many works by other artists.

John would stare at each piece for what seemed like hours. He had the time. His schedule was never, ever tight. The admission price always appealed to him as well; it was free. The museum was located in the La Candelaria neighborhood, which made it convenient to visit other landmarks like libraries and other museums.

John spent hours at Simón Bolívar Park. It was one of his favorites. It was also one of the most popular parks in the vast city. He would run, or sometimes sit and read a novel. He also loved to read people. He studied the families playing all around him. He watched kids run and parents chase them. Families picnicked and paddle-boated. He'd used to feel a pall of depression about his lack of family, but just like he'd learned to live with a chronic, dull headache, he'd learned to live with that, too. The loneliness was just another ringing in the ears.

John's favorite pastime in Bogota, aside from drinking, was to visit Monserrate, the beautiful mountain just over 10,000 feet high. He wasn't interested in the crass commercialism of the place or even the lovely Catholic Church. It was the views he was after—the experience itself. The incredible panorama of the city kept bringing him back. He loved to sit alone and watch the sunset. He always sat alone.

When he first started going, he had no alternative but to ride the aerial tramway to the top. The altitude precluded any attempt of physical assent on his part. However, as his lungs adjusted over time, he began to take the steps. He progressed to the point where he could do it in just about an hour and a half. On occasion, he would even take the steps back down, as well.

John was in the country on a tourist visa. Not only was he a high-functioning drunk tourist—he also was proficient at being a friendly American to his neighbors. His hotel was unusual because there were standard hotel rooms, but other rooms served more like permanent apartments for locals. No one could ever quite explain this to him. He knew many of his neighbors by name and loved to engage in conversation—or at least try. There was safety in these types of relationships. It was mainly surface stuff. He didn't have to ingrain himself into their lives or stories. He could be both present and temporary. When his door shut, he did not have to be bothered by anything or anyone other than his thoughts.

There was one particular neighbor with whom he had a complicated relationship. It was the lady two doors down, Señora Alvarez. He'd never learned her first name because she had never offered it. He only knew her by Señora Alvarez, and she let him know early on where she stood with *El Señor*, the Lord. She was proud to be a *Católico Carismático* – a Charismatic Catholic.

He mostly enjoyed Señora's upbeat and friendly greetings, though this depended on his mood. He would avoid her on occasion if he were, as his grandmother used to say, "in a bad humor." It felt to him that this neighbor had somehow made John her mission, but he didn't know what the mission consisted of, per se.

John got out of a little yellow taxi with three plastic grocery bags. He reached his hand into the passenger window to tip the driver, and when he turned around, there was Señora Alvarez. He cringed a little bit, happening not to be in the mood for her company.

John was always trying to improve his Spanish, and Señora Alvarez was trying to improve her English. This fact had impressed John in the past. He could not help but admire someone in their mid-seventies being proactive in enhancing such a life skill.

In a very thick accent, she said, "How are you today, Mr. John Wright?"

"*Muy bien, Señora.*"

Immediately Señora pushed back. "No Spanish! English, *por favor.* . . . I mean, please."

Her little mistake put John in a better humor. "Yes ma'am. I am fine. How are you?"

"I am good feeling, and I thank you for the question. It is a beautiful day. I am feeling blessed."

John smiled and said, "Good for you, Mrs. Alvarez."

Señora Alvarez stopped before going into the hotel and grabbed his bicep. "John, do you feel blessed today?" Her gaze bore into his eyes for a long, uncomfortable time.

The only answer he could muster was, "Why, thank you, but I have to get these groceries into the refrigerator before they start melting."

He loosened himself from her grip and quickly went inside, forgoing the elevator for the steps. He didn't want to bump into her at the elevator and get another interrogation about his current level of blessedness.

He put the fruit into a bowl. He may have been a heavy drinker, but it did not diminish his fastidiousness. He was tidy to the point of bordering on obsessive compulsion. He'd lost control of so much in his life that he demanded—at least when sober—that everything within the tiny square footage of his existence be perfectly ordered. The fruit had its place.

The hotel refrigerator was small, but not as small as the ones in the United States. He put a six-pack of the popular Postobón soda inside. He enjoyed the drink and indulged in it about once per day. He stuck the deli meat inside. He put the bread in the bread place, the mustard in the mustard place, the chips in their space, and a couple of miscellaneous items into their places.

The last thing John pulled out of the plastic bag from the corner market was a new, shimmering bottle of Hennessy cognac. He sat the bottle down prominently on the little table in the corner of the room. He stared at it for a long time. The light gave it a different color than he was used to on his evening binges. It was strangely lovely to him on this particular day. He put the cognac in the cognac place. He liked to be organized and to be able to locate items when he needed them. He was confident that he would need that bottle a little later on.

Later that night, the ancient Westclox wooden hotel alarm clock read 4:09 a.m. It was bright enough to illuminate an airport landing strip. John slumped in his chair with four objects in front of him on the faded wooden table. There was a legal pad with nothing written on it just yet. There was an old Bic pen and a loaded nine-millimeter Glock pistol, which he had acquired in a slightly nefarious negotiation a few weeks earlier.

Finally, there was a half-empty glass of Hennessy. He fidgeted with the pen. He pulled the pad towards him. Then he spun the pistol on the table. He took a long drag from the cognac. He repeated the cycle many times. He contemplated his life as one does during such existential crises. There were a few good memories that fought to bring a smile to the corners of his mouth. But the bad memories quickly overtook them, like lava erupting from a volcano. Bad memories outnumbered the good ones twelve to one. His life had had so much potential and so much loss. He gulped the cognac, then fiddled with the pen. Another memory came to mind. And so it went.

At exactly 4:13 a.m., his cheap cell phone rang, rattling the cheap wood on the bedside table. He nearly jumped out of his skin. On the second ring, he answered. "Hello! Wait, slow down. What the heck are you talking about? Start over. Oh, no. When? How? She was doing great at her last check-up. . . ."

The semi-hysterical voice on the other end was Sandra, his baby sister and only sibling. She was calling to inform him that their mother had unexpectedly died. Mom was old, but by all practical markers and medical information, she was doing great. She was in excellent health for one her age. Sandra explained that their mom had fallen on the way to the restroom and hit her head. Before she lost consciousness, she'd had the presence of mind to call her daughter, who immediately called the attendant on call at the assisted living facility. When they rushed to her room, they'd found her unresponsive.

After that horrific report, Sandra's next call was to her big brother in Bogota. The phone call shook him away from the emotional precipice on which he had been standing. Ironically, his mother's sudden passing was the jolt he needed to prevent his premeditated one.

He promised to come back to Florida as soon as he could book a flight. He hung up the phone. All of his fiddling with the objects on the table ceased. He put his face in his hands and wept for a good long time. Tonight would be another memory in the bad column. This experience would move towards the very top of a list of excruciating ones.

CHAPTER FORTY-TWO

John sat in a crappy, old green Ford Taurus wearing a pathetically ill-fitting dark gray suit. The suit used to fit perfectly. Then, an alteration changed the fit. It was not a garment alteration but a lifestyle one. It had caused noticeable weight loss. It wasn't the trail running so much as his diet consisting of more and more alcohol and less and less actual food.

He donned a crisp, white dress shirt and a black necktie. His dress shoes were out of style, now considered fashionably retro. He dug the clothing out of an old box that his mother had stored in a unit provided by the facility as part of her lease agreement.

For the life of him, John didn't know why his mother had kept any of his things. He didn't want them and could only think that his mother wanted them to remind her of better times. In the box were a few practical items of clothing, such as what he now wore. There were also some memorabilia. He now found himself needing the practical and tabling the nostalgia. Another time, perhaps. Perhaps not.

This occasion was a matter of honor for John. After all, he was burying his very own mother. The miles may have been difficult for this former clergyman, but it was time to pull himself together and honor her well-lived life. He had gathered the suit, shirt, tie, and shoes from the mothballs. He had the dry cleaners do their best and fastest work. The results were surprisingly effective.

He found a tiny, hole-in-the-wall place in downtown Tallahassee that still polished shoes. He was fascinated by their artistry and dedication to the craft. They even brought out a blowtorch at one point. When his shoes were finished, John thought he might even be able to see his reflection in them enough to shave his face.

The car was a loaner from Bart, his boisterous and gregarious brother-in-law. Bart had always wanted to pal around with a big brother, and he'd resented John's move to Colombia. But despite the circumstances that brought them together, he was delighted to see John and was anxious to facilitate anything he might need.

Sandra, the responsible sibling who had been regularly checking on their mother, was the one attending to details. She asked if John wanted to be a part of the myriad of arrangements, the estate, and other matters. She offered this to be courteous. John respectfully declined for the same reason. He had complete trust in her decisions to this point and felt it unnecessary to play the "big brother is here now" card. She had been doing an outstanding job of caring for Mrs. Wright, and there was no reason to think she would not continue to do so.

While Sis worked on the particulars, John needed transportation to get himself to the funeral home and cemetery. He'd sold his truck and almost every other possession before moving to Colombia. What John hadn't sold, he'd given to a mission or tossed in the garbage. He still had enough money to live for a while, including funds to rent a car. However, with all expenses and no income, the math would not work in his favor forever.

Bart had the old green Taurus as a backup for when one of their new family cars or his small business van might need to be in the shop. He offered the car, and John was grateful to borrow it. He may not have been able to do anything about the color or the dents, but John could undoubtedly have the vehicle detailed, which was precisely what he did.

There he sat in the battered, old car with his old, floppy suit. He had done his best to do right by his mother for this dignified day. He held the folded newspaper obituary in his hands and gently shook his head. If he'd had any idea that there was such an abrupt end on the horizon, he would have been back without question. He suddenly longed to sit and ask his mom a thousand questions. He'd continued to make anonymous payments to the facility, although his sister was certainly savvy enough to know the money came from John. She also knew that John was running from something, and the payments were his attempt not to run from his responsibility.

John had a two-hour drive right into the heart of responsibility—the burial of his mother. Many years earlier, his parents had fallen in love with each other and then, shortly afterward, had fallen in love with the part of the Florida Panhandle known as "the Forgotten Coast." Before his father "took ill" years later, they'd often traveled down to that coast to picnic, explore trails in the Apalachicola National Forest and eat fish. They claimed the best fish in America could be eaten in those forgotten parts.

On one such trip, they came upon a beautiful cemetery in the middle of nowhere. More accurately, it was located in a relatively desolate spot between Port St. Joe and Mexico Beach. The views at this cemetery were stunning. Older folks tend to think about things that younger ones do not. Perhaps, like John, they thought about things like turning in the proverbial hotel key and checking out of this life for the next one. As soon as the elder Wrights saw the cemetery, they were oddly drawn to it as a final resting spot—they could be together for eternity, overlooking a lovely river that would eventually run into the beautiful Gulf of Mexico.

John had been so distracted with busying himself—in a quest to not be too busy with anything—that he had not taken the time to see the place. That is, until this day. This was the day to take the time. Alone on a two-hour drive, he was accompanied only by his thoughts. His thoughts were like emotional neuropathy; there was a dangerous numbness to them. The thoughts dulled him. The danger with actual neuropathy is that one could cut himself and bleed profusely yet never feel and address it. With actual neuropathy, sharp, shooting, debilitating pains came seemingly out of nowhere. This was John's emotional experience as well.

Oh, how he loved his mother. She was so proud of his accomplished life. That's why she'd kept the accolades he'd collected so many years ago. Her affirming words made him smile. His utterly disappointing life made him weep. The thought of not living up to his potential saddened him. The fact that he'd never given her a grandchild grieved him nearly as much as her passing. He knew that she'd wanted John to be the progenitor of the family name.

The shooting pain would stop long enough to think of something sweet. Mom's genteel Southern cadence and elegance made him smile. She'd practically never said a bad word about anyone. Even when she found out the crushing truth about Layla, the worst adjectives she could spew towards her were "disappointing" and "dissipated." She was one-of-a-kind.

John's tears did not impede his ability to drive his brother-in-law's Taurus. He was determined to be at the funeral home well before anyone else so that he could spend intimate time with his mother and sister. He'd left plenty early. Part of his motivation was boisterous Bart. John was accustomed to closing his hotel door and not hearing a voice for hours or even days if he liked. Bart was like a puppy—adorable and incessant.

What did impede John's drive was a loud pop. It sounded like a balloon popped an eighth of an inch from his eardrum. The pop was followed by a whooshing noise and then a flopping sound. "Bart!" was the only thing he could muster. He used the name as a cuss word.

Bart's green backup car had sat unused for so long that the tires had developed dry rot and were no good. Neither grown man had thought that contingency through, and John felt stupid, alone, and isolated. He looked at his phone. There was no signal.

The flat tire happened miles and miles from any residential area or commerce. Sitting there in the Florida heat on a two-lane road in a broken-down car with no signal was a perfect portrait, a factual microcosm, representing the last several decades of his life.

CHAPTER FORTY-THREE

John smacked the steering wheel with the heel of his hand. He exhaled and leaned his head way back. Then, inexplicably, he began to laugh. The complete and utter absurdity of his current situation washed over him. Thirty years ago, he had been an up-and-coming success. He'd been on everyone's radar as the next-one-up on the launching pad for greatness. Everyone in the region had had their eyes on him—at least everyone in the ministry world.

However, time—the great examiner of life's exams—had graded him as most definitely *not* a shooting star. In fact, the grade had been distinctly opposite of that. As recently as two weeks ago, he'd been flying under the radar, living in obscurity on another continent. So here he sat in the deep South of North America, the country of his origin. The South was what he'd loved so much and understood so well. These were his roots. He sat simultaneously as one utterly familiar with the environment and as a total alien. So he laughed and laughed. There was a release somehow. It was a necessary and involuntary expression, like the pressure that builds up until an explosion.

When the laughter was over, there was an oddly joyful sigh that morphed into another season of weeping over the loss of his mom. It was all too much. Dad was gone. Now Mom. His potential was gone. These moments create an awareness of the impossibility of personal immortality. He didn't weep as long as he had laughed.

When that little jag was over, he got down to the business of the moment. It was time to wipe his eyes and solve a problem. The problem at hand was how to get to the funeral home. He had a steely determination not to let his mother down—at least, not again.

Fortunately for John, his breakdown—emotionally and literally—happened on a hill. Hills are relatively rare in the flat state. It was fortunate because, when the car came to a stop in the middle of the lane, John had turned off the engine impulsively. It now, inexplicably, would not turn back on again. So he put the gear shift into neutral and tested the brakes, making sure they'd work without a running engine. Content with the answer, he let gravity do her work.

With the absence of shoulders, aside from a small section of real estate with grass a foot high, his main priority was getting the car off the road. The grass looked like a perfect place for snakes or other horrific creatures. He wanted no part of the edge of the pavement. Halfway down the hill, a dirt road presented itself on the right. The tiny road was a refuge in a barren wilderness.

He built up enough speed to navigate off of the blacktop and onto the small dirt lane. The road continued at a steep enough decline to provide gravity the opportunity to keep doing her job. Once he was far enough off the road, John looked for two things, the first of which was a place to change a tire safely. Of course, he didn't even know if there *would* be a spare in the old green boat of a car. He also hoped to stumble upon a cell phone signal. He found the first, but the second eluded him.

John discovered that the dirt road wasn't so much of a road as it was a long, dead-end driveway. It led to the Antioch Redeemer House of God, a white clapboard church much like those often found in this region. This one seemed a little out of place, however. This church had been meticulously maintained. The gorgeous, green shrubbery, interspersed with colorful flowers, contrasted with the dirt road leading to it. Their small parking lot was organized and packed with cars. The whole scene looked like it had a fresh coat of paint on it. Cars, grass, bushes, church, steeple—all of it seemed starkly fresh.

No parking was available for any newcomer—that is, with one exception. All of the spots were occupied by vehicles except for one area right in front of the church steps. It was as if a divine valet had reserved it. John thought it might just be a cosmic coincidence.

John got out of the vehicle to the sound of raucous music spilling out of the open windows and the back door, which was halfway open. He walked around the Taurus and observed the flat pancake tire. The rot was now as evident as the source of his predicament. The rim had destroyed any chance of redeeming the tire.

As he stood there, two young African American men came out of the church and approached him. The taller man reached out his hand and said, "Hi, I'm Avery." Avery had a contagious smile.

"Hi, Avery. I'm John."

The other man stretched his hand out and said with an equally contagious smile, "I'm Andre. It looks like you've had better days."

"You could say that, Andre." John smiled. Their demeanor almost demanded a smile.

Looking down at the tire, Andre observed, "Yikes. That stinks. Looks like you could use a little help. You look too fresh to mess up that suit."

"You guys look a lot fresher than I do," John replied.

It was a factual observation. The men were in perfectly-fitting suits. Avery had on a black pin-striped suit, and Andre was wearing a beautiful royal blue ensemble. Neither wore a tie, but they looked as if they'd just stepped off the cover of a fashion magazine.

"We'd be happy to take off our jackets and lend you a hand," Andre said.

"That is so kind of you guys." John was almost emotional about their offer. "Honestly, I haven't worn a suit in many, many years. Not used to it—or used to flat tires, either."

"Gotcha," Avery said.

"I'm on my way to a funeral."

"Oh, man. So sorry, man. Someone close to you?" Andre asked.

"Mom."

Andre put a hand on John's shoulder. "Wow. Sir, we are so sorry. Let us help you."

John cried about his deep loss initially, but he hadn't in the last couple of days. This stranger's sincere expression of condolence caught him by surprise. No one knew about the death in his tiny circle. For this reason, no person had shown an ounce of tenderness towards him, and he hadn't expected any. Andre's words created a lump in his throat and he consciously forced himself not to cry in front of these Samaritans.

"I hate to admit it, but I could use the help. Not only do I not want to get this suit greasy, but honestly, I'm not sure I even remember how to change a tire."

Andre held out his hand. "Let's see the keys, sir. We got this."

Avery agreed. "Mr . . . " He paused, having not received the stranded motorist's last name.

"John is fine."

"Okay John. The service just started, and it's hot out here. Believe it or not, it's nice and cool in there. The ceiling fans, the open windows, and all the shade over the building work to create a nice, cool space. It can even get downright nippy in there at times. We call it God's A/C."

Andre concurred. "Good idea, Ave. There are some good seats near the back, and it's cooler back there, anyway. We'll figure this out and come and get you when we're finished."

"Thanks, Andre. You and Avery are lifesavers. I owe you both big time. I really need to get to the funeral home."

CHAPTER FORTY-FOUR

John slowly walked up the simple, wooden steps of the church. Before he got to the door, he paused. It had been so many years since he had walked into a church for a service. There was so much water under the bridge between that last service and whatever was going on in this lovely building. Sure, he had finally caved in and gone to churches over the years for weddings, christenings, and funerals. But the last time he'd actually attended a typical worship service had been in Clary, when he'd said goodbye to his tiny congregation in the woods. He just wasn't sure that he could do it.

He looked over his left shoulder at the men as they carefully put their suit coats on the hood of an immaculate BMW. Andre wiped his brow with the back of his hand and looked at the steps. He could sense John's reluctance. "Go on ahead, John. We got this. Nobody will pay any mind about you goin' in during worship. Happens all the time."

John doubted that a white, fiftyish, former preacher in an ill-fitting suit entered this house of worship late "all the time"—especially one who had not darkened the door of a church in decades. But he knew what the man meant, and it meant something to him that they were sacrificing their time and sweat to get him out of this jam. So John smiled, took a deep breath, and disappeared into the clapboard cathedral.

Andre opened the trunk of the Taurus. He found a spare tire and gave it a little punch with his right fist. His hand sank into it like a pillow, so he knew the tire would not solve the man's problem in its current condition.

"Flat, too," he said to Avery.

"Let's get some air in it. We'll run it down to my cousin Henry. He's got a little shop behind his house with an air pump."

Andre pulled the tire from the trunk and tried to roll it to Avery's car. The flatness created a bit of a challenge. "Fella looked pretty sad, didn't he?"

"Well, his momma just passed, so. . . ."

Andre cut him off. "Nah. We see that kinda sad all the time. Man looked deeper sad. Know what I mean?"

"S'pose you right," Avery said. "Jesus, do something good for that poor man."

"Amen."

John had cautiously walked into the sanctuary. His trepidation instantly gave way to awe. First of all, it did indeed feel ten to twelve degrees cooler than it did outside, even with so many people there. Then there was the electric atmosphere. He had never experienced anything like this. Not in seminary. Not in Clary. Not in Columbia. Not in Smithville. It felt as if he had just stepped into unbridled joy. The look on the worshipers' faces was nothing short of sheer exuberance.

About a half dozen people turned his direction when he walked inside. Each person smiled at John and immediately returned to their active worship. That was the thing that caught John off-guard. This was not a perfunctory experience for these people. They were participants and not spectators. He looked around, and of course, there were a few small children coloring or sleeping, seemingly oblivious to the spiritual activity. Those were the few exceptions. The rest of the children were singing, clapping, smiling, and even bouncing to the music. Everyone was on the beat, and everyone was on key.

John didn't sing. He only knew the words to one song, but he did not participate. He hadn't been a participant for a very long time. In the midst of about a hundred adult participants, he stood alone as a spectator. He did find himself caught up a bit in the music, though. He even caught himself swaying a time or two.

Between the songs, there were a few "amens" and shouts. The whole thing was sort of amazing to John. He'd never thought he would find himself back in a church—and if he did, he never in his wildest dreams imagined that it would be like this.

He surveyed the crowd. Of course, he didn't know a soul. He wasn't the only white face in the building, but he was undoubtedly a distinct minority in the room. It didn't seem to matter to them, and it honestly didn't matter to him. It wasn't the faces or races that made him uncomfortable. It was what was invisible that made him apprehensive.

Elaine Wagstaff, an elegant and authoritative woman, walked to the pulpit. She gave a quick and powerful exhortation and then once more led the song that the congregation had just sung. She wasn't quite as exuberant or charismatic as the man who had been singing when John walked in. She had strength and noticeable depth.

Avery and Andre were trying their best to help out the stranded traveler-turned-reluctant-worshipper. Cousin Henry wasn't at home. He was not a churchgoer, so the men just knew he would be on his couch with a beer and the remote control, switching from pre-game show to pre-game show.

His lady said someone had invited him to a church on the other side of the county. The two good Samaritans were astonished at this.

Time was of the essence, and they didn't have time to track Henry down. By the time they got to the church, the service would already have been dismissed, and Henry would be on his way to lunch somewhere. They texted Henry's phone, but he'd either left it in his truck, turned it off, or allowed the battery to die. The two men pressed Henry's live-in girlfriend, asking if they could go on a scavenger hunt to find a key to the shop in order to get the tire pumped up.

Pastor Wagstaff was now nearly halfway through her sermon. This was not a superficial, shallow, or apathetic speech. This woman wasn't drawing a check to remodel a pool house by preaching something she didn't believe. John had never met her but could tell that one of two things was true: she either believed what she was saying to her core or her performance was worthy of an Academy Award.

"You can't outrun Him. Go on ahead and try," she said into a hand-held microphone.

"Well? Preach, Pastor," shouted someone in the congregation.

She did exactly that. "Paul said, 'For the gifts and calling of God are without repentance.' Y'all know what that means."

"Tell us, Pastor," someone else shouted.

"'Most every other reliable translation of Holy Scripture says, 'The gifts and callings of God are....' Now, y'all ready?! 'His gifts and His call are irrevocable.'"

Several stood at that exact moment. "Say it!" "Preach!"

The people shouted other things that John couldn't quite make out.

The pastor said, "Touch and agree with your neighbor. Tell 'em, 'It's irrevocable.'"

The congregation heeded the instruction. John was glad he was sitting alone, because he didn't feel like touching and agreeing with anyone.

"Irrevocable means, 'not to be revoked or recalled; unable to be repealed or annulled; unalterable.'"

These words caused some others to stand to their feet.

She continued to deliver her homily authoritatively. "Why are you running, lady? Sir, where you going? God ain't changed His mind. He doesn't call us and then say, 'Oh, I was just kidding.'"

"Amens" erupted all over the sanctuary.

"We don't serve that kind of God. Now watch this. When that old man Samuel poured oil all over David's head, the Bible says, 'Yet from that day forward, the Spirit of the Lord came upon him.' Touch and agree. Say, 'That day forward.'"

All around him, people obeyed their leader's admonition. They touched, agreed, and declared, "That day forward."

Pastor Wagstaff continued. "When David grew up and ran from crazy King Saul, that oil was on him. Not recalled. Not annulled."

A man yelled, "Not recalled." Another shouted, "Not annulled."

"When David's mean-spirited wife didn't like the way he danced, that oil was dripping off him. Irrevocable!"

The congregation seemed to be in a frenzy as they shouted almost on cue, "Irrevocable!"

"When the man was running for his life, hiding out in caves and having to scrounge for food, longing for a drink from the well of his youth, the call was running with David. God's Spirit was chasing him down. Not recalled. Not annulled."

As if it was a responsive reading in an ecumenical church, the people declared, "Not recalled. Not annulled."

Pastor Wagstaff continued. "When his own family, Absalom, was stabbing him in the back, sabotaging his leadership, perverting God's ways . . . THAT. CALL. WAS. IRREVOCABLE."

The crowd was simply beside themselves. They stood and shouted for what seemed like five minutes. "IRREVOCABLE! IRREVOCABLE! IRREVOCABLE!" Even the children were shouting. Some stood on the pew and shouted. The whole scene felt surreal to John.

The shouting died down, and the people eventually sat down. The whole thing seemed to be scripted and rehearsed somehow. But John knew in his heart that it was neither.

Pastor Wagstaff now spoke much more softly. It wasn't quite a whisper, but it was dramatically different in volume and tone.

"I'm calling all the runners. No, that's not right. *God* is calling all the runners. He didn't call you to go and change His mind. It's not too late. Take one step back to your call, and He'll take three steps up to you. If you want that peace, it's what this pastor wants. Just join me down here."

That line was too much. It took John back to his ministry roots. He had a vivid memory of saying the exact words verbatim to congregations that he had loved:

"He's calling all the runners."

An organ began to play a soft spiritual. People started trickling to the front. In a staggered fashion, a couple dozen people made their way toward the preacher. Some knelt at wooden benches in the front. Others walked near the walls and raised their hands. Women wearing large hats and their Sunday finest earnestly bowed while standing. A couple of men in suits stretched prostrate on the floor.

"That's right. There is peace for you. You've run right back to the God of your calling. We're gonna pray."

Pastor Wagstaff bowed her head to pray. "I want to pray, but the Spirit of God won't let me, not just yet. He's so strong on me. There's another runner. Where are you? His love is calling you off that run. He wants you to get back to the right race he chose all along. His call is irrevocable. But so is His love."

John felt hot tears roll down both of his cheeks. This was all too much. He wanted to run out into the hot Florida sun and keep running, but he felt like he had landed in a divine trap and couldn't get out of it.

CHAPTER FORTY-FIVE

The blow that cut John's eye in this celestial boxing match was the line Pastor Wagstaff delivered about "this is what your pastor wants." That blow took him right back to the beginning. He'd heard old bishops in his past describe his current predicament in their sermons. When the old preachers talked about Peter, they depicted precisely what he was feeling at this moment.

During Peter's rebellion, Jesus took him back to the beach where he'd first called him. The bishops described how Jesus made breakfast in or near the spot where he had called Peter. It was the "table of restoration," he remembered one of the bishops say.

But the punch that had knocked John clean out was the line from the articulate Pastor Wagstaff: "Jesus is holding out His hand and wants to help you back over the fence to the right race—the right racetrack—and then your run's gonna mean something." Boom. Knock-out. He was on the mat. It was not a technical knock-out. He was done and undone. Emotionally, physically, spiritually, and in every single way, he was o.u.t. He had no more fight and no more run.

Relief actually swept over John at that moment. It was the relief of decision. Psychologists point to momentary euphoria over suicidal individuals just before they end their lives. It is not a release from the depression as much as it is a relief that the final and horrible decision has been made. People have misunderstood it and have later lamented their own misreading.

What John was experiencing was the decision to die. He had not awakened intending to die that day. John had not written it on his daily planner. But he decided to die in this shaded African American church, and he was satisfied with the decision. He knew that even Jesus "gave up" when he "gave up the ghost" on the cross. John had given up differently years ago, and that decision created a host of problems that he was either unaware of or unconcerned about. That decision had not been good for the world at large or for him personally.

The relief at this moment was that of giving up on the give-up. John didn't know what it might mean to give up the race he was currently running. He didn't care what it might mean. He was exhausted from running. John didn't know where he was running or exactly what the prize might eventually be. He was done with the run. He didn't know if that meant he would die literally, if he would be exposed as a reprobate and fraud, or just what exactly. At this exact moment, in a rural church in the forgotten coast of Florida's Panhandle, he simply did not care what it meant. He was tapping out.

As all of these realizations were settling into him, he realized something else. He had been gripping the pew in front of him so tightly that his hands hurt. As he loosened his grip on the bench, it was as if that action loosened his position in the pew. Before he knew it, he was walking down an aisle he had never walked on to a minister he had never met amongst people he knew nothing about.

He had experienced this sort of "altar call" many times, except from the vantage point of standing on the stage. Now he experienced it not as a salesman, per se, but as a customer. He'd heard many testimonials about what it was like. In this moment, for John, it was like the first time he had ever ridden a roller coaster. Descriptive words about a coaster ride fail to adequately depict what the experience is actually like.

John had heard that people felt light as they approached a spiritual moment at a consecrating altar. John's experience was just the opposite. Each step did not get lighter. Each step felt like he was pulling a foot out of poured concrete in various stages of drying. The further he walked, the dryer the cement was, and the harder it was to take a step. Physically, John was involuntarily wrenching, twisting, and even slightly shaking.

With each step he took, it seemed as if the concrete of his past was partnering with the gravity of his present. It was pulling him down. People in the aisle stood aside as he slowly and deliberately made his ascent to God and his descent into full self-realization. Tears were streaming down his cheeks. He had a determination to quit—and gloriously quit—whatever he was doing with his life.

He got to the old altar bench near the pulpit. It had been stained over decades by the tears of the saints, and no one had had the heart to paint it. The faded wood served as a holy remembrance of profound challenges and even deeper grace. It was about to get some more stains, but not from a saint. The invisible concrete on his feet was now simply too heavy for John to go another inch. He collapsed across the wood—and as he did, he had an involuntary reaction similar to his response to the flat tire.

It was similar and yet completely different. He did not laugh. John Wright did something that could only be characterized as wailing. It was a sob so deep that it was very close to a howl. It was so loud and stark that it momentarily alarmed a few folks. The abruptness and spontaneity of it even alarmed John himself. He quickly dismissed that alarm and was utterly unconcerned about optics or even audio. Quitters aren't concerned about optics, and he was quitting the quit.

The weeping and wailing were a holy and complete decompression. This decompression lasted a long, long time, because there had been so much pressure accumulated over so much time that needed now to be released. After a bit, John tried to control the emotion, but the release and relief were simply too satisfying for him to end it abruptly.

Pastor Wagstaff smiled to her congregation and said softly into the microphone, "Saints, keep seeking Him. Keep speaking to Him. We thank God for what the Spirit is doing in our new friend here. This is why we gather. This is why we open our doors—that we may encounter His presence."

People continued their praying, lamenting, and interceding as the music played softly in the background. Pastor Wagstaff slipped from behind her pulpit and came down the steps toward John, who continued to weep. The wail had subsided, but the intensity had not. John's shoulders shook as he deeply grieved, now with hardly a sound.

"Let it out, my friend," the pastor said as she approached. She placed her hand on his right shoulder. "You must have been the runner." At the touch and words of this reverend, his wailings produced a sound. It was a groan. "That's right. I got a feelin' that you gonna switch back to the right race today, friend."

John was familiar with what the charismatics called "prophetic gifts." He had never been on the receiving end of any such gift, unless this classified as such. He'd heard the gift described as someone "reading your mail." John was about to have his mail read to him by a complete stranger.

"Friend, I don't know you," Pastor Wagstaff began, "but I hear the Holy Ghost tell me to tell you that our Lord Jesus is opening His hand to help you over the fence. He is gonna help you get back on the right track, the right racetrack. You been running in the woods and all over creation. But now, all you got to do is take His hand."

John's shoulders continued to shake.

"He says all you got to do now is take His hand. He'll put you on that track. It ain't too late, and you ain't gone too far. He just whispered the verses in my ear for me to tell you, and He wants you to listen very close now."

John's shoulders stopped shaking. He looked up towards the pastor through tears that precluded good vision. An usher handed him a handful of tissues. He wiped his eyes and nose a couple of times. He concentrated on the pastor's words.

"What is your name?"

"John. John Wright. John Mark Wright."

"Well, my new friend, Mr. Wright, he has given me two words for you. Here they are. The old prophet said something thousands of years ago that the Spirit is saying to you right here and right now: 'I will whistle for them and gather them. I will redeem them; and they shall increase as they once increased.' Here is the other word to you: 'He brought me up also out of a horrible pit, out of the miry clay, and set my feet upon a rock, and established my goings.'"

As the pastor quoted Zechariah 10:8 and Psalm 40:2 from the Old Testament to the former pastor, John began to tremble. He had no idea why. He had no idea why any of this was happening. Slowly, the congregation stopped their individual petitioning. A hush fell onto the people. Something powerful, unexpected, and unprecedented in their church in the woods was happening. A white man appeared out of nowhere. Angels do that, but this man was no angel. If he was an angel, then he was one burdened to the core. He was in the process of getting unburdened, and their pastor was skillfully helping in the navigation of that process.

Every eye was on the action at the old, tear-stained altar bench in front of the wooden pulpit. Pastor Wagstaff seized the moment. This was not some kind of show to observe. It was neither some oddly-ticketed event to attend. Instead, it was a leadership opportunity for this pastor and a learning opportunity for her congregation.

"This is how the Body of Christ responds, Antioch. We bear one another's burdens. Red and yellow, black and white, all God's children are precious in His sight. This man right here is what this house is all about. It is in our name. Redeemer. Antioch Redeemer House of God."

The people made sounds in agreement. The sounds were muted, hummed "amens" more than articulated ones. Some people took off their shoes, like the Old Testament story of Moses and the burning bush. There seemed to be an unusual holiness or uniqueness to whatever was happening on this warm Florida afternoon.

"Church, this man's name is John Mark Wright. He is in the right place today. John Wright, God is doing two things for you today. He is whistling, and He is grasping. He whistled for you to be in this house on this day, and He is holding out His mighty and tender hand to help you back over the fence to the right race and the right racetrack."

John had been spiritually knocked out for a while, and his knees were a little shaky as he tried to stand. Pastor Wagstaff embraced the man and then turned to her left. "This is my husband. He is my Mr. Wright. His name is Earnest."

Earnest opened his arms and gave John a firm embrace. The tenderness, warmth, and acceptance of these folks opened the gates once again for John's tears to flow. Several more men and a few women lined up to greet the visitor to the service that day. The sincerity of the welcoming group, and the one welcomed, moved them all.

Pastor Wagstaff grabbed the microphone and, from the floor, spoke into it. "Well, we have been in His presence. Well, well, well."

The mood shifted into a subtle yet building jubilation. The organ kicked up, and the feeling did, too. The people spontaneously sang a familiar, old spiritual. Again, it was as if this had been rehearsed. Everyone was on the same sheet of music in this church, and it was all gloriously impromptu.

When the singing subsided, Pastor Wagstaff turned to John and said, "Mr. Wright, is there anything you would like to testify about today?"

Testify? How would one who had been on a thirty-year run even begin to testify? He put his right hand over his necktie, which was wet from tears, and uttered the only thing that he could manage to say, "Thank you." It was the shortest sermon he had ever preached—and possibly the most powerful one.

He looked at his watch. He could not believe that an hour and twenty minutes had passed since he'd walked into this clapboard church. He now felt the press of time to get to the funeral home. He still had time to arrive early, if no further delays happened. This delay had been both divine and devastating. The tire rot was awful. The Antioch Redeemer House of God was awesome in the truest definition of the word.

As John walked out of the church into the bright sunshine that day, an odd thought hit him. *Oh, there is the light.* It wasn't the quantum phenomenon that hits the eyeball. It was the opposite of heaviness. The concrete was gone. There was a lightness in his step. *This must be what they meant.* He knew that the mystics and monks debated the concept of whether it was possible to be born again, *again*. But that is exactly what he felt like. He felt like he had been born again, *again*. The air smelled better, the birds sounded louder, and his outlook was thoroughly different.

CHAPTER FORTY-SIX

J ohn took a look back into the church. He wanted to remember every detail. The tiny narthex gave way to a bright room that had a beautiful wood floor. He stood just outside the door and looked at the people still hugging, laughing, some still praying, and kids still playing. A child dressed in her Lord's Day finest held her mommy's hand and looked at him. She smiled and waved, and the life-hardened former preacher waved back. The simple act reflected a kind of purity that was a balm for John's soul. To John, the slight wave was God's way of saying, "I see you. I know you, and I love you."

He now looked to the parking lot—as if on cue, the trunk of the Taurus shut. Avery and Andre wiped their hands on some rags and wiped their brows with the backs of their forearms. Their shirt sleeves were rolled up, and sweat stains were evident down their spines. They looked up at him, and Avery said, "Back in business, John."

John descended the steps with his hand patting his chest. As he walked, he shouted, "What do I owe you, Avery and Andre?"

"Not a single thing on this earth," replied Andre.

"We were happy to help out, John. It's what brothers do." Avery knocked knuckles with John, not wanting to get grease on his new brother. "But I gotta tell you that you might need to replace all of these tires and get a spare once the funeral is over. For sure do it before you head back to wherever you're goin'."

"You guys are lifesavers. I will never forget this."

"How was service?" Andre asked. "Not too boring, I hope."

"Far from it." John swallowed and took a deep breath. "Far, far from it."

An older man walked up to the group at that moment. His curly white hair was starkly juxtaposed against his dark skin. He was wearing a brown suit that was a little too big and slightly ill-fitting, just like John's. He wore a yellowish shirt with a brown-and-gold-striped clip-on tie.

"'Scuse me, fellas," the old man said.

"Hello, Mr. Timmons," both men from Antioch said in greeting.

"Mr. Timmons is our prophet in residence," Andre said.

"Nice to meet you, Sir," John said, offering his hand.

"Nice to meet you, son," Mr. Timmons responded. "But I am no prophet in residence. Just an old, retired preacher." He leaned into John and said, "But you know, real preachers don't know the word, 'retire.'"

"Is that so?" John smiled.

"That's a fact. Well, just like Pastor Wagstaff said. My voice is weak, and there isn't a pulpit for me 'cept a class now and again to teach for Pastor. But I write myself a sermon every week. Don't even know why, but it keeps the mind sharp. Irrevocable, I s'pose."

"Good for you," John said.

"They good, too," Avery affirmed. "I read a bunch of 'em. Young bucks should take notice."

Mr. Timmons handed John his brown Bible. John took it into his hands and looked Mr. Timmons directly into his eyes, which were dimming with age but brimming with love. Mr. Timmons sensed his curiosity.

"God is a Spirit, Mr. Wright. That Spirit told me when you walked past me a while ago that I was s'posed to give you this Bible. This isn't my good preaching Bible. That's in my study. This is the newest one. I call it my fun Bible. I've had it about two years, and now you have it."

The Bible was well-worn. The cover looked like it had been stained by the natural oils of a human hand over many, many years. John thumbed through it, and there were neatly-underlined passages and highlights from front to back. There were neat pencil markings in the margins.

"Mr. Timmons, you've only had this book for two years?" John asked incredulously.

"You can believe that," Andre answered for him. "Man knows his Bible."

Mr. Timmons smiled and said, "Like they say, if your Bible is falling apart, chances are you are not."

John actually laughed for the first time since the catharsis he had just experienced inside the building. It felt good to laugh. "I would believe you, Mr. Timmons."

"I'm an old man. After all these years, there are so many marks in that book because that book is alive, and so is the Author. You are alive too, son, and you are walking now on a fresh race with the Author. Preacher Wagstaff kept talking about running. At my age, we just walking the race, but we racin' nonetheless."

The men all laughed.

John asked, "Mr. Timmons, are you sure you want to give me this?"

"Never been more sure of something."

"Fellas, I can never thank you enough for your enormous kindness to me. I would hug you, but it is too stinkin' hot. So I'll just shake your hands and give a raincheck on hugs."

John shook hands all around. He got into the Taurus and pulled through the dirt parking lot onto the dirt road. He turned right at the top of the hill onto the blacktop. So far, so good. No shaking, whooshing, or rattling. Just rolling. When he got to the first four-way stop sign, John looked at the passenger's seat beside him. In it sat his new gift, bestowed upon him by an elderly retired—or rather, a not-retired—preacher named Mr. Timmons. Just to the right of the Bible, he saw the top of a half-pint of Wild Turkey whiskey peeping out from underneath the obituary of his beloved mother.

He stared at the bottle for a long time. There were no cars behind him blasting their horns, as he often experienced in Bogota. In that city, they laid on the horn as the light was literally turning green. It was as common as breathing. In this desolate place, no one would be pushing him for a long time. He could have sat there for thirty minutes looking at the Bible, obit, and whiskey if he wanted to before another car approached any of the four stop signs.

This entire day was so marvelously curious to him. On his way to the Forgotten Coast to honor and remember his mother, he'd unexpectedly buried himself in a clapboard church in the middle of nowhere. But he didn't feel dead. He felt alive—more so than he had in many years.

Something had just happened to John Wright. It seemed so much more than some mystical religious experience. It was so much more than a psychotic or cathartic encounter. He had been to ballets and symphonies that moved him to tears. This was a disparate happening. This was not an outside/inside thing. It was a deeply inside/outside thing. Something had happened inside of him. It did not feel to him like it would fade with time, as a beautiful artistic performance might.

The quandary facing him at this intersection was what to do with the items within his reach. He had a dilemma. John did not like to waste anything. He inherently knew that the bottle and the Bible lying on the seat next to him were incongruent. One of them needed to go. He didn't like to re-gift things, and of all things to re-gift, Mr. Timmons's Bible seemed a profane option.

On the other hand, it didn't seem logical to donate whiskey to the local food pantry. Nor would it be appropriate to give it to the panhandlers that hung around the intersections near the Tallahassee airport. He did not want to contribute to the delinquency of a minor—or of an adult, for that matter. If John Wright was to run a new race, many things must be new in his life. For years now, the bottle had been a trusted companion.

John reached over and rubbed the brown, worn leather of the Bible. How many hours had this book been in Mr. Timmons' lap? How many insights from the living literature had impacted his life? He reached past the book and grabbed the obituary. He held it in front of his face and looked at the picture of his mother. It was a twenty-year-old picture, and it was beautiful. This was the image of their mother that his sister said she wanted to remember.

He gently opened the Bible and carefully put the obituary inside it. Then he reached over the Bible again and grabbed the bottle. He unscrewed the top and deeply inhaled the aroma of the bourbon. He hit the button to roll down the window. It moved down about an inch.

"Not making it easy, huh?" John said to his deity, to the devil, to himself, or perhaps just to the wind. He chuckled and opened the door.

He poured the entirety of the bottle onto the steaming hot blacktop. The bottle was nearly full. He poured until it was utterly empty. He shut the door and tossed the empty bottle into a trash receptacle Bart kept in the back floorboard. He glanced left and right and proceeded through the intersection to honor a woman that he couldn't help but think would be proud of the choice he had just made.

CHAPTER FORTY-SEVEN

Fourteen months later

John fidgeted in the leather chair. Life had been different for the last few months. It hadn't been perfect, but it had been peaceful. That is, until right now. He kept his hands in his lap and looked around the office in which he was waiting. There were beautifully-bound classic books on tastefully-decorated shelves. Right next to the elegant books, some things looked out of place.

There was a surfboard leaning against the end of one of the shelves, NBA-autographed basketballs, and even a framed poster of the Rolling Stones signed by Mick Jagger himself. "To Preacher Paul" was written just above the signature. *This isn't like any bishop's office I've ever seen*, thought John.

The door abruptly opened, and entering the room was an energetic thirty-nine-year-old minister named Paul Thompson. "Mark Wright, as I live and breathe!" he said as he thrust out his hand for a vigorous shake.

"That's right. Nice to meet you, Bishop Thompson."

"No, sir. Just call me Paul."

"All right. A pleasure to meet you, Paul."

"The pleasure is all mine, Pastor John."

That greeting stung John. *Pastor.* That was not a pleasant and nostalgic call back to a bygone era. It physically affected him. He had not been addressed with that salutation in so long, and it seemed so painfully odd.

"John will do just fine, Bish . . . um, Paul."

"Okay, fine. Please take your seat, John." John obliged, and Paul took a seat near him instead of the ergonomic chair behind the modern desk.

John had been summoned to the bishop's office just as in his former days of ministry. He had been in his mid-to-late twenties then, and he could now see the onramp of sixty. Since that time, the district had relocated the office of headquarters to a more commercially progressive part of town closer to the interstate: the location better served the convenience of the clergy who came from all corners of the state.

For the life of him, John could not imagine why he was needed. Had he forgotten to pay his ministerial dues the last year of his service? He pondered what the penalties and interest might be for this oversight after this many years.

He had no idea if there were any people left in the churches where he served. If there were, he probably didn't know a soul. He'd had no contact with any colleagues for years. No one had reached out to him when he went off the grid. He harbored no ill will towards any of them—he'd made it profoundly difficult to reach him.

He wondered if there was some legal entanglement concerning the properties connected to his service. Perhaps there was a lawsuit regarding accusations of fiscal misconduct—or worse. Maybe he was being called to testify. His mind had been racing since he was summoned, and the more it did, the readier he was to get this meeting behind him.

"Hey, thanks so much for coming. I've been looking forward to sitting down with you for so long," said the new bishop as the two men sat next to each other in the office. John awkwardly squirmed while Bishop Thompson seemed completely at ease.

"Thank you," was the sum total of creative response John could muster.

"No, thank YOU!"

Trying to appear less awkward, John added while looking around the room, "This is a far cry from the old Bishop's office. This place is pretty cool."

"Does it bring back memories, Pas . . . I mean, John?"

"Not really. Everything is so different. Well, maybe the queasy feeling of being in a bishop's office. The PTSD feels familiar."

They both laughed a bit, and it relaxed John a tad.

"Why exactly did you ask me to come, Paul?"

"Where do I start? Let's begin with this: Dude, you are a rock star! And I know rock stars." Bishop Thompson pointed to the Rolling Stones poster as he said this. "You have no idea what you have meant to my whole family, and to me, all these years."

John sat there with a completely puzzled look on his face. "I'm sorry, Bishop Paul," he winced as he said it for breaking the "just call me Paul" rule, but he couldn't help it. Now that he was old, he realized that he was a bit old-school. "Have you and I met?"

"We sure have, Pastor John." Bishop Thompson winked good-naturedly, breaking the "just call me John" rule—tit for tat. "I suppose you don't remember. I grew up in Smithville. I was a nine-year-old little boy in a trailer park." He paused for effect. "Anything coming to your mind?"

"Go on," John said, genuinely interested in the beginning of this story.

"You and your wife were in ministry transition to Springfield. Even though you were leaving the church in just a few weeks, you still launched this huge Vacation Bible School for the community."

John said, "Okay, I think I do remember that."

"My parents were poor, John. They did a great job raising us, but to be honest, Dad was an alcoholic, and he sometimes got a little mean. Not awful, mind you, like some war stories. Just mean when he drank. Mom was a bit of an enabler. He never beat us, but it was still kind of a brutal upbringing."

"I'm sorry," John said sincerely.

"Don't be. This sad story has a happy ending, thanks to Pastor John Mark Wright." Bishop Thompson was beaming as he said this. John was now completely mystified. The bishop discerned that and continued.

"You drove your old yellow Toyota truck through the trailer park one afternoon. That day, Dad was on a tear inside the trailer. My buddy Patrick and I were outside waiting for anyone to come out and shoot some ball with us—anyone or anything to get us away from the combat fields that we called home. You pulled up beside us. . . ."

Bishop Thompson paused as the emotion caught in his throat. It both surprised him and didn't surprise him at the same time. He gathered himself and continued. "I have told this story two hundred times over the years, and I don't know how this part keeps punching me in the mouth. I should expect it, I suppose. Probably because you are right here in front of me."

Offering him an emotional life preserver to relax the moment, John said, "Well, if we were boxing, I'd say you have me on the ropes, my new young friend. I'm hanging on every word."

Bishop Thompson smiled and exhaled. "Well, you pulled up beside us, and you invited us both to the VBS. You made it sound so exciting, like some kind of master salesman. It was like you were selling us the greatest puppy on earth for a quarter. It was a no-brainer, as they say."

"And you guys went to the VBS?"

"Yes, we did. You told us to make sure we got permission from our parents. Patrick's folks never cared where he went or what he did. He forged the permission slip. He did that kind of stuff a lot."

"Oh, wow."

"Yeah, wow," Paul agreed. "I ran into the trailer, and Mom was glad to get me a reprieve from the chaos. We climbed into your Toyota and went to the VBS that day. We had the time of our lives. We went back every single night. I kept begging Mom to take me back to the church on Sunday—all the Sundays. She finally got worn down and did. You were gone by then."

"Oh, my," John said softly. He was swept back decades. Memories that he believed had evaporated presented themselves in wave after wave. They didn't just show up—they came back like some kind of restored film. They were vivid. He remembered it all. All. Layla. The kids. The people. The joy. The fact that his former vocation—his "calling"—had made this kind of difference in a person was simply overwhelming.

"You left, John, but I never did," the bishop said. "Well, eventually—as an adult—I did leave, in a way. The church in Smithville rocked my life. I became a revolutionized, radical little kid. I got so on fire for God that my folks got freaked out. They thought that I might be in a cult or something. So they decided to go and check it out to protect me."

John now sat on the edge of his seat, literally and metaphorically. His eyes were moist.

"So they went to church, and then guess what?" He was too impatient to wait on the reply, so the question became rhetorical. He was too excited to wait. "They never left either! Dad eventually got on the board and was an awesome board member, and Mom became the assistant women's leader and one of the secretaries."

John just shook his head. "Well, that is pretty wonderful. Inspiring, actually. You have made my day, Bishop Paul."

"So maybe you can understand why you are something of a folk hero in the Thompson Clan history. I've been looking for you, my friend, and you have proven to be as elusive as the white rhinoceros."

"Well, I kinda spent a few years . . . a few *decades* . . . off the grid."

"Yeah. I'm just glad that I found you. I've wanted to thank you personally, and now I can. Thank you, John Mark Wright, for caring for a broken-down kid in a broken-down trailer park on that incredible day."

"Oh my." John exhaled deeply again. "That is so thoughtful of you." He closed his eyes and took deep breaths in a valiant attempt to maintain his composure.

CHAPTER FORTY-EIGHT

"**A**nd I have a job for you, John," Bishop Thompson said. This statement abruptly shifted the mood altogether.

John had no problem maintaining his composure now. "Did I mention PTSD earlier?" John responded.

Holding up his hands, the bishop sympathized, "Hey, I get it. People have filled in the gaps for me on your resume a little bit."

"Gaps?" John responded incredulously. "Resume?"

"You have navigated some rough water, no doubt, but I have a church where I need you to do some interim work."

When John had taken high school English, his teacher, Mrs. Roman, had taught him that the "but" in specific sentences was the only thing that mattered. It was an extraordinarily important conjunction. Nothing mattered before the "but," and the only important thing that mattered was what came after the "but."

This was the biggest "but" John had ever encountered in his life. "Navigated rough water?" Bishop Thompson's "but" was the Hoover Dam of all conjunctions. If that word could stop all of the "rough water"—sabotage, depression, loneliness, abandonment, ambush, addiction, vice, and suicidal ideations, for starters—then it would be a miraculous conjunction. He sat and wondered, at his age, how the words following, how the days following, could mean more on this side of the "but."

"The church is called Grace Fellowship. It has rafted down some rapids, as well." The bishop's words snapped him back into the present moment. "If your work as the interim pastor goes well, it could become permanent. If that doesn't work out, I still need a man like you in our tribe."

John sat there paralyzed. He stared. Paul smiled, content with the silence and situation. John was in no way content, honored, complimented, or intrigued. He was, in fact, nearly offended by the suggestion. The goodly portion of his adulthood defined the angst which came from the very thing this smiling, young man now suggested he restart.

John finally broke the silence. "Respectfully, please pick a better man or better woman to help you out. Bishop, I have a history. I don't think you want nor need a guy like me."

"Let me be the judge of that. I may be young, but I am told that I have a keen sense of character." There was a gentle authority in the young minister's voice. It was almost like he shifted into another spiritual gear, and John noted that this gear seemed perfectly natural in him.

"I don't even hold credentials with any organization anymore. I've been out of all this for thirty years. Please don't allow the sweetness of nostalgia to interfere with your responsibilities to your territory. You really don't need a washed-up old guy like me."

Now Bishop Thompson seemed slightly offended and pushed back with a little more authority. He leaned forward and said, "On the contrary. I am not mistaking nostalgia for duty. Look, people make assumptions about me—'the youngest bishop in the state's history' and all of that. I don't care about any of that stuff. Frankly, I know I need all the help I can get. I embrace the wisdom of the gray-heads. Some of the junk I have to navigate in this state . . . well, people like you have expertise in navigating it. It's the real-life, nitty-gritty asphalt of existence."

John sat silently. He was impressed by the authority of this man. The more he talked, the more John realized the bishop had much more substance than surfboards and Stones posters.

"I am moved in my emotions today," Bishop Thompson continued. "It is a significant day. But make no mistake, my request is not about nostalgia. It is about seasoning. I deal with stuff today in my windshield that you see in your rearview mirror. You can give me and my team wisdom on how to navigate it. We have a systemic problem in this state—heck, in this nation for that matter. The problem is the epidemic of preachers bailing on their calling. Ministers are jumping ship in record numbers for a variety of reasons. I need you to jump back *on* the ship and help us keep the rest of us on board."

The words stung. John thought, *You want a quitter to give a scared-straight seminar to other potential quitters.* Although he bristled at the notion, it made sense to him. There was not a hint of insult in the words, tone, or demeanor of this bishop. Instead, his frankness was refreshing. John recalled the last bishop he'd dealt with who had come at him with all kinds of hidden agendas and manipulation. This new bishop was coming at him straight on and seemed to have a good and compassionate heart. John had sensed the same sort of heart in old Bishop Johnson so many years earlier.

"John, I need your wisdom. What you did changed my life. Methods and trends have changed, but football is football."

John looked up quickly. "Huh? Paul, run that by me again."

"Sure. Pass routes and defensive schemes change in the game of football, but the game ultimately comes down to blocking and tackling, just like the first day they rolled a pigskin out onto a field. Some stuff doesn't ever change."

The leader let that sink into his middle-aged recruit.

"Let me switch metaphors with you. I tend to do that a lot."

John smiled, "Go for it."

"It's like riding a bike. Come on, John!" Bishop Thompson clapped loudly as he said it.

The intensity of that statement indeed reminded John of the passion a football coach possesses. It startled John, actually.

"Get back on the bike. Get back in the pulpit. You'll remember how to ride. Yeah, you'll be a little rusty at first, but I promise it will come back to you, and will come back faster than you can imagine."

The bishop thought he now truly had John on the ropes—he never ran out of metaphors. John was trying to fight back, but his punches were softer—they weren't landing. John was trying his best to cast off this "offer."

"I'm not trying to make excuses, but I got pretty beat up doing what you are now asking me to do again. This stuff drudges up a lot of pain, and..."

Bishop Thompson held up both hands. "I read the file. I'm sorry, John, I didn't mean to interrupt you." John nodded his forgiveness. "I am so sorry for the damage done to you. You changed the course of my life. I want to be a part of your change, and a part of your healing. I have a couple of guys I want you to meet. I would like them to join us, with your permission. I want to do something special, John. Would you mind meeting my friends?"

"Of course not. This is your office and your meeting."

"Good!" said the bishop as he jumped to his feet.

CHAPTER FORTY-NINE

Bishop Thompson walked to his office door and opened it. He motioned for two men to join him. John Wright stood up from his chair but not nearly as quickly as the bishop had jumped up from his. The two men smiled respectfully as they walked across the office to the middle-aged former preacher.

Bishop Thompson began the introductions. "Pastor Wright, I'd like you to meet..."

"John. Just John, remember?" He wasn't being obstinate as much as advocating for his mental and emotional wellbeing.

"Of course. Forgive me. I would like you to meet my friends Rob and Rex. Rob, Rex, this is John Mark Wright."

Rob, a man in his early forties, extended his hand to John first. Rex, some ten years younger than his companion, followed suit and shook John's hand.

"Nice to meet you, gentlemen," John said politely.

"Let's all take a seat," Bishop Thompson said. Becoming more serious in tone, he continued, "This might be out there, John—and as I recall, your style was kind of out there, too—but, I feel very strongly about this. I want to reinstate you to vocational ministry. I want to do something symbolically, also."

"I've noticed you have never met a metaphor or a symbol that you didn't like," John said.

"Ha! Right. But this symbol is more than a metaphor. It is downright biblical. You ready for it?"

"Doubt it, but hit me with it anyway."

"I want to, well, wash your feet like Jesus washed His disciples' feet. I have asked these men to be witnesses and to share with you from their hearts."

John looked pale. He looked up at Rex, who stood there beaming, and then looked at Rob, whose face was more subdued. John's eyes lingered on a curious scar that adorned the man's face.

Rob spoke next. "John Mark, I cannot say that it is nice to meet you." He let the statement hang in the air for just a beat. "The reason I cannot say that is because I have met you before." He let that settle in the room as well.

"You don't say," John responded. "This is beginning to feel like an episode of 'This is Your Life.' Oh, you guys are way too young to have ever heard of that show. See, Bishop, I can't read audiences anymore."

He attempted to lighten the atmosphere with jokes, but the atmosphere remained thick with the substance of the moment.

Shifting nervously, John said, "I am sorry, Rob. I am drawing a blank. I can't recall meeting you. Forgive me."

"My last name is Nella. My name is Rob Nella."

John's eyes narrowed, and his attempt at smiling disappeared.

"My father's name is Bill. Bill Nella."

John fidgeted in his seat but remained silent.

Rob continued. "I love my dad, but he had a way of making the lives of preachers miserable, and I never really understood why. He had a very complicated upbringing, but that is no excuse to treat people horribly. I actually found out about this stuff later in life. I don't know all the details—and I am not asking to know them. I'm just here today to officially apologize to you for any and all damage that my family caused—damage to you personally or to your ministry."

John Mark became visibly uncomfortable. He felt his face become hot. A wave of nausea hit him. He felt a little dizzy. He desperately wanted to escape, but there was nowhere to go.

"I don't really know what to say, Rob," was all he could manage to say in the moment. He touched his own cheek and then pointed to Rob. "I do remember you, Rob."

Rob smiled kindly and touched his scar. "We all have them, don't we? Some scars might go away, and some stay with us."

"What happened?" John asked. He then quickly added, "I apologize. None of my business. I may have known at one time, but perhaps I forgot."

"Apologies not necessary. I was riding my bike down an old logging lane when I was about ten or eleven. A stupid truck ran me off the road, and I landed in some barbed wire."

"I'm sorry to hear that," John said.

"I read in a book somewhere—and I wish I could find the source, but I'll never forget the line—'Wounded people are dangerous because they have learned that they can survive.'"

"I like that," Bishop Thompson said.

Rob continued. "When I see this scar, it reminds me that I survived something. I am so glad that you have survived, too. Sometimes, our scars are invisible, but they are there nonetheless."

Rex Grossman spoke for the first time since the introductions. "Do I look familiar, John?"

"Now come on, fellas!" John answered.

"Well, if I do, it would be a little weird, because I truly have never met you."

Everyone laughed. Rex's humor was the perfect levity to make an emotional situation a little more bearable. It gave the room a chance to breathe.

"I am here because the church Bishop Paul told you about is my church. I am a volunteer, and we need some help. I run a law practice for underprivileged people in our city. At our church, we don't need a polished orator to be our leader. Lord knows I see enough of those in courtrooms."

"I'm sure you do," John said.

"We've been pretty beaten up. We need someone who's real and maybe even a little raw. We are looking for someone who has been beaten up by life and survived, like Rob said. We need a shepherd who will show us how to win, how to overcome."

"I'd be your man on the first part," John said. "I've had the crap beaten out of me by life . . . but I don't think I qualify for the second part. I'm most definitely not a winner."

Bishop Thompson pulled a chair close to John. "You may have stumbled in the dark for a year. . . . or thirty. The fact that you made it out of the darkness and into the light tells me that you are indeed a winner. You are an overcomer. Rex is in a church full of people who've been beaten to a pulp by life. They could use a seasoned example."

The other men pulled chairs up around the former preacher. Bishop Thompson directed his attention to Rex. "Rex, would you mind getting the basin?" Rex immediately walked out of the office.

Bishop Thompson turned to John and began to roll up the pant legs of this minister who, so many years before, had driven a yellow truck through a future bishop's trailer park and forged destiny as he did so.

"Jesus set for us an example to follow. He showed us how to be His humble servants. Today, we follow that example as we wash the feet of the Lord's humble servant, Pastor John Mark Wright." As he said "Pastor," his piercing gaze locked onto John's eyes, and there wasn't an ounce of apology in it. It was too much. John looked to his right, breaking the stare.

CHAPTER FIFTY

Rex returned with a basin of water and a couple small towels. He placed the basin between the bishop and the "recruit." Bishop Thompson looked directly into John's eyes. His voice became authoritative but in a very even-keeled manner. There wasn't a hint of phoniness in his tone or demeanor. "The Bible says that Jesus left for us an example that we should follow in His steps."

The bishop opened a well-worn Bible and turned to the Gospel of John. "Do you recognize this Bible, Pastor John Mark?" Bishop entirely dismissed John's request to be called only by his first name.

John's eyebrows burrowed a little as he looked at the book. "I can't say that I do."

The bishop smiled and said, "This is Bishop Johnson's Bible. His dear widow wanted me to have it. In fact, she brought it to the presbytery for my installation service."

This information moved John. "That is quite precious. I had a great fondness for the old bishop. He was one of the purest fellows I have ever met."

"I happen to know that he had a great warmness for you, as well. If he is in that big cloud of witnesses in the sky, I know that today is a delightful scene to him," the new bishop said.

"One of the examples Jesus left us was to stoop down and serve. John, *He* did this, even though there was a man named Judas in their midst. In fact, the chapter I am going to read from says that Jesus knew who was going to betray Him."

Bishop Thompson let those words hang in the air. "Betray." It was a cocktail of betrayals that had spun John into thirty years of wandering and weeds. This entire scene felt simply surreal. John was right back in a bishop's office, negotiating the influence of his authority. The betrayers were not in the room; however, the son of one of them sat nearby. On a small table was a Bible that had belonged to the benevolent bishop from John's past.

John sat there in, as they say, a perfect storm. A cacophony of emotions swirled in his heart. Bishop Thompson began speaking, and his words momentarily stopped the swirl of emotion and brought focus. "Before we do this, I want to read a few verses from John's Gospel." He began reading the fourth verse of chapter thirteen.

"'So he got up from the meal, took off his outer clothing, and wrapped a towel around his waist. After that, he poured water into a basin and began to wash his disciples' feet, drying them with the towel that was wrapped around him.'"

Bishop Thompson stopped reading and put the Bible on his lap. "Pastor, this is what we are going to do today. Regardless of your ultimate decision to help us with this important assignment, I strongly feel that what we are doing now is an assignment that I have from the Lord. I must obey this assignment."

He picked the Bible back up and continued to read. He skipped down to the twelfth verse.

"'When he had finished washing their feet, he put on his clothes and returned to his place. "Do you understand what I have done for you?" he asked them. "You call me 'Teacher' and 'Lord,' and rightly so, for that is what I am. Now that I, your Lord and Teacher, have washed your feet, you also should wash one another's feet. I have set you an example that you should do as I have done for you. Very truly I tell you, no servant is greater than his master, nor is a messenger greater than the one who sent him. Now that you know these things, you will be blessed if you do them."

Putting the Bible on the floor near the basin, but far enough away to ensure it would not get splashed with water, Bishop Thompson took a knee and began to remove John's shoes. He spoke as he worked.

"I'm glad that you have consented to this for several different reasons. One is that, if we want to be like Jesus, we must follow His radical example." He put John's right shoe near the Bible with the sock tucked neatly inside.

"Another reason is selfish. That book just said that we would be blessed if we did this. I do feel blessed, but would like all of the blessings I can get." He placed the left shoe adjacent to the right and tucked the other sock inside.

He had not made eye contact during the removal of the shoes. He spoke matter-of-factly and like a friend. However, as he grabbed the basin, the authority and the confidence returned to his timbre. He methodically rolled up John's pant legs to mid-calf and placed his feet into the large basin.

"Pastor John Mark Wright, in the name of Jesus and following His holy example, I now wash your feet." The bishop poured tepid water over John's feet but not all of the water in the wooden pitcher. "I serve you, and I esteem you more significantly than myself."

John closed his eyes and worked diligently to keep his emotions in check. These words washed over him. The bishop continued, "The Lord Jesus Christ forgives all sins and brings about wholeness, holiness, and restoration."

Bishop Thompson handed the pitcher to Rex Grossman. He knelt and looked up at John, who had opened his moist eyes. "Pastor Wright, I wash your feet as a lowly penitent in need of God's mighty grace. I wash your feet believing that His mercy will manifest in your future and in ours." With that, he poured more water over John's feet and into the basin.

Rex handed the basin to Rob. Rob knelt and started to speak. He said, "Pastor. . . ." That was the only word he was able to utter before being completely overcome with emotion. He knelt for at least two long minutes inhaling through his nose and exhaling deeply from his mouth.

Finally, he was able to continue. "Pastor, I wash your feet with a great desire and expectation that God will wash away your pain; that God will wash away the pain caused by every Judas in your life. . . ." There came the emotion again. With a catch in his voice, he continued, "I am so sorry, dear pastor, for every injury caused by my own family. May God wash away your pain." He poured more water on his feet, stood, and went to an oversized, blue chair in the corner. He sat down, put his face in his hands, and wept deeply.

Bishop Thompson took Rob's place at the basin. John could not contain the tears that now quietly streamed down his life-weathered cheeks and onto his lap. The bishop poured the last little bit of water—perhaps a cup's worth—on John's feet. "As an agent and ambassador of our Lord

Jesus on the earth, and by the authority of His church, I restore you into full-time vocational ministry."

With those words, a deep guttural groan came out of a pastor who referred to himself interchangeably as "washed out" and "washed up." His response surprised him. It was a very similar response to the one he'd had at the Antioch Redeemer House of God.

The atmosphere of the room completely changed. It was undeniable to all four men. The light streaming through the windows seemed brighter. The air seemed sweeter. Rex sat in a chair and gently rocked back and forth. He looked a bit like a Jewish rabbi at the wailing wall. Rob continued to weep. In fact, there were tears all around.

The tears from Rex were induced by the absolute and undeniable power of the invisible Presence in the room. Rob's tears were inspired by a loyal love for his father, a recognition of the hurt and shame that his father caused, and a compassionate empathy for his childhood pastor.

Bishop Thompson sat and quietly cried while simultaneously smiling. It was an odd combination to witness. There was no shame or sadness in his tears. There was an inherent joy in them. Sure, the moment offered a tinge of nostalgia. More than anything, though, there was an inherent "rightness" about it. Bishop Thompson believed this moment was supposed to happen, and was honored to have a front-row seat in it.

A buffet of emotions caused John's tears. The Presence, certainly, stimulated his response. He used to experience this Presence, this atmosphere, regularly—monthly and even weekly—a few decades earlier. He hadn't realized how much he had missed it.

Shame. Shame was also a contributing factor to John's weeping. He was ashamed of all the years he had squandered running from his immutable assignment. On the heels of the shame came a tangible sense of grace, acceptance, forgiveness, and beautiful connectivity with the Divine. He wept at the shame this young man, Rob, must have been feeling. That emotion was accompanied by compassion and even love for the man. That deep and divine love for his former child congregant brought a fresh wave of tears.

While Bishop Thompson had tears of joy, John also wept tears of hope. There was this little hope sapling in his soul—a seedling of potential for his future. Growing was a sense that, perhaps, this calling and destiny may not have been entirely shipwrecked. Perhaps, just perhaps, it was still to be fulfilled. He wept at the possibility of honoring an irreversible, change-less, unrepealable, unalterable, irremediable, indelible, and irrevocable calling placed upon his life so long ago.

If a journalist had walked into this meeting to write a report, the story would have words in it such as "bizarre" and "ludicrous." There were four grown men in a moderately sized office weeping as if they had just received horrible news. Yet one was smiling through his tears. One of the men had his pants rolled up with his feet in some type of washbasin. Water spilled onto the carpet next to the weeping man.

What happened next, a journalist might not even have found the right words to report—at least not that would have rendered it believable. What happened next, no one had ever experienced before. However, John and Bishop Thompson had both studied accounts of it in seminary.

It started with John Mark Wright. He wept for a long while and then took a deep breath. A chuckle followed the deep breath. The other men continued to emote but made a note of the quiet chuckle. His laughter was followed by about a half dozen other closed-mouth chuckles. If the imaginary reporter had found a word, it would have been "absurdity"— and it was about to get more absurd.

John Mark's chuckles morphed into a deep and sustained laughter. Next on the laugh train was Rex. His face concurrently laughed and looked puzzled. Next was Bishop Thompson. He laughed hard. He was closer to laughing than any of them anyway because of the resident joy he was soaking in. Getting on the train last was Rob. Like the good book says, the last shall be first. He came late to the laughing party, but he was the most boisterous.

Outside the closed doors, denominational office employees looked up towards the office and then looked at each other. The noise was boisterous and sudden. One young intern even made a gesture, tipping an invisible flask to his lips. The motion communicated to the curious employees, "They must be drinking."

As hard as the weeping had come, the laughter now came even harder. Bishop Thompson was on his literal side against the arm of the chair. Rex and Rob stood, grabbed each other by the shoulders, and looked at each other in the eyes as they both guffawed. John Mark walked over to the window and looked out. He laughed as he had never laughed at any time in his memory. John had wept until his head hurt. Now, he laughed until his stomach hurt.

The peculiar conference ended with four grown men in the middle of a bishop's office hugging one another, slapping one another on the back, and simply celebrating whatever had just happened there.

Bishop Thompson concluded the meeting. "Gentlemen, good conference!" He clapped his hands together one time. "If I tried to explain the results of the meeting in official minutes, number one, I wouldn't know what to say. Number two, if I figured out what to say, no one would believe it." That caused the other three to laugh naturally and not supernaturally—or whatever it was they had been doing before.

John Mark extended his hand to shake the hands of the others. "I'm not sure I believe it, but I desperately want to!"

CHAPTER FIFTY-ONE

Rex Grossman stood beside a lovely woman named Lisa Forsman. Lisa was an anesthesiologist at Grady Hospital in Atlanta, GA. She was also the new chairperson for the personnel committee at the inner-city church where they were now standing. She had replaced Rex, who'd recently rotated off the leadership committee. Grace Fellowship was in full swing as they stood in the back, swaying to and fro.

The burgeoning congregation sang, swayed, and clapped. Rex leaned over and spoke to Lisa loudly enough to be heard over the music. "Pastor said that this is his favorite service."

Lisa yelled back, "It sure seems like it. He just lights up!"

The music got softer, and so did the voices of the two leaders as they spoke.

"He loves the English services too. You can just tell," Rex said.

"Rex, a year ago, we were dying. We didn't have even fifteen percent of our current attendance—even if you threw in every nationality."

Rex added, "And that includes every stray cat that walked across the parking lot. Now, look at this!"

Lisa and Rex could barely contain their enthusiasm.

"The multiple services each week are wearing me out, and I've never been happier," Rex said. They both laughed a little at that.

The final worship song concluded, and a fifty-five-year-old pastor walked up four steps towards the old wooden pulpit. He was smiling ear to ear, as the expression goes. He was wearing a crisp, black, short-sleeved shirt with a white clergy collar, a pair of faded Levi jeans, and some dark brown hiking boots. He greeted the congregation with loving and encouraging words.

Rex and Lisa stepped out into the small lobby of the church to deal with a problem. It was a "good problem," like so many of the issues during those days. There were too many children in the children's church, and one of the departmental leaders dispatched a volunteer to see if there were any more chairs. The two church executives happily pointed the worker to a room storing the solution to their problem: more small folding chairs.

When they stepped back into the sanctuary, the sermon was heating up. Pastor John Mark Wright was addressing this Hispanic congregation in nearly flawless Spanish.

"*Gente hermosa de Dios, la vida puede ser un poco brutal.*
Sí hay es algo que aprendí en mi viaje, nunca se acaba.
Hay una luz en el Fin del túnel por una temporada pensé.
La luz era un tren que se dirigía hacia mí."

The congregation broke into laughter at this. The pastor told a loosely-translated version to this beautiful congregation: life could be brutal, but there was light at the end of the tunnel. The laughter was elicited by the preacher's reflection that, for a while, he'd thought that the light was a train heading straight for him!

The text he was preaching was about the prodigal son in the New Testament. He told the people that the Light of the world comes for all of them. The Light is not intimidated by pig slop, nor by the foolish squandering of resources. Destiny is destiny. Calling is calling. The Light doesn't stop coming for us, even when our decisions are unwise.

Just like in the old days, Pastor John Mark had the congregation's rapt attention. But his ministry was different somehow. There was seasoning to his sermon. There was a simultaneous sense of freshness and an element of being weathered by life.

In Spanish, he continued. The English translation was: "The Light of the world is tenacious. It doesn't give up. The Father runs off of the porch and runs to us with His light and His love. He will kill the fatted calf to celebrate us, and He will put a ring on our fingers. God erupts in jubilee when we come back into the light!"

Many people streamed to the front as the minister invited them to walk in the Light. So many beautiful Hispanic souls were happily receiving the Light that the preacher was promoting. Many were crying. Some were kneeling. A few simply bowed their heads, and some bent at the waist. Weeping gently, the people prayed in their native tongue and asked God for all manner of things, but mainly asked Him for Light.

Rex and Lisa joined Pastor Wright in the "green room" following the service. The loosely-called green room was a former large storage closet equipped with a small table, two wooden chairs, and an old, brown leather loveseat. It was simply yet tastefully decorated. A bowl of fruit, a coffeemaker with individual pods of different flavors, and assorted healthy snacks sat on the table. The room was clean and pleasant. A few lamps illuminated the space.

Rex and Lisa knocked and entered the room, bouncing. Each hugged the pastor. "Great sermon," Lisa said.

"Oh. Thanks, but when did you learn Spanish, Lisa?" John Mark asked.

"I watched a couple of videos last night, and I think I have it," she answered with a smile.

"*Uno mas*," Rex chimed in.

They had just finished the second service of the morning, and there was one more to go. The next one would be an English service.

"*Muy bien, Señor Rex*," Pastor John Mark said.

"*Gracias*."

Lisa was beaming. "You have exceeded our wildest expectations, Pastor."

"I appreciate the deference, but you know I'm just John Mark."

"All the same, I can't bring myself to call you that so casually," Lisa countered. "I respect the office, but I also have enormous respect for you personally."

"Suit yourself, Lisa. Whatever you feel most comfortable with," John Mark rejoined. "But I have to say that I don't feel comfortable with receiving any credit for what is happening at Grace Fellowship."

Rex jumped in. "Yeah, yeah, yeah—it's all the Lord and all that; but, come on. He has to use somebody, and He is using y.o.u."

"Well, Rex, He is using us a.l.l. All of us are servants that the Lord is using. You know, I'm not just a salesman of this grace; I am also one of the biggest customers. I just spoke about the prodigal son. I know there was a language barrier in the last service, but you'll hear it in this one if you stick around. I'm just a prodigal that squandered so much and came out of slop only to be clothed in Daddy's robe."

John Mark looked at his watch and abruptly ended his conversation. "Speaking of! This prodigal has to get back to work. Love you both so much. You're great leaders, and I mean that."

Lisa said, "We love you too. And remember, Pastor, we don't say 'going to work' if you love what you do. It's obvious you do. What you do comes across as pure joy."

Pastor Wright winked and was out the door and into yet another service filled with hungry worshippers. They may have been in an English-speaking service, but the diversity was apparent and stark. There were Caribbean citizens, Africans, and more Hispanics. Many attendees were from India. There were congregants from twenty-one countries who sang joyfully and robustly, much like in the previous service.

Lisa and Rex sat closer to the front during this worship service. John Mark took the pulpit and preached the exact text, this time in flawless English.

"The Light is named Jesus. Not only is He Light, but He is also Peace. He is the Prince of Peace. He baptized me with His mighty peace when I thought I would never experience it again." Erupting across the room were hearty "amens" and a few that said, "Amen, Pastor."

"Before we conclude the service, I would like Taylor Jenson to come and recite what the young folks call a 'spoken word.' To me, it is just a beautiful poem. After this beautiful piece of art, we will have a time of commitment."

Taylor, a young woman majoring in African Studies, came to the steps. She might have been considered a quintessential African American, having moved to the States from Ethiopia as a young teenager and currently being entrenched in studying her native continent. She walked elegantly across the stage to the microphone. She carried no notes, but carried herself with a certain grace. She projected a unique combination of both confidence and humility. She stopped in front of the microphone, took a breath, smiled, and flawlessly recited the piece. She enunciated her words with enthusiasm and passion.

Tainted

Out of the ashes of a devastated soul,
Through the smoke clearing vistas of sinful toll—

Steps the Preacher written off long ago.
Publicly disgraced for his prodigal show.

He landed on the heap of preachers tainted;
His shame was broadcast and the faithful fainted.

No one gets a pass from this nebulous shadow.
How's he even standing in this infamous meadow?

Settling in this sediment of black despair,
Barely could the Preacher gasp hope's sweet air.

But a voice settled with him, though he could barely hear it.
The whisper of one dwelling with a contrite spirit.

And the voice said, "Stand, Grace has come for you . . .
Grace has brought life, the way, and the truth."

By faith, he took one step on broken reputations.
Each step that followed brought kind confirmation.

Like Samson at his end, a glory has returned.
Redemption is delivered to a man once spurned.

Walking back to a ministry, though not the same—
Chiseled to simplicity by despair and shame.

The Preacher, now humbled, walks out from the ashamed.
God's mercy has re-clothed him, and he has been renamed.

Outcast he is no longer, for he has been rescued.
A minister once more—a man for God to use.

When Taylor finished, Pastor John Mark Wright, lead minister at Grace Fellowship in Atlanta, GA, walked to his pulpit. "Beautiful, Taylor. Thank you so much. Jesus is the Prince of Peace. I have experienced His peace once again in the very depth of my soul, and it is precious. If you want this peace that your pastor is talking about, then join me here. Let's ask Him to give it to you even now."

Music began to play while dozens and dozens of men, women, and teenagers of every background walked to the front of the sanctuary.

The End

CPSIA information can be obtained
at www.ICGtesting.com
Printed in the USA
JSHW012352210623
43461JS00005B/19